# The Charming Quirks of Others

## ALEXANDER McCALL SMITH

Little, Brown

LITTLE, BROWN

First published in Great Britain in 2010 by Little, Brown

A CIP catalogue record for this book
is available from the British Library.

Hardback ISBN: 978-1-4087-0256-7
C format ISBN: 978-1-4087-0257-4

Typeset in Bembo by M Rules
Printed and bound in Great Britain by
Clays Ltd, St Ives plc

Papers used by Little, Brown are natural, renewable and
recyclable products sourced from well-managed forests and certified
in accordance with the rules of the Forest Stewardship Council.

**Mixed Sources**
Product group from well-managed
forests and other controlled sources
www.fsc.org  Cert no. SGS-COC-004081
© 1996 Forest Stewardship Council
FSC

Little, Brown
An imprint of
Little, Brown Book Group
100 Victoria Embankment
London EC4Y 0DY

An Hachette UK Company
www.hachette.co.uk

www.littlebrown.co.uk

This book is for Robin Straus, in gratitude.

# 1

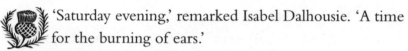'Saturday evening,' remarked Isabel Dalhousie. 'A time for the burning of ears.'

Guy Peploe, seated opposite her in the back neuk at Glass & Thompson's café, looked at her blankly. Isabel was given to making puzzling pronouncements – he knew that, and did not mind – but this one, he thought, was unusually Delphic.

He stirred his coffee. 'I'm not quite with you, Isabel. Not quite. Burning ears?'

She smiled. She had not intended to be opaque and it was Guy, after all, who had brought up the subject of Saturday evenings; she was merely picking up on the theme. He had mentioned an opening he had attended last Saturday, a show featuring a Scottish realist painter who had been ignored in his lifetime but who was now lauded as a genius. Everybody had been there; which meant, he said with a laugh, everybody who went to Saturday-evening openings at galleries. The remaining four hundred and eighty thousand people who lived in Edinburgh and its immediate environs had presumably been doing something else.

That had triggered Isabel's remark about burning ears, which she now went on to explain. 'What I meant is that on a Saturday evening,' she said, 'there are always a number of dinner parties in Edinburgh. The same people go to dinner with the same people. Backwards and forwards. And what do they talk about on these occasions?'

'Those who aren't there?' suggested Guy.

Isabel agreed. 'Exactly. And there are certain people who are talked about a lot. This is not a particularly big pond, you know. In some ways it's a village.'

Guy nodded. 'All cities have their villages,' he said. 'Even the big ones. London claims to be full of them. New York, too.'

'But New York *has* a village,' said Isabel. 'It's called The Village. Which is helpful, I suppose.'

Guy laughed; Isabel's wry comments, dropped as asides, could seem so arresting even if, when you analysed them, it was hard to say why: this was an example. There was nothing exceptional about what she had said − not on the face of it − but the comment about helpfulness tripped one up.

'Of course,' Isabel continued, 'to use the definite article about one's village demonstrates − how should one put it? − a good conceit of oneself. That clan chief called The MacGregor: does he correct people who call him *a* MacGregor? Would he have to say "No, *The* MacGregor, please"?'

'I'm sure he wouldn't,' said Guy. 'People like that are usually very modest. If you've been on the go for five hundred years, you're usually fairly low key about it.'

Isabel thought that was quite true. She knew a Nobel laureate who referred to 'a little prize they were once kind enough to give me − totally undeserved, of course'. That took some doing, and some strength of character too; how many of us, she wondered, would hide a Nobel prize under our bushel? Her friend had heard the news, she remembered his telling her, through a message left on his telephone answering machine. *This is the Nobel Committee in Stockholm and we are delighted to inform you that you have been awarded the Nobel Prize this year for . . .*

But there was something else to be said about MacGregors. 'You do know that their name was interdicted?' she said. 'James the Sixth, I'm afraid, reacted rather harshly to some bit of bad behaviour by the MacGregors and made their name illegal. It's an odd notion, don't you think? Making a name illegal. They had to start calling themselves things like Murray and so on.'

Guy knew that. Isabel had spoken about it before; she often brought up the Stuarts, for some reason that completely escaped him. People had their historical enthusiasms, he supposed, and the Stuarts were not exactly a tedious dynasty. It might have been better, he thought, if they had been; better for them, that is.

'Mind you,' said Isabel, 'it has to be said that James the Sixth was a somewhat miserable piece of work. I've tried to like the later Stuarts, you know, but I have to say it's an effort. Charles the First was such a weak and self-indulged man, and by the time we get to Bonnie Prince Charlie the genes had gone pretty bad. James the Sixth, I suppose, was far brighter than most of them, but he must have been rather difficult company much of the time. Interesting, though: gay kings usually are.'

'Didn't he have a wretched childhood?' said Guy. 'That's sometimes an excuse, isn't it? The fact that one has had an awful time as a child can explain so much, can't it.'

Isabel reached for her cup of coffee. 'Does it? I wonder. I

3

think that there's a case for putting your early years behind you. Plenty of people have done that. They grow up and then draw a line.'

Guy considered this. 'Yet the early years won't necessarily go away. If you're desperately unhappy when you're young, aren't you damaged goods?'

Isabel was prepared to concede this of James VI. 'He had that awful tutor, that Buchanan man, who intimidated him.'

Guy nodded. 'An inhumane humanist. Very grim.'

'And James,' Isabel continued, 'was brought up in such a love-less atmosphere. A major case of maternal deprivation. Then his mother had her head chopped off, we must remind ourselves. That hardly leads to happiness. And his father was blown up, wasn't he? Again not a good thing for a parent, or for anyone, actually.' She paused, warming to the theme, which was a favourite one of hers. She thought Henry Darnley, Mary's husband, was vain and scheming, a narcissist, and even if one would not wish an explosion on anybody, there were some who did seem to ask for it. 'And even before he was blown up he would hardly have been a particularly good father, murdering Mary's secretary, for heaven's sake, and having all those affairs.'

She glanced about her. A woman at a nearby table was listening, and not bothering to disguise it; did she realise, Isabel wondered, that they were discussing events of four hundred years ago? But let her listen. 'Then, of course, when some light comes into James's life at last, it is taken away from him.'

'Light?'

'His cousin,' said Isabel. 'Esmé Stuart, his cousin from France. He turned up in Scotland when James was thirteen, and James fell in love with him. He was very beautiful, by all accounts, and James at last had a friend. Poor boy.'

The eavesdropper's eyes widened involuntarily.

He wrote poetry, Isabel continued. This sad, boy-king of Scots wrote poetry. After Esmé Stuart had been forced out of Scotland by scheming nobles, James had written a poem about a rare Arabian phoenix coming to Scotland and being persecuted. 'That was Esmé,' she said. 'The boy he loved. He disguised him in the poem as a female phoenix because, well, in those days . . . It was so sad. And they are lovely lines – full of sorrow and loss.' And well they might have been, she thought. What sorrow there must be in loving somebody who does not love you back; or to love somebody whom the world says you cannot love?

They both fell silent. Then Guy said, 'You were talking about ears burning.'

Isabel toyed with her cup. 'Yes. There are a few people in this city who know that every Saturday their names are going to be mentioned at numerous dinner parties. They know it. Imagine that, Guy. Imagine knowing that there are ten, maybe twenty tables at which you are being taken to pieces and then put together again – if you're lucky.'

Guy made a face. 'Uncomfortable.'

'Yes. Deconstruction always is. And that's where the burning of ears comes in. If there's any truth in the idea that your ears burn when somebody's talking about you – and there isn't, of course – then imagine the ears of these unfortunates. They must glow like beacons in the night.'

'Gossip,' said Guy. 'Nobody should worry about gossip. There's no need for ears to burn.'

Isabel looked up sharply. 'Oh really? Don't you think that gossip can be pretty wounding?'

'Yes,' said Guy. 'Malicious gossip can. But a lot of gossip is mild – and really a bit pointless.'

Isabel agreed. 'Utterly pointless,' she said. 'Look at those glossy magazines that publish tittle-tattle about the doings of celebrities. None of these people actually *does* anything of any worth to anybody. Not really. But do people like to read about their private lives? Yes, they do. And how. He breaks up with her. She buys a house in France or is seen on so-and-so's boat. She goes to the gym, and is photographed coming out of it. And so on and so on. Why do people read that sort of thing?'

'Do you read them?' asked Guy.

'Me? Of course not,' said Isabel. She paused. Even as she gave her answer, she realised that this was not true and would have to be corrected. One should never mislead a friend, or an enemy for that matter, she thought. We owed the same duty of truthfulness to everybody, no matter what we thought of them. 'I don't buy them, but as for reading – well, never, that is never unless my teeth play up.'

Again Guy looked at her blankly.

'I read them when I go to the dentist,' she said. 'There are some magazines that we read only when we go to the dentist. Mine has all of them in his waiting room. He also has those ritzy fashion magazines with advertisements for expensive designer sunglasses and so on, and magazines about boats. He has a boat, he told me. So I read these magazines from time to time. But only at the dentist's.' She looked at him apologetically. 'Should I feel ashamed?'

Guy shook his head. 'No. We all have guilty pleasures. Yours is harmless enough.' He paused. 'But back to burning ears. Who are these people whose ears burn?'

Isabel smiled. 'The principals of schools,' she said. 'Listen next time you go to a dinner party. People talk about the principals of their children's school. They do it all the time.'

Guy digested this. He frowned. 'Strange.'

Isabel shrugged. 'It keeps people going. Not that these teachers do anything dramatic – or not usually, although there was a good bit of gossip doing the rounds last year when one of the schools appointed a new head of French and then unappointed – or, should we say, disappointed him – before he even arrived to take up the job.'

Guy said that he had heard about that – vaguely.

'The rumour mill went into full-time operation,' said Isabel. 'There were all sorts of stories going the rounds.'

'Such as?'

'Amazing things. One I heard was that he had applied under a false name and was wanted by the French police. The French police! I suppose to be wanted by the French police is somehow more exotic than being wanted by other police forces. It can't be very glamorous to be wanted by the Glasgow police – rather ordinary, in fact – but the French police – now there's a cachet.'

'And the truth?'

'The board had a change of heart. They had their reasons, no doubt, but these were probably pretty prosaic, and no reflection on the candidate. The French police wouldn't have come into it, I would have thought.'

Guy changed the subject. He had a catalogue that Isabel had expressed an interest in seeing, and he had brought it to show her. There was an auction coming up at Christie's in London and there were several paintings, including a Raeburn that Isabel said she had heard about. Now, as he put the glossy publication on the table, Isabel went straight to one of the pages he had marked with a small, yellow sticky note.

'Sir Henry Raeburn,' said Guy, as Isabel opened the

catalogue. 'Look at it. *Portrait of Mrs Alexander and her Grand-daughter.*'

Isabel studied the photograph that took up most of one of the pages. A woman in a white-collared red dress was seated against a background of dark green. Beside her was a young girl, of eight perhaps, half-crouching, arms resting on the woman's chair.

'His colours,' said Isabel. 'Raeburn used those fabulous colours, didn't he? He occupied a world of dark greens and reds. Was that the Edinburgh of his day, do you think?'

'Their interiors were like that, I suppose,' said Guy. 'Those curtains. Look.'

Isabel reached out and touched the photograph, her finger tracing the line of the fabrics draped behind the sitters. 'I find myself thinking of what their world was like,' she said. 'When was this painted? Does it say?'

'It's late Raeburn,' said Guy. 'Eighteen-twenty? Something like that.'

'So this little girl,' said Isabel. 'Might have lived until when? Eighteen-seventy, perhaps. If she was lucky.'

'I suppose so.'

'And then her own daughter – the great-granddaughter of our Mrs Alexander – would have lived from, let's say, 1840 until 1900, and *her* daughter from 1870 until 1930 or even 1940. Though she was actually a bit older when she died.'

Guy looked at her enquiringly. 'Oh?'

Isabel sat back. 'My paternal grandmother,' she said. 'Which makes her . . .' She pointed to the girl, 'my four-times great-grandmother.'

Guy's surprise was evident. 'So that's why you asked me about this. You'd heard?'

'Yes. I knew that one of my ancestors had been painted by Raeburn – two, in fact. My father told me about it when I was a teenager – he showed me some of the Raeburns in the Portrait Gallery, and he said that on his mother's side we were Alexanders. The painting was mentioned in one of the books about Raeburn, but its whereabouts were described as unknown.' She pointed to the catalogue. 'Until now.'

Guy nodded. 'I see. Well, that makes this sale rather important to you. Do you want to go for the painting?'

Isabel reached out to take the catalogue. Opening it, she turned to the full-page photograph. 'What do you think?'

Guy shrugged. 'It's a fine double portrait. Everything that makes Raeburn such a great portraitist is there. The ease of it – he painted very quickly, you know, which gives his paintings a wonderful fluidity. That's there. And the faces . . . well, they're rather charming, aren't they? The girl has a rather impish look to her. Perhaps she was planning some naughtiness, or Raeburn was telling her an amusing story to keep her still while he worked. It's very intimate in its feel.'

Isabel thought that this was right, but it was not what mattered to her. What mattered was the link that existed between her and two people in the picture. My people, she thought. My people.

'How much do you think it'll go for?'

There could be no clear answer to this, and they both knew it. 'It depends. It always depends in an auction. You never know who's going to be in the room. You never know who's going to take a fancy to a painting. Some people have deeper pockets than others.'

She wanted him to put a figure on it, and she pressed him.

'Forty thousand pounds,' he said. 'Something like that. But

you could be lucky and get it for twenty-five or thirty. Interested?'

Isabel had forty thousand pounds. Not in cash, of course, but she could raise that if she needed it by selling shares. That year she had bought two paintings – one for three thousand pounds and one for eight hundred. She was not used to spending much larger sums on art, although she had done so before. This, though, was special. She nodded her assent. 'Will you try?'

'I'll do my best,' said Guy. 'I'll get a condition report and check that everything's all right. Then we can go for it, if you like. Give me an upper limit.'

She closed her eyes and saw, rather to her surprise, her mother, her *sainted American mother* as she called her. 'Don't miss your chances in this life,' her mother had said to her. And now she was saying it again.

'Thirty . . .' she hesitated. Her sainted American mother had something to say. *Thirty-eight.*

'Yes?'

'A hammer price of thirty-eight thousand. Let's not go any higher than that.'

Guy took the catalogue and made a note in the margin. 'We should be all right,' he said.

Isabel looked at her watch. Grace was looking after Charlie for a couple of hours; she had taken him to see her friend who had a child of the same age. She would be back, she said, at two, and Isabel wanted to be at home when they returned.

'I have to get back,' she said, rising to her feet. 'When is the sale?'

'Six weeks from now,' said Guy. 'Plenty of time. It's down in London, and so we'll bid by phone. If you change your mind, let me know.'

10

'I won't change it.'

Guy knew that she would not. He knew Isabel reasonably well, and he had noticed two things about her. She told the truth, and she was as good as her word. He too rose to his feet, and as he did so, an elderly woman who had been sitting at a nearby table leaned over and addressed him.

'Mr Peploe? You are Mr Peploe, aren't you?'

Guy inclined his head. 'Yes.'

'I just wanted you to know how much I like your paintings,' said the woman. 'Those lovely pictures of the island of Iona. And Mull too. So striking.'

Isabel bit her lip.

'I'm afraid they're not mine,' said Guy politely. 'My grandfather. Samuel Peploe. He painted them.'

The woman looked surprised. 'Really? Well, doesn't time pass? My goodness. Well, I still want you to know that I like them very much indeed, even if it was your grandfather, not you.'

Guy thanked her politely; he avoided catching Isabel's eye. Once outside, he looked at her, his eyes bright with amusement. 'Well!'

Isabel was thinking of the Raeburn, and of the woman and her granddaughter. We were all tied to one another – ourselves and those who came before us; this had been their city too, these streets their thoroughfares, these stone buildings their homes. The curious, anachronistic mistake of the woman in Glass & Thompson merely showed that the barriers between present and past could be porous. Isabel had closed her eyes and seen her mother; as easily might she look into the mirror and see something in the shape of her nose, or the line of her brow, that she might discern in the two sitters in that Raeburn portrait. We were ourselves, but we were others too; our past written on us like lines drawn on a palimpsest, or the artist's rough sketch beneath the surface of a painting. And little Charlie – she saw herself in him sometimes, in the way his mouth turned when he smiled; and her father was there, too, in Charlie's eyes, which were like two sparkling little pools of grey and green.

She looked at her watch; she would have to rush to be home when Charlie arrived. She wanted to be there in the hall, to take him from Grace and to hold him tightly against her, which he allowed, but only for a few seconds, before he began to struggle to escape her embrace. That was the lot of the mother of sons; one embraced and held them, but even in their tenderness they were struggling to get away, and would.

# 2

The next day was a working day for Isabel. As editor –
and now owner – of the *Review of Applied Ethics*, she
could determine her own working patterns, but only to an
extent. The journal was quarterly, which might have led outsiders to think that Isabel's job could hardly be onerous. Such
outsiders would be wrong – as outsiders usually are about
most things. Although three months intervened between the
appearance of each issue of the journal, those three months
were regulated by a series of chores that were as regular as
the tides, and as unforgiving. Papers had to be sent out for
review and, if accepted for publication, edited. The professors
of philosophy who wrote these papers were, as Isabel had discovered, only human; they made mistakes in their grammar –
egregious mistakes in some cases even if in others only minor
solecisms. She corrected most of these, trying not to seem too
pedantic in the process. She allowed the collective plural: *if you
wish to reform a person you should tell them* – Isabel allowed the *them*
because there were those who objected strongly to gendered

pronouns. So you could not tell *him* in such circumstances, but would have to tell *him or her*, which became ungainly and awkward, and sounded like the punctilious language of the legal draughtsman. She also allowed infinitives to be split, which they were with great regularity, because that rule was now almost universally ignored and its authority, anyway, was questionable. Who established that precept anyway? Why not split an infinitive if one wanted to? The sense was as easily understood whether or not the infinitive was sundered apart or left inviolate.

But it was not just the editing of papers that took up her time. An important part of each issue was the review section, where four or five recent books in the field of ethics were reviewed at some length, and a few others, less favoured, were given brief notices. Then there was a short column headed *Books Received*, which listed other books that had been sent by publishers and were not going to be given a review. It was an ignominious fate for a book, but it was better than nothing. At least the journal acknowledged the fact that the book had been published, which was perhaps as much as some authors could hope for. Some books, even less favoured, got not even that; they fell leaden from the presses, unread, unremarked upon by anyone. Yet somewhere, behind those unreadable tomes, there was an author, the proud parent of that particular book, for whom it might even be the crowning achievement of a career; and all that happened on publication was silence, a profound and unfathomable silence.

That morning, four large padded envelopes were sitting on Isabel's desk in her large Victorian house in Merchiston. She closed the study door behind her, and looked at her desk. The four packages were clearly books – they had that look to them – and several other envelopes which her housekeeper, Grace, had

14

retrieved from the floor of the hall were just as evidently papers submitted for publication. It would take her until lunchtime to deal with these, she decided; Jamie had a free morning – no bassoon pupils and no rehearsals – which meant that he could devote his time to his son. They were going to Blackford Pond, where the ducks were a source of infinite fascination to Charlie. Then they would go somewhere else, he said, but he had yet to decide where. 'Charlie will have views,' he said. 'He'll tell me.'

Charlie now spoke quite well, in primitive sentences with a subject – as often as not himself – and a verb, usually in the present tense but occasionally in the past. His past tense, Isabel had noticed, had a special ring to it. 'It is a special past tense he uses,' she said to Jamie. 'It is the *past regretful*. The past regretful is used to express regret over what has happened. *All gone* is a past regretful, as was *Ducks eaten all bread*.' He still talked about olives, of course; *olive* had been his first word, and his appetite for olives was as strong as ever. *Olives nice* he had said to Isabel the previous day, and she too thought that they were nice. They had then looked at one another, Charlie staring at his mother with the intense gaze of childhood. She had waited for him to say something more, but he had not. They had said everything there was to say about olives, it seemed, and so she bent forward and kissed him lightly on his forehead.

She thought of that now as she surveyed her desk. She sighed; she was a mother, but she was also an editor, and a philosopher, and she had to work. Settling herself at her desk, she opened the first of the book parcels. Two books tumbled out, accompanied by a compliments slip on which a careless hand had scribbled *For favour of a review*. Underneath was the date of publication and a request that no review should appear

15

before then. That, thought Isabel, was easily enough complied with, given that journal reviews were sometimes published as much as two years after publication. She herself had reviewed a book eighteen months after publication and had only discovered after her review had been published that the author had died six months previously. It was not a good book, and in her review she had written that she felt that the author's next book on the subject would be much better. Worse than that, she had commented on a certain lifelessness in the prose. Well, he was dead; perhaps he was dying when he wrote the book. She shuddered at the memory. She had tried to be charitable, but she had not been charitable enough. Remember that, she said to herself; remember that in your dealings with others – they may be dying.

The two books looked interesting enough. One was on the moral implications of being a twin; the second was on the notion of fairness in economic judgements. She was not greatly excited by the economics book – that would be *received*, she thought . . . unless the author was dying, of course. She turned to the back flap and looked at the photograph of the author. He looked young, she decided, and healthy enough to write another book, which might get a full review. He could be placed in the *received* pile without risk of . . . she was about to say *injustice* to herself, when she realised she was being unjust. Just because she was not particularly interested in discussions of fairness in economics, that did not mean that others would not be. No, she would promote the book to the *Brief Notice* section. That was fair. As for the twins book, on opening it, she saw this sentence: 'Because moral obligation comes with closeness, there is a case for saying that the twin owes a greater duty to his or her twin than is owed by non-twins to their siblings.' She frowned.

16

Why? She flicked through several pages and read, at random, 'Of the many dilemmas confronting the twin, a particularly demanding one is the decision whether or not to tell one's twin of a medical diagnosis received. If one twin is diagnosed with a genetic disease, for example a form of cancer in which there is a strong familial element, then the other twin should know.' That, said Isabel to herself, is not a dilemma. You tell.

The twins book would have to be reviewed, and it occurred to Isabel that it would be interesting to have it reviewed by somebody who was a twin. But the twin would have to be a philosopher, and she was not sure if she knew any person answering that description. The author, perhaps, might know; she would write to him and ask him. Of course she could not commit herself to any name that he suggested – authors could not choose their reviewers – but it would be a start.

She opened the next parcel and extracted from it a slender book bound in blue. Tucked into it was a folded letter, which she extracted and opened. She saw the heading of the note-paper first and caught her breath. Then she read it.

The letter came from Professor Lettuce, the previous chairman of the *Review*'s editorial board and friend and collaborator of Professor Christopher Dove, the closest thing to an enemy that Isabel was aware of possessing. She had not chosen Dove as an enemy – he had assumed that role himself, and had revealed a ruthless streak in the process. He had recently accused Isabel of publishing a plagiarised article, but had been seen off. Lettuce had initially backed him, but had been persuaded by Isabel to change his ways – 'I have been a foolish Lettuce' was his memorable remark on that occasion. Now, it appeared that Dove and Lettuce were friends again, because here was Lettuce sending Isabel a new book by Dove and offering to review it.

Dear Isabel (wrote Lettuce),

I hope that this finds you well and that the *Review* is thriving in your capable hands. Our mutual friend (*our mutual friend,* Isabel muttered *sotto voce*) Chris Dove (*Chris!*) has, as you may know, written a rather interesting new book. I'm not sure if the publishers have sent you a copy – perhaps they have – but at the risk of burdening you with numerous copies, here is another one. I thought I might offer to review it for you, and have started penning a few thoughts, if that's all right with you. I'll do about two thousand words because I think that this is a work that deserves a decent discussion. I'm a bit pressed at the moment – this wretched research assessment business is such a burden – and Dolly (*Dolly Lettuce, his wife,* thought Isabel. *Poor woman. Dolly!*) is in the middle of making redecoration plans for our house at Wimbledon, so all is rather fraught on the domestic front – but I should be able to get it done by the end of the month and will send it along then. Thanks so much for agreeing to this, and please – *please* – do get in touch with me when you wrench yourself away from the provinces and come to London. Lunch will be on me.

All best,

Robert Lettuce.

Isabel felt the discomfort of being outraged but not being sure of which cause of her outrage was the more significant. Lettuce had casually insulted Scotland – which was *not* a province of England, but a country – and an old one at that – within a union with England. Nothing could be more calculated to annoy a Scotswoman, and Lettuce should have known that. But that was merely a matter of personal pride, which Isabel could swallow easily enough; it was more difficult for her to deal with the breathtaking arrogance of his assumption that he could write a review without being asked. He thanked her for agreeing to publish his review – well, she had not agreed and felt highly inclined not to do so, and she would not be bought off with a breezy invitation to lunch in London.

She would write to Lettuce, she decided, and thank him for offering to review Dove's book, but would say that she must – very reluctantly – decline his offer because . . . She thought of reasons. It would be tempting to say that it was because Dove's book was not of sufficient interest to merit a review – that was *very* tempting. Or she might say that she had decided to review the book herself. That was perhaps even more tempting, because it would give her the chance to cast Dove's book into the outer darkness that it undoubtedly deserved. 'This slight contribution to the literature,' she might write, 'is unlikely to find many readers.' Or, 'An effort to elucidate a difficult topic – courageous, yes, but unfortunately a failure.'

She stopped herself. Such thoughts, she told herself, were crude fantasies of revenge. Dove had plotted against her and would have succeeded in hounding her out of her job had she not had the resources to buy the *Review* from under his nose, and then get rid not only of him but also of Lettuce, who had been his co-conspirator. Dove had planned her removal, but that did not mean that she should stoop to his level and seek revenge by writing a critical review of his book. That would be quite wrong.

She looked up at the ceiling. One of the drawbacks to being

a philosopher was that you became aware of what you should not do, and this took from you so many opportunities to savour the human pleasure of revenge or greed or sheer fantasising. Well might St Augustine have said *Make me chaste, but not just yet*; that was how Isabel felt. And yet she could not; she could not let herself experience the pleasure of getting her own back on Dove because it was, quite simply, always wrong to get one's own back on another. It was her duty to *forgive* Dove and, if one were to be really serious about it, to go further than that and to *love* him. Hate the acts of Doves not Doves themselves, she muttered; they said that about sin, did they not? Hate the sin, not the sinner.

She put aside Lettuce's letter and picked up Dove's book. She read the title, *Freedom and Choice: the Limits of Responsibility in a Role-Fixated World*. She wrinkled her nose. Was the world really role-fixated? Freedom of choice, though, was a subject in which she was interested and indeed she had written on the subject when she was still a graduate research fellow. Turning to the end of the book, she found an annotated bibliography. She could see that Dove had been assiduous in his marshalling of the literature, and there, yes, there were her two papers on this subject. And after the first of these – a paper that had been published in the *Journal of Philosophy*, and which had been fairly widely cited – was Dove's annotation. He had used only one word: *Unreliable*.

Jamie returned at twelve. Charlie had fallen asleep in his pushchair – a tiny bundle of humanity in Macpherson tartan rompers and green shoes. The rompers were damp across the chest with orange juice and childish splutterings; the shoes had a thin crust of mud on them. She smiled; an active morning with his father. She kissed them both; Charlie lightly on his brow so as not to awaken him; Jamie on the mouth; and he held her, prolonging their embrace.

'I've missed you,' he said.

She looked surprised. 'Missed me this morning?'

'Yes. I wish that you had been with us. We saw the ducks. In fact we had a really intense time with the ducks. We watched them for half an hour.'

She smiled. 'They're obviously fascinating when you're . . .' She pointed down at Charlie. 'When you're that size. Think of what they must look to him. Massive.'

Jamie followed her gaze. 'He's out for the count. Should we leave him?'

'Yes, let him sleep.' She drew Jamie aside. 'I wanted to ask you something.'

She took him into her study and showed him Dove's book. Jamie took it from her and looked at the title on the cover.

'Christopher Dove,' he said. 'Your friend.'

'It was sent to me this morning by Professor Lettuce. Can you believe that?'

Jamie shrugged. 'I've never been able to tell them apart. Lettuce is the large, pompous one, isn't he? And Dove's the tall one with the creepy manner?'

'You describe them very well,' said Isabel. 'Yes, that's them.'

'Oh well,' said Jamie. 'So Dove's written this book. You don't want me to read it, do you?'

Isabel explained about Lettuce's letter and his completely unwarranted assumptions. 'He shows the most amazing brass neck,' she said. 'And I really don't know what to do. That's what I wanted to discuss with you.'

Jamie lowered himself into one of the easy chairs in Isabel's study. 'Say no. Send the book back and tell them that you decide which books are to be reviewed. Be polite, but firm.'

She knew that was perfectly sound advice. Lettuce should not be left in any doubt as to the position; a fudge of any sort would simply mean that he would proceed to write the review regardless and it would then be difficult for her to turn it down. And yet, and yet . . . She looked at Jamie. She could not imagine his being involved in a fight of any sort – he was just too gentle for that. And too nice. He was also truthful: he said what he was thinking and rarely agonised – as she did – before coming up with a view.

'You're probably right,' she said. 'But I'm afraid that I'm worried about something.'

Jamie raised an eyebrow. 'You're not scared of Lettuce, are you?'

'Of course not. No. But I'm worried about my reasons for turning him down. What will he conclude? Don't you imagine that he'll think me petty and vindictive? And others might think that too. If Dove goes around saying that I ignored his book for reasons of personal spite. And he could say that, you know.'

'Yes, he could. But do you really have to worry about what Dove says? People won't necessarily believe him.'

She thought about this. She wanted it to be true, but she did not think it was. People were only too ready to believe things that were manifestly untrue. When it came to remarks that showed others in a bad light, people were happy to believe things that showed others to be weak or flawed in some way; we believed that of them because it made us feel better; it was as simple as that.

'You see,' said Isabel, 'Dove describes one of my papers as

unreliable. He says so in the bibliography to this new book of his.'

Jamie looked surprised. 'Unreliable? Dove said that?'

Isabel nodded. Her dislike of Dove was growing; the slow-burning qualities of anger meant that she was only now beginning to feel the impact of that one, dismissive word: unreliable. How dare he? And what did he mean by it?

She closed her eyes. Anger disfigured. She told herself that, took a deep breath, and then told herself it once more. We are disfigured by anger and must avoid it. We must, no matter how much we seethe.

'I think I should let him write it,' she said.

'In spite of this unreliability business?'

'If I show him that I am happy to publish criticisms of my own work, maybe that will make him think again.'

'Think again about you?'

'Yes. About me.'

Jamie rose to his feet. He put Dove's book down on the table and walked across the room to Isabel. He embraced her. He kissed her with a sudden, urgent passion. What have I done, she wondered, either to provoke this or to deserve this? She returned his kiss. It did not matter about Dove; it did not matter about Lettuce; they were nothing to her, now that she had this exquisite, gentle young man who had come so unexpectedly into her life. She had everything, while Dove and Lettuce had nothing. So she should forgive them and publish Lettuce's review, even if it turned out to be – as she thought it would - a paean of praise to Dove and all his works. Let him do that; she had everything and could afford to be generous.

She disengaged from their embrace. 'I'll publish it,' she said. 'I've decided.'

'If that's what you want to do,' said Jamie. He looked at her tenderly. 'You know, you're a tremendously kind person. It's one of the reasons I love you. Your kindness.'

She was taken aback. 'There are many people much kinder than I am.'

He looked doubtful. 'Name one.'

'You,' she said.

He cooked lunch – a light bowl of pasta with a few mushrooms; a salad. They ate in the kitchen, talking about a concert that he was due to be playing in the following week. She was beginning to know her way around the politics of music; she understood now the quirks of conductors, of concert hall managements, of temperamental, prickly administrators. Not enough effort, Jamie said, had been made to advertise this concert.

'And then, when they get a disappointing turnout, they wonder why,' he said.

'People can't attend things they don't know are happening,' said Isabel. And then laughed; it was such an obvious thing to say.

Jamie agreed.

She suddenly thought of something. 'Have there been occasions when the players forgot to go?' said Isabel.

Jamie's smile disappeared. 'Don't,' he said.

She looked at him inquisitively. 'You?'

He looked down at his plate. 'I can't even bring myself to think about it,' he said.

She could see that he was distressed; what had started as a light-hearted conversation had become serious.

'You mustn't let it worry you,' she said quietly. 'Who

amongst us hasn't inadvertently done something awful?' She thought of her review of the dying man's book. 'We have to forgive ourselves, you know.'

He nodded. 'They had to cancel. They had to refund the ticket money.'

'Forgive yourself.'

'Really?'

'Yes. People punish themselves – sometimes for years. But it's not always necessary. Forgiveness allows everybody to start again, not to be burdened with a whole lot of old business.'

She thought of those studies of conversion that showed how people turned to a new faith or a new ideology to get rid of the burden of the past. They became new people, they thought, and could forget about what they had done before. She was not sure whether that was self-forgiveness or self-invention; they were different things, really, and she could not help but feel that self-invention was an easy way out. *Not me*, it said. *A different person did that.* Which could be quite true. We did become different people as we grew; the child is not the same person as the man.

She looked at Jamie thoughtfully. 'What were you like as a little boy?' she asked.

He shrugged. 'A little boy,' he said. 'You know . . . A little boy.'

She tried to imagine him at the age of seven. 'Your hair?'

'Same. And you?'

'I wore my hair in pigtails,' she said. 'I had a doll called Baby Isabel and we had matching dresses. If I put on a gingham dress, then Baby Isabel wore the same.'

Jamie smiled. 'Baby Isabel! What a lovely name. You must have loved her. Did you?'

25

Isabel looked away. 'Baby Isabel was left on a bus,' she said. 'I cried and cried. They tried to get me to pay attention to one of my other dolls, but it was Baby Isabel I wanted.'

He was silent. Then Jamie spoke. 'You know something, Isabel? I murdered my teddy. I threw him over the Dean Bridge – you know, right over the Water of Leith, where the suicides jump. I threw my teddy over the edge. I don't know why I did it. I suppose I might have wanted to see him fall, but the parapet was too high and I couldn't. That was the end of him. My mother said, "Now you've done it. That's the end of Teddy."' He paused. 'I've never talked about it. Never.'

She reached out to touch him. 'I think you can forgive yourself for that, too.'

He rose to clear the lunch things away. 'All right, I forgive myself.'

'Good.'

She went out into the hall, where they had left Charlie to continue his sleep. She lifted him up gently; she would transfer him to his bed. She was aware that she and Jamie had experienced a moment of intimate disclosure in the kitchen, talking about their childhoods, about the little things that might seem inconsequential but that were obviously buried somewhere in the mind where they could be far more powerful than one might imagine. The possessions of childhood are sometimes loved with astonishing intensity; precious to their owners in spite of their simplicity or raggedness. Baby Isabel was a cheap little doll, but adored with passion, as, no doubt, was that betrayed teddy.

As she carried the still sleeping Charlie upstairs, Isabel found herself wondering why Jamie had thrown his teddy over the Dean Bridge. He was punishing him no doubt – or perhaps he was punishing himself. And if he was punishing himself, what for? She would ask a psychotherapist friend who knew all about such things. This friend had once said to Isabel that we punished ourselves for all sorts of reasons, but, for the most part, we did not deserve it. 'In fact,' Isabel had said, 'I wonder who truly deserves punishment anyway. What good does it do to punish a person? All that does is add to the pain of the world.'

Her friend had stared at Isabel. 'Yes,' she said. And then, after a further few minutes of thought, she had said yes again. 'That sounds so right,' she said. 'And yet I suspect, Isabel, that you are very wrong.' And Isabel thought: yes I am. She's right; I'm wrong.

# 3

Cat had asked Isabel to help out at the delicatessen the next morning, and Isabel, as she always did, agreed. She knew that her niece only asked for her assistance when she really needed it, and in this case it was the best of reasons: a medical appointment.

Isabel could not help but sound anxious. The news that anybody has a medical appointment is often taken as a sign of the worst; that was entirely natural, even if people saw doctors for all sorts of innocent purposes. 'Is everything all right?' she asked. And thought, *I could not bear to lose you.*

'I'm seeing a dermatologist,' said Cat. 'I have a spot and the GP said that . . .'

'Oh, Cat . . .'

'Listen, don't panic. People have spots. She said that it looked absolutely fine to her but she suggested that I have it checked.'

'I know, I know. It's just that . . .' And here she almost said *I could not bear to lose you*, but did not. 'It's just that I always worry when people have medical appointments.'

'Well don't,' said Cat. 'Anyway, could you . . .'

'I'll be there,' said Isabel. 'Do you need me to open up?'

Eddie would do that, explained Cat, but it would be helpful if Isabel were able to arrive shortly thereafter. 'He's all right to begin with, but he gets really anxious if he's in charge by himself for too long. You know how he is.'

Isabel did know. She was fond of Eddie, whom she had known for some years now, and she was used to his vulnerability, even if she had never been able to understand it. It seemed strange to her that a young man who looked robust enough should be so lacking in confidence as to be incapable of being left in charge of a delicatessen. But she realised that this was what anxiety was like – it knew no rhyme or reason; just as a fear of the dark cannot be assuaged by the pointing out that there was nothing there, anxiety could be without foundation.

Something had happened to Eddie – some dark thing – that Cat knew about, but that she would not explain to Isabel. Isabel had not pressed her; if Eddie had told her in confidence, then she would not want Cat to break that confidence. She could guess, though, and she assumed it was to do with sex, and with the shame that went with that. Her heart went out to Eddie; she wanted to wrap her arms about him and say to him that he should not feel ashamed, that whatever had happened to him was not his fault, it was no doing of his, and was no reflection on him. She wanted to say to him that such things happened to both men and women and that it did not mean he was less of a man for it. But she realised that there must have been people who had already said all these things to Eddie and it had made no difference. You did not erase horror and shame with a few words; it did not work that way.

Eddie had made some progress, of course. There had been a

girlfriend, and even if she was not what Isabel might have wished for Eddie – she was a Goth, a follower of a fashion for pallid looks and dark clothes – he seemed to grow while she was with him. She had gone, Isabel understood, and she did not think that she had been replaced.

'Isabel?'

'Sorry. I was lost in thought.'

Cat was used to this. Isabel thought too much, she felt. 'I said: will Jamie be able to look after Charlie?'

Isabel was moderately surprised by Cat's question. Her niece had experienced great difficulty in coming to terms with the fact that it was her aunt – even if Isabel was a very young aunt – who had taken up with her former boyfriend, and there had been a time when she would have scrupulously avoided any mention of Jamie's name. But that had seemed to become much easier, as this question revealed.

'Yes,' she said. 'Jamie will do it, or Grace can if Jamie is teaching. Either way Charlie will be entertained.'

Arrangements were made, and that morning shortly after nine Isabel made her way along Merchiston Crescent to the delicatessen on Bruntsfield Place. It was a warm morning – June had eased itself into July with a grudging rising of temperature – and the foliage in the gardens along her route was in riot. She dodged a particularly ebullient climbing rose that had sent tendrils into the path of pedestrians; indeed, on one of these tendrils, snagged on a vicious-looking thorn, was a small fragment of blue material. A passerby had been caught, Isabel decided, and had lost a bit of a blouse or a shirt. She stopped, and gingerly took the piece of cloth from the thorn. No, she decided, if the owner of the garden was not going to cut back this impediment to the safe use of the pavement then she would, before anyone lost an eye on one of those thorns. Reaching up, she took hold of the rose where it crossed the iron railings of the fence and bent it sharply to one side. The plant gave, but not enough; now the tendril pointed down towards the ground, discouraged but not detached.

'Excuse me!'

Isabel gave a start as she heard the voice from the garden.

'Excuse me, what do you think you're doing?'

A man came into view in the garden; a man somewhere in his fifties, she thought, holding a garden rake.

'Your climbing rose had sent a shoot out over the pavement,' said Isabel. 'It's a bit dangerous, I'm afraid. I was just pruning it for you.'

The man took a step forward. He was wearing a khaki shirt and there were large damp patches under the armpits. His complexion was florid, rather puffed. She thought that he looked as if he had suffered a stroke at some point, perhaps not all that long ago.

'You can't do that and that,' he said gruffly. 'That's my rose and rose. You can't break its stems like that. Who do you think you are, are?'

'It was over the pavement. It's already caught somebody. Look – here's a piece of cloth I've taken off one of the thorns. And it could cause real damage. Somebody could get poked in the eye.'

The man took another step forward. She could hear his breathing now; it was shallow and rather fast. He was not healthy, she thought.

'Rubbish,' he said, his voice rising. 'Rubbish and rubbish. You can't take other people's and people's roses and break and break them. You can't and can't.'

31

Isabel said nothing. The curious repetition of words that marked his speech was strangely unsettling.

'So, so just you leave my roses and roses alone,' said the man.

Isabel took a step backwards. She looked at the garden rake in his hand. 'I'm sorry,' she said. 'Maybe you could prune them just a bit.'

The man frowned. 'Prune and prune,' he said. 'Yes.'

She walked away. She felt raw after the encounter; he was clearly suffering from a neural condition of some sort, and she should not blame him for remonstrating with her, but it still left her feeling uneasy. The speech difficulties suggested that somewhere in his brain there were lesions or misplaced connections, or perhaps connections that were not there any more. She looked about her, at the stone buildings and the metal shapes of the cars parked along the road. All that was so solid and resilient, while our brains were such soft and living things. A few cells went out of order, forgot their function, or died, and that marvellous gift of language went awry. A few more cells might go, and then a blood vessel, and that brought the hammer blows of death. Just a tiny membrane, the sides of a fragile vessel, stood between us and annihilation and disaster.

When she reached the delicatessen she found Eddie behind the counter. He smiled cheerfully.

'Cat left a note,' he said. 'Thanks for coming.'

She told him about what had happened on the way in. 'There was a rose that had grown across the pavement – sent out one of those long shoots. It was full of thorns, and so I tried to break it off. Its owner got very excited about it. He spoke rather strangely – repeated himself.'

'Oh, I know him,' said Eddie. 'He comes in here. He asks for cheese and cheese. And when I give him his change he says, "And thank you and thank you and you." It's weird.'

'Who is he?' asked Isabel.

'He told me his name once,' said Eddie. 'I just remember the first part. Gerald, I think. Something like that. He told me his life history, but there were people waiting to be served and they started looking impatient. He worked in Amsterdam for many years, he said. He was something to do with the bank.'

'Which bank?' asked Isabel.

Eddie shrugged. 'Some bank. His wife is Dutch, he said. But I've never seen her.'

'It's a very strange speech disorder,' said Isabel. 'Very curious.'

'It's like echolalia,' said Eddie.

Isabel looked at him in surprise. 'What's that?'

Eddie wiped some crumbs of cheese off the cutting board. 'My grandfather had it. He repeated everything you said to him. If you said, "I've been to town" he would say, "To town". Or if you said, "It's raining hard," he'd say "Raining hard". He was like an echo, you see.'

'You see.'

'Yes,' said Eddie. 'That's the idea.'

'Strange,' said Isabel.

'Strange,' echoed Eddie, and then laughed. 'He wasn't unhappy. I don't think he knew that he was doing it.'

Isabel wondered whether the man with the garden rake was unhappy; she thought that he probably was. But there was no time to speculate about that, as two customers had walked in at the door and both, it seemed, wanted attention.

Cat arrived at half past eleven. The early part of the morning had been busy but it had slackened off and the delicatessen was

33

now quieter. Isabel looked at her niece, hoping to see some sign of how the medical consultation had gone.

'Is everything all right?' she asked, lowering her voice so that Eddie should not hear.

Cat shrugged. 'Yes, fine.'

Isabel smiled with relief. 'So they were not worried about the spot?'

'I don't think so,' said Cat. 'They sliced it out – it was pretty small. He injected novocaine so I felt nothing.'

'And everything was fine?'

'They've sent it off to the pathology lab,' said Cat.

Isabel's heart gave a lurch. 'Oh . . .'

'It's standard procedure, Isabel,' said Cat. 'You mustn't worry. They have to do that if they take anything off. Just to be sure. He said that it looked fine to him but they just make sure.'

'Of course.'

Cat began to undo the strings of Isabel's apron. 'So why don't you give me this and you go and sit down. I'll bring you coffee. There's yesterday's *Repubblica* on the rack over there. You can practise your Italian.' Cat was given the newspaper by one of the staff from the Italian Consulate who called in every day on the way back from work. She did not read it herself, but quite a number of the customers who dropped in for coffee read it, or pretended to read it. 'One or two of them can't read Italian,' Cat had said. 'They'd like to, but they can't. So they sit there pretending to read – it makes them look sophisticated, I suppose. Or so they hope.'

Isabel did read Italian; if she had any difficulty with *La Repubblica* it was with understanding the complexities of Italian politics. But that, she suspected, was the case with everybody's politics. And it was not just a linguistic difference; she could never understand how American politics worked. It appeared that the Americans went to the polls every four years to elect a President who had wide powers. But then, once he was in office, he might find himself unable to do any of the things he had promised to do because he was blocked by other politicians who could veto his legislation. What was the point, then, of having an election in the first place? Did people not resent the fact that they spoke on a subject and then nothing could be done about it? But politics had always seemed an impenetrable mystery to her in her youth. She remembered what her mother had once said to her about some American politician to whom they were distantly related. 'I don't greatly care for him,' she said. 'Pork barrel.'

Isabel had thought, as a child, that this was a bit unkind. Presumably he could not help looking like a pork barrel. But then, much later, she had come to realise that this was how politics worked. The problem was, though, that politics might work, but government did not.

She picked up *La Repubblica* and went to sit at the far table. A few minutes later, Eddie brought her a large cup of milky coffee. 'Just as you like it,' he said.

She thanked him and continued to read the newspaper. A magistrate in Naples had been found floating in the sea; the Government in Rome announced that it took a very serious view of this and would be dispatching further judicial resources. 'We are not going to be intimidated by the Mafia,' a spokesman said. And also in Naples, an unidentified source close to 'powerful interests' was quoted as saying that this unfortunate event had nothing to do with anybody in the city and merely underlined the need for swimmers to take great care when entering the sea. Isabel winced at the cynicism. And yet such people –

such powerful interests – were everywhere getting closer and closer to the seats of power. There was corruption at every turn, and those who stood for honesty and integrity were more and more vulnerable, more and more isolated amongst the hordes of people who simply had no moral sense. And it was not just Italy; it was everywhere, even here in Scotland, that the lines between integrity and compromise were being eroded. Even here in Scotland, with the moral capital of Presbyterian rectitude in the bank, there were rich businessmen who thought they could buy the attention of those in power, and who did so, sometimes quite openly. And then, when people queried this or protested, the politicians in question simply brushed off suggestions that there was anything improper in the arrangement. Perhaps they were simply being honest; money spoke in every dialect, in every language, and it was rare that anybody said that they could not hear it. All human affairs, Isabel thought, are rotten; perhaps political morality was just a question of trying to limit the rottenness.

She put the paper down and reached for her coffee cup. She gave a start. There was a woman standing in front of her; she had not seen her from behind the paper, and it was a shock.

'Isabel Dalhousie?'

She racked her brains to remember where she had seen this woman.

'Yes,' she said brightly. It was an unusual, rather angular face, not one that was easy to forget. 'Hello.'

She feared that her lack of recognition would show, and it did. 'You may not remember me,' said the woman. 'Do you mind if I join you?'

Isabel indicated the empty seat on the other side of the table. 'Please.'

The woman lowered herself into the chair. She was well-dressed, Isabel observed, with an understatement suggestive of both good taste and funds: it was not ostentatious clothes that were really expensive, it was quiet clothes that exhausted the credit card.

'Forgive me for interrupting,' the woman began. 'Jillian Mackinlay. We met at . . .'

It came back to Isabel. 'At the Stevensons'. Yes, I remember. Sorry, I was having difficulty.' People could tell when you were having difficulty placing them; it was best, Isabel thought, to be frank and apologise. And apology was usually necessary; *I can't for the life of me recall who you are* may have the virtue of honesty, but it was no balm to the injured feelings that a failure to be remembered may otherwise cause. If we remember somebody, then how can they forget us? Are we that forgettable?

Jillian nodded. 'I saw Susie the other day at a concert. She spoke about you, actually. She said something about how you had helped somebody she knew.'

Isabel was uncertain what to say. She helped people occasionally, but it was not something she proposed to wear on her sleeve.

'Yes,' Jillian continued. 'And I wondered . . . well, I was going to get in touch with you. And then I saw you here and I thought that it might be easier to speak face to face rather than to telephone you.' She paused, and looked at Isabel as if she was waiting for encouragement.

'It's better to see the person you're speaking to, I think,' said Isabel, adding, 'as a general rule. So often today one is actually speaking to a machine somewhere – a very sympathetic machine, of course, but a machine none the less. Do you mind if I ask – are you in some sort of trouble?'

Jillian blushed. 'No, good heavens, no. Not me. Not personally.'

Isabel felt relieved. It had crossed her mind that Jillian was about to make some sort of personal disclosure — of an errant husband, perhaps, or some other domestic difficulty, and she would have to explain that she would like to be able to help, but . . . Jamie's words came back to her, 'Listen, Isabel, I know that you feel you have to help, but don't get involved — please don't — in other people's matrimonial problems. It rarely helps.' He was right. People with matrimonial difficulties usually wanted allies, not advisers.

'Well,' said Isabel, 'I don't know whether I can do anything, and of course I don't know what the problem is. If you'd care to tell me.' She smiled encouragingly at Jillian; there was awkwardness in the other woman's manner and she wanted to reassure her. At the same time she thought, *I have enough on my plate. I have Charlie. I have the* Review. *I have Jamie. Brother Fox* . . .

Jillian signalled to Eddie, who came to take her order for coffee. As Eddie left, she lowered her voice and said, 'That young man — there's something lost about him, don't you think?'

Isabel was cautious. 'Eddie?'

'Oh, you know him?'

'Yes. My niece owns this place, you see. I occasionally work here.'

Jillian blushed again. 'I've been very tactless. Sorry.'

'Not at all. You're right about Eddie. But I think he's making progress. He's more confident. He's a nice young man.'

This seemed to please Jillian. 'Good. I see so many young people because of my husband's involvement with a school.

Teenage boys. And I think we sometimes don't realise just how hard it is for them these days. It's much easier for girls, I think. Boys are more confused. They've lost the role they used to have – you know, being tough and so on. Brawn means nothing now.'

'Quite.'

'So you often come across boys who are quite lost. They retreat into themselves or their cults. Skateboarders are an example of that. Or at least some of them are.'

Isabel thought about skateboarders. It was not an attractive group, with their lack of interest in anything much except their repetitive twirls and gymnastic tricks. They tended to be teenagers, though, and teenagers grew up, although sometimes one saw older skateboarders, almost into their thirties, overgrown boys stuck in the ways of youth. She shuddered. Certain groups of people made her shudder: extremists, with their ideologies of hate; the proud; the arrogant; the narcissistic socialites of celebrity culture. And yet all of these were *people*, and one should love people, or try to . . .

'Skateboarders are typical of the refuge cult,' said Jillian. 'They retreat into the group and don't really talk to anybody else.'

Isabel said that she thought that many teenagers did that, and not just skateboarders. Yes, that was true, Jillian said, but skateboarders were an extreme example. 'They block out the rest of the world, you know. They think that there are skaters and then there are the rest. It's that bad.' She waited a moment, and then added: 'I know about this, you see. Our son became one. He didn't talk to us for two and a half years. Just a few grunts. That was all.'

'But he came back?'

'Yes. He came back. But he had wasted those precious years

of youth. Think what he might have seen and done, instead of spending his time on streets, skating aimlessly. Just think.'

'We all have our ways of wasting time,' said Isabel. 'Think of golf . . . What's your son doing now?'.

'He works for a hedge fund.'

She could not help but smile. 'Oh.'

'Yes, it sounds ridiculous,' said Jillian. 'But one's children don't always turn out exactly as one hoped. Do you . . .'

'I have a son. Still very young. He has yet to . . . to disclose his hand.'

Eddie returned. He had made Isabel another cup of coffee too. On the top of the foam he had traced in chocolate powder the shape of a four-leaf clover. She studied the clover design and then looked up at him. 'It's good luck,' he said, and winked.

'Sweet,' said Jillian, after he had left them. She dipped a spoon into the top of her coffee and licked it. 'Do you mind if I call you Isabel?'

Isabel did not, although she was not sure about this woman. There was something imperious about her, something high-handed that made her doubt whether they could ever be close. If there was a clear division between friend and acquaintance, then Jillian, she decided, would remain an acquaintance.

'My husband, Alex, is on any number of committees,' Jillian said. 'He was a businessman before we retreated to a farm near Biggar, and he's been co-opted on to virtually every public body in Lanarkshire. I put up with it, and he seems to like it. He's pretty busy, as you can imagine.'

'What's the popular saying?' asked Isabel. 'If you want something done, ask a busy person.'

'True. And he gets things done. He's really good at that.'

40

Jillian paused to take a sip of her coffee. 'One of the things he does is serve on the board of governors of Bishop Forbes School. You know it? It's just outside West Linton.'

'Of course I do,' said Isabel. 'I was at school in Edinburgh. We used to get the boys from Bishop Forbes shipped in for school dances.'

'They still do that,' said Jillian. 'They send them in to dance with girls. Being a boys' school, they try to arrange some female contact for the boys. Not that the boys need much help in that respect.'

Isabel looked out of the window. She was remembering a school dance where one of the girls had claimed to have seduced a boy in the chemistry lab, having slipped away from the hall with him. They had not believed her, and had pressed her for details. She had burst into tears and accused them of ruining a beautiful experience for her. 'You're such a liar,' said one of the girls. And 'Wishful thinking,' said another. The cruelty of children.

Isabel brought herself back to what Jillian was now saying.

'Alex is the chairman of the board of governors, as it happens. It's his second term; I tried to get him to hand over to somebody else after he had done three years, but you know how some people are – they think they're indispensable. That, and a sense of duty.'

Isabel was trying to remember Jillian's husband. There had been a dozen or so people at the Stevensons' house that night, and she found it difficult. There had been a tall, rather distinguished-looking man who could well have been the chairman of a board of governors. He had talked to her about art, she thought; about Cowie. Yes, they had talked about a Cowie retrospective that the Dean Gallery had put on.

41

'Not that I would want him to give everything up,' Jillian went on. 'I can imagine nothing worse than having one's husband underfoot all day. So he carries on with my blessing, and I fulfil the role of chairman's wife as best as I can, although frankly I find school politics pretty stultifying. It's the pettiness. Any institution is like that, I suppose.

'The Principal is a very good man – Harold Slade. Maybe you know him. He rowed for Scotland in the Olympics years ago. Rather like that politician – what's his name? – Ming Campbell. He was an Olympic runner, wasn't he? Well, Harold announced that he wanted to take up the headship of an international school in Singapore. He wasn't going for the money – I think he was just ready for a change, which was fair enough. He had been Principal for twelve years, which is quite a long time for one person to hold the job. So we advertised, and Alex was the chairman of the appointment committee – naturally enough.'

Jillian sipped again at her coffee. 'We had rather more applications than we expected. Some of them were very good. One or two withdrew for various reasons, but eventually they put together a rather strong shortlist of three candidates, all of them from Scotland. We had expected to get some impressive applicants from England, but for some reason the English candidates were rather weak. So it's pretty much a local list, which makes it easier to get in references and so on. Alex likes to talk to referees face to face if he possibly can, and he's been able to do that since all three are Scottish.'

Isabel nodded. 'I suppose it's important to talk to people,' she said. 'It's hard to be honest in a written reference. You expect that the candidate will get hold of it one way or another. And then, if you've written something damning, there's all sorts of trouble. It's rather like doctors' notes. They can't write what they really think any more – the patient can see what's there.'

Jillian had views on this. 'And a good thing, too,' she said. 'Doctors used to write terrible things in the past. I had a friend who found out that she was described in her medical notes as a "dreadful woman".'

'And was she?' asked Isabel. She spoke quickly; it slipped out, and she immediately apologised. 'No, I don't really mean that. I mean . . .' She trailed off. There *were* dreadful people, and doctors had to deal with them.

'Not at all,' said Jillian. 'Maybe she's a bit *demanding*, but that's not the same as being dreadful.'

'No, of course not.'

'Anyway,' Jillian continued, 'it looked as if we'd find no difficulty in getting a very good person to take over, but then my husband received an anonymous letter. Normally he would throw such a thing straight into the wastepaper basket, but in this case there was something that stopped him from doing so.'

'It was about the candidates?'

'Yes. Well, yes and no. It was about one of the candidates. Unfortunately, it didn't say which one. It merely said that there was something about one of them that would cause the school considerable embarrassment if he were to be appointed. But it gave no further details.'

'A shot in the dark,' suggested Isabel. 'The writer of this letter could be trying it on, surely. It could just be a spoiler. Perhaps from one of the unsuccessful candidates. People get pretty upset about these things.'

'I thought that,' said Jillian. 'But there was something significant about this letter. It gave the names of all the candidates. So the person who wrote it must have seen the shortlist. And I can't imagine there were many of those. There were the members of the committee – and it's hardly likely to have been one of them. And . . . well, the school secretary, Miss Carty. She's one of those people you find in schools who never seem to have a first name, but it's Janet in her case. A rather mousy woman, probably unhappy about something or other.'

One might say that about most of us, thought Isabel. Most of us are unhappy about something or other.

'Anything else? Was there anything else in the letter?' she asked.

Jillian shook her head. 'No.'

'Typed?'

'No. Handwritten. In green ink.'

Isabel smiled. 'There's a popular view that green ink is favoured by the insane. No truth to it, no doubt. But people say that. They say that real cranks like green ink.'

Jillian reached for her cup again. She had said all she wished to say, it appeared, and she was waiting for Isabel's reaction.

'It must be rather worrying,' said Isabel. 'I can see that. But I don't know if I can say more than that.'

'Would you look into it?' asked Jillian.

'Well, I don't really see what I can do. I really don't.'

Jillian leaned forward. 'Please,' she said. 'We have to make an appointment. But we just can't risk appointing somebody who is going to come unstuck because of their past. We can't afford scandal – you do see that, don't you?'

Isabel said that she understood that reputation was important. But this did not seem to satisfy Jillian, who returned to the theme. 'I can't stress enough how important it is to avoid scandal,' she said. 'Education is competitive these days. Parents have

44

a choice. A whiff of something not quite right and we would lose students – we really would.'

'I understand. But, really, what do you expect me to do?'

Jillian lowered her voice. A young couple had come into the delicatessen and had taken a seat at a neighbouring table. The woman was looking at them in a way that suggested more than casual interest. 'We need a very discreet person – and I gather that you are just that. We need somebody to make enquiries and find out which of these three has . . . well, has a past.'

'We all have a past.'

Jillian brushed this aside. 'There are pasts and pasts.' She paused. 'Please help us. The last thing we could do is to get professional enquiry agents involved – imagine if that ever got out. So we need somebody like you – somebody who knows her way about Edinburgh, who understands the issues. You'd never be suspect. And I *have* done my homework on you – you have a reputation, you know, for helping people.'

Isabel stared down at the table. She had more than enough to do over the next few weeks. And yet she had never turned down a direct plea for help. Jillian was not to know it, of course, but Isabel found it very difficult indeed – practically impossible – to say to somebody in need of help that they would get no assistance from her.

'All right,' said Isabel.

Jillian reached out and took Isabel's hand and squeezed it. 'You're an angel.'

I'm not, thought Isabel. I'm weak.

'Look,' said Jillian. 'I'm not sure how you do these things, but why don't I send you a photocopy of each candidate's application? There's a curriculum vitae with each of them – that'll tell you all you need to know.'

'And more than I *should* know,' said Isabel.

Jillian looked blank. 'I don't see . . .'

'Confidentiality,' said Isabel.

Jillian laughed dismissively. 'Oh, we never bother with that.' She paused. 'Do you?'

Isabel looked at her in a bemused fashion. 'But you yourself said that you wanted me to do this because you didn't want it to get out. That suggests that you attach at least some importance to confidentiality.'

Jillian was brisk. 'Where necessary,' she said. 'But not otherwise.'

# 4

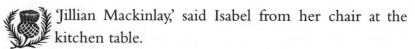'Jillian Mackinlay,' said Isabel from her chair at the kitchen table.

Jamie barely looked up from the stove. He was cooking dinner that night, and with Charlie safely tucked up in bed and asleep by now – he had been tired out by five o'clock and had had been given an early supper and bath – the house seemed quiet. Any sudden absence of children, Isabel noted, made the normal silences of the evening seem more pronounced; a small child could be a centre of noise, like a cyclone moving across the weather map, until suddenly, at bedtime, the storm subsided and quiet returned.

'Jillian who?'

'Mackinlay,' said Isabel. 'We met them at the Stevensons'. It was some time ago . . .' She thought quickly; in the lives of most of us there is a time before our partner and a time after our partner: in her case, BJ (before Jamie) and AJ (after Jamie) although AJ suggested that Jamie was in the past, which he was not, and so DJ (During Jamie) might be more appropriate. She

47

was sure that this meeting at the Stevensons' had been in the DJ years.

'Can't remember,' muttered Jamie.

Of course he could not, thought Isabel; they met so many people on the social round – such as it was – and one could not be expected to remember every conversation at every drinks or dinner party. Most such conversations were instantly forgettable anyway, merging into one another, smoothed out by banality.

'There's no reason for you to remember her. I almost didn't when I saw her this morning, but then she helpfully told me exactly who she was. People sense it when you haven't got a clue who they are.'

'Garlic,' said Jamie.

She looked at him quizzically. 'Garlic?'

'Sorry. I'm trying to get this right. I haven't put any garlic in and she said that I should. Or I think that she did.'

'She being?'

Jamie dipped a spoon into the contents of the pot and tasted the result. 'Mary Contini.'

'Check the recipe.'

He put down the spoon, shaking his head. 'I don't know where I put the book. It's somewhere, but I don't know . . . Do you think garlic makes a difference?'

Isabel smiled. 'Yes, of course. Garlic in a dish makes it taste garlicky.' She paused; what was wrong with Jamie this evening? 'Don't you agree? Whereas, dishes without garlic . . .'

Jamie sighed. 'Don't taste of garlic.'

She looked at him. The sigh was uncharacteristic; it suggested that he had found her comment tiresome, a weak attempt at humour.

'Do you want me to take over?' She had not asked him to

cook that evening – he had volunteered. He was a good cook, she had discovered, and unlike many men he seemed prepared to stick closely to the recipe – or most of the time at least. Men, she had noticed, were inclined to be slapdash in their measuring of quantities and even choice of ingredients; her father, who belonged to a generation of males who rarely ventured into the kitchen, had occasionally cooked but had been gloriously cavalier in his methods, substituting mint for basil and, on one famous occasion, onions for potatoes.

Jamie declined Isabel's offer, but not very graciously, she thought. He was rarely irritable, and there seemed to be something on his mind this evening. Should she ask him? She watched him at the stove. Yes, his body language gave it away; there was something tense about his position, as if he were feeling hostility to the task he was performing, as if he were poised to move away. He was standing, she thought, in the way of an opera singer about to stride off the stage in a display of high dudgeon.

'Should I . . .'

He did not let her finish. 'I'm fine. It's just that I wish I had the recipe to hand . . . Garlic.'

'Put it in. You can't go wrong with garlic.' You could, of course.

He mumbled something she did not catch. Then he gave the casserole dish a final stir, replaced the lid and turned to face her. 'This woman, Jillian what's-her-name – what about her?'

'Jillian Mackinlay. I met her today at the delicatessen. She came to sit at my table.'

Jamie walked over towards Isabel and pulled out a chair. 'Oh? Did you mind? I find it a bit irritating when I want to read something or just sit and think and somebody comes up.'

Isabel shook her head. 'No, I didn't mind.'

'And?' He hesitated, watching her closely. 'She didn't . . .' He sighed. 'She asked you to do something? Is that it?'

Isabel did not reply for a moment. She knew exactly what Jamie would think – and say – about this. He had advised her to stop what he called meddling – but it was *not* meddling, she felt. Meddling was interfering unasked; she was always asked. And there was another difference: a meddler did not necessarily interfere for the good of somebody else – meddlers as often as not had their own interests in mind, or were driven by vulgar curiosity. And what, she wondered, was the difference between vulgar curiosity and acceptable curiosity? Was it just that our own curiosity was perfectly understandable, whereas the curiosity of others was vulgar? She smiled at the thought; that sort of distinction lay at the heart of many of our acts of discrimination. What I like is art; what you like is kitsch. My old car has character; yours is a wreck.

Jamie frowned. 'What's the joke?' He sounded peevish, and Isabel stopped smiling.

'I was thinking of something,' she said evenly.

'You haven't answered my question.'

She raised her glass to her lips, looking at him over the rim. 'Yes, she did ask me to help her. And before you say anything, I don't see why I shouldn't say yes to requests of that sort. I am, after all, a moral philosopher by trade, and if I feel an obligation to help, then it's difficult to stand back. You do see that, don't you?'

To her surprise, Jamie did not argue. He shrugged. 'All right. Fine.'

She waited. He was looking away from her now, out of the window, and she knew at that moment, she knew with a

50

conviction and certainty that took her by surprise, that there *was* something wrong. She knew, too, that she had to ask him now.

'There's something wrong, isn't there?'

It was as if he had not heard her question, as he continued to look away fixedly, saying nothing.

'Jamie?'

He turned round and she saw that there were tears in his eyes. She rose to her feet and came round the table to be beside him. She fumbled; she knocked over her glass, but it was empty now, and it simply described a half-arc on the table and then came to rest unharmed.

'Jamie, what's wrong? My darling . . . What is it?'

He took her hand. 'It's been a horrible day,' he said.

'Why? Tell me about it. Go on.'

She felt the tension in his hand; even there.

He wiped ineffectively at his eyes. 'You know that new group I've been playing with? The chamber group?'

She nodded. He had told her a little about it. 'The one that meets down in Stockbridge? In St Stephen's Street?'

'Yes. Tom lives there. He runs it. We've got a concert in August, on the Fringe. We've been doing one or two other things too. A wedding reception. And there's a possible engagement in Stirling . . .'

'Yes? Isn't it going well?'

'No, it's going fine. It's just that there's this girl in it, Prue. She's a cellist.'

Isabel tensed. 'Yes?'

'A couple of weeks ago she told me that she was ill. She said she had something that they could do nothing for. She said she had a few months left – that was all.'

51

Isabel continued to hold his hand, and put her other arm around his shoulder. 'Oh Jamie!'

'She has this condition, you see. I knew she wasn't well because she had talked to me about going to see a doctor in Glasgow, a specialist of some sort. I had the impression that what she had was quite rare. Anyway, we were rehearsing today and she looked so ill – really pale and thin. I found it so . . . so upsetting. I walked with her down St Stephen Street. She lives in Leslie Place, just over the bridge, and she asked me whether I would come back with her to her flat. She said that she needed to talk to somebody and there was nobody in the flat. So I went with her and she made me some tea and . . . and I just found it so difficult.'

Isabel did not say anything. There was nothing to be said. She felt that in the face of something like this, words of comfort could be platitudinous and even inflammatory. She had once lost a friend at school in a car accident and her father, in an awkward attempt to comfort her, had said something like *At least she didn't suffer*. His words had been well meant, but they were inappropriate and had merely served to make her angry with him. The absence of suffering was not the point; the point was the untimely loss.

But she could say that she was sorry to hear this, and she did. Jamie acknowledged her with a squeeze of his hand. He said, 'Thanks' and then he rose to his feet; the casserole needed attending to, and it was getting late. She watched him as he served the potatoes that would go with the main dish. He put two on his plate and two on hers, then like a server in a school kitchen determined to be scrupulously fair, he placed a further one and a half on her plate and the same number on his.

She watched him, and the thought came to her: the actions

52

of the beautiful could be strangely fascinating, could assume an almost sacramental nature. Any one of us might do something simple, like tying a shoelace or combing our hair, or, as now, putting potatoes on a plate, and our acts would seem unexceptional. But when Jamie, or somebody like him, did such things the act became something more than its mundane essentials. Artists sensed this, she thought, and captured the significance. Through Vermeer's eyes we could look for hours at a young woman reading a letter. We knew that it was simply a young girl reading a letter – but it was more than that, far more.

He sat down, and they ate in a silence that was punctuated only with desultory exchanges. Halfway through the meal, she reached out and touched him on the arm. He paused, and looked at her, and briefly closed his eyes. She touched him again, lightly, and they resumed their meal.

He spoke with lowered eyes. 'I'm sorry, I'm just not myself.'

'I understand.' She did. She imagined, too, how he felt; there would be the rawness that came with the hearing of bad news, the feeling of hopelessness that comes from the knowledge that we all must die, and some sooner than others. The only time this did not hurt was when we still had about us the immortality of youth, and Jamie would be far beyond that now.

She told him at the end of the meal that he should not bother to help with the clearing of the table and the stacking of the dishes.

He offered. 'No, I will.'

'No. Go and play the piano. Leave the door open. I'll listen.'

He did not insist, and left the room. She heard him open the door of the living room and a few moments later there came the sound of the first notes. Schubert.

Jamie played for half an hour or so. Isabel finished in the

kitchen and went into her study, where she picked up an article she had been reading earlier and had abandoned. It was tough going, and she knew that she could not accept it for the *Review*. Yet there was something dogged about the author's argument, and in spite of herself she found herself reading it to the end. There the author concluded: 'Ultimately we act for the good because we see it to be there – like the sun. We cannot judge the sun, and there is no point in trying to do that. The sun is there. We are here. We cannot either explain or deny these facts.'

She set the paper aside. She was not convinced. The suggestion that we acted for the good because it was there was no answer, except, perhaps, in an intuitive system of ethics. How did we know that what we thought of as the good was, in fact, good? That was the job of the moral philosopher, and it did not help merely to say that the good was there, like the sun. She felt her irritation growing, but then, quite suddenly, she thought: unless . . . unless the good was indeed something like the sun, something that we *felt*, just as we feel the sun upon our skin. Goodness would be a glow, a source of energy, a radiating force that we might never understand but which was still there. Gravity was there, and we felt it, but did anybody, other than theoretical physicists, actually understand it? What if goodness were the same sort of force: something that was there, could not be seen or tasted, but was still capable of drawing us into its orbit?

She felt almost dizzy at the thought. Perhaps there was a force of moral goodness, every bit as powerful, in its way, as any of the physical forces that kept electrons in circulation about the nucleus of an atom. Perhaps we understood that, even if we acted against it, even if we denied it. And that force could be called anything, God being one name that people gave to it. And we knew that it was there because we felt its presence, as the religious believer may be convinced in his very bones of the presence of God, even if we could not describe the nature of it.

Or was it just a brain state – something within us rather than outside us, a trick of biochemistry? The feeling of recognition experienced on encountering this force of goodness might merely be an entirely subjective state brought about because some region of our brain was stimulated by something we saw – or even thought we saw. The perception of goodness as a force, then, might be nothing more significant than the warm feelings brought about by alcohol, or by a mood-enhancing drug. Those insights, it was generally agreed, were unimportant and solipsistic – a chemical illusion that signified nothing.

The moment passed. She thought she had come to some understanding of goodness, but it had been illusory, a quicksilver flash of vision, nothing more. Perhaps that is how goodness – or God – visited us: so quickly and without warning that we might easily miss it, but perceptible none the less, and transform-ing beyond the transformative power of anything else we have known.

The following morning, while Isabel was in her study, Jillian Mackinlay walked up the front path of her house, an envelope in her hand. Grace, who was entertaining Charlie in the garden, intercepted her as she approached the front door.

'Yes?' she said. 'Good morning.'

Jillian gave a start. 'Oh, sorry, you gave me a bit of a fright. I hadn't expected to find anybody lurking . . .'

Grace's nostrils flared. 'I was *not* lurking. Charlie and I . . .'

The visitor blushed. 'I'm sorry. I didn't mean it like that. I was just a bit surprised.' She paused to smile at Charlie, who was looking up at her with unblinking eyes. 'This is Isabel Dalhousie's house, isn't it?'

Grace reached for the large envelope that Jillian was clearly in the act of delivering. 'It is. I'm the housekeeper.'

'I see. Then could you give this to Isabel?'

'That's what I was proposing to do.'

There was a short silence. Jillian looked down again at Charlie. 'Well, you are a very serious little fellow, aren't you?'

Charlie returned her stare, and then, without warning, began to cry.

Jillian seemed confused. 'Oh dear, I seem to have upset him.'

Grace, holding the envelope in her left hand, scooped Charlie up with her right. 'He'll recover,' she said. 'I'll take the letter in now.'

Isabel was at her desk when Grace delivered the letter. 'This came by hand?'

Grace nodded. 'Why do people deliver by hand?' she asked. 'To have a look round, if you ask me.'

Isabel chuckled. 'That's understandable enough. Most of us are interested in other people's houses.'

From her expression, Grace made it clear that she was not. She gestured to Charlie, who had found the wastepaper basket and was busy emptying it of its contents. 'She frightened Charlie. He started to cry.'

'Children sometimes take against people,' said Isabel vaguely, slitting the flap of the envelope with the paperknife that Jamie had found in an antique shop in Stockbridge. Peering inside, she paged through the top of the papers without taking them out. It was what she had expected. She looked up; Grace's eyes were on the envelope.

'No,' said Isabel. 'It's not what you think. She hasn't written an article for the *Review*. It's not that.'

Grace raised an eyebrow.

'It's something quite different,' Isabel went on. 'It's . . .' She stopped. Grace obviously wanted to know, but she was not sure whether she wanted to tell her. Grace had a tendency to pry, apparently believing that she had a right to know Isabel's business. But did she? There were some things that she would find out about, just by being in the house and witnessing Isabel's life at close quarters, but that did not give her the right to know everything.

She wanted to say, 'It's private,' but it would have seemed so petty, so unfriendly. So instead she said, 'I've offered to look over some applications for a school principal's post. Nothing exciting.'

The effect of this was to make Grace all the more interested. 'Where?' she asked. 'What school?'

Isabel hesitated. 'It's confidential, I'm afraid.'

Grace stared at her. 'I can keep a secret,' she said, adding, in an accusing tone of voice, 'You know that.'

Isabel did know that. Grace would never reveal anything that happened in the house; she trusted her on that. 'All right, Bishop Forbes. You see it if you drive out past West Linton.'

'I know,' said Grace testily. She leaned forward, looking pointedly at the envelope. 'How many?'

'Three,' said Isabel. 'This is the short leet.' She used the Scots word for list, as many still did. 'I really don't think I should say any more about it, though.'

Grace turned. 'Come on, Charlie. We're not wanted here.'

'I don't want to sound rude,' said Isabel hurriedly.

'And I don't want to know things you don't want to tell me,' said Grace. 'Even if I happen to know who one of them is anyway.'

Isabel held up a hand. 'Excuse me?'

Grace affected insouciance. 'I happen to know, now that I think of it. There's a man called Fraser. He's one of them, isn't he?'

Isabel looked in the envelope; the names were clearly written at the top of the first page of each application. Grace was right. John Fraser. 'How on earth did you know?' she asked. The envelope had been sealed; Grace could not have opened it on its short journey from the garden path to Isabel's study, and even if she could, she would not have done such a thing. She might be nosy at times, but she was utterly correct in her dealings with others.

'Yes,' said Grace, not without an air of satisfaction. 'John Fraser is the cousin of a woman who comes to our meetings. I sit next to her sometimes. She told me. He told her, and then she told me. He said he wanted the job because at the moment he's an assistant principal at some school near Stirling. He's ambitious, she said.'

Isabel digested this. The meetings to which Grace referred were, of course, her spiritualist sessions. All sorts of people went there, it seemed, as Grace often mentioned contacts she had made at some seance or other. She remembered her conversation with Guy Peploe about villages; not only was Edinburgh a village, but so was Scotland.

'You haven't met him, have you?' asked Isabel.

'No. Not him. As I said, his cousin sometimes sits beside me.'

Isabel nodded. 'Has she said much about him?'

Grace thought for a moment. 'I don't think so. She likes him a lot, though. They were quite close as children, I think, and they've kept up with one another. He's . . .'

Isabel waited. 'Yes?'

'He's a mountaineer, I think. He . . .'

A shadow moved outside; Isabel noticed it out of the corner of her eye. Brother Fox? He sometimes slunk through the gardens during daylight hours, leaving the path he had created for himself under the rhododendrons and venturing out into the middle of the lawn, blinking in the direct sunlight. What did foxes see? she wondered.

'So he's a climber. Interesting.'

'I think he's one of these people who climbs Munros. You know – they collect them.'

Isabel did know. Munros were Scottish mountains above three thousand feet, named after a famous Scottish mountaineer. There were several hundred of them, and the real Munro-baggers tried to climb them all in as short a time as possible; sometimes that was a few years, sometimes it was a lifetime.

Isabel thought for a moment. She, too, had had a cousin, Delia, who was a mountaineer, a cousin of her father's generation who had been a staunch member of the Scottish Ladies' Mountaineering Club. Cousin Delia had taken the eighteen-year-old Isabel to climb in Glencoe, and they had stayed in a bothy belonging to the club. It had been during the high summer, with its white nights, and Isabel had awoken early, not long after four, and the tops of the mountains were already touched by the first rays of the sun. She had ventured outside, startling a couple of sheep grazing at the side of the small whitewashed building, and they had scurried away up a slope, sending scree trickling down the hillside. The experience had remained in her mind, as some moments can, like a photograph filed away in an album, a captured moment of her life.

And later that day, when they were coming down the mountain, for a while they followed the course of a river that was joined at one point by a burn tumbling off the mountainside. At this confluence there was a pool, bounded by smooth rocks that sloped gently under the water. Delia had turned to her and said — Isabel remembered her words so clearly, again one of those curious memories that lodge in our minds for no particular reason: 'This is where the men swam; the lady mountaineers bathed in a pool just a little further down.' And in her eighteen-year-old's imagination she saw the men in the water, swimming purposively, as men might do, while round the corner, in their concealed pool, the Scottish ladies stood half-submerged, like Diana and her nymphs caught by some passing artist and fixed for ever in paint.

She looked at Grace, who had picked up Charlie again and was bouncing him up and down, to his evident pleasure. 'Do you think I could meet the cousin?'

Grace continued to bounce Charlie. 'Him?'

'No, her. Your friend. The woman who goes to . . .'

'The Psychic Centre?' It was the name of the organisation that ran Grace's meetings.

'Yes. I'd like to meet her.'

Grace shrugged. 'She's not there every week. Most weeks, but not every week.'

Isabel assured her that this would be perfectly all right and asked when the next meeting would be.

'Tomorrow night,' said Grace. 'There's a man from Denmark coming to speak to us.'

'I'd be most interested in coming,' said Isabel. 'A medium?'

'Another of these psychic locators,' said Grace. 'He finds missing people. He goes into a trance and sees people. He was very effective.'

'That reminds me,' said Isabel. 'Have you seen my Chambers Dictionary? I had it somewhere and I can't . . .'

Grace responded quickly. 'In the morning room. Beside that green chair.'

Isabel smiled. 'You saw it?' she asked.

Grace looked at her suspiciously. 'Don't joke about these things, please. They are not for laughing at.'

'But I wasn't joking,' said Isabel. 'I simply asked you if you saw it. The trouble with English is that words mean so many different things.' And that was true, she thought. English was such a strange language, one in which even the words *please* and *thank you* could be used as stinging weapons in arguments.

Grace raised an eyebrow. 'Oh yes,' she said, meaning, in fact, that she did not believe Isabel's protestations of innocence.

Charlie began to niggle. He was bored with all this, and meant exactly what he said.

# 5

She did not talk to Jamie about the cellist; every couple has areas into which they know it is best not to venture. Isabel sensed that Jamie did not want to discuss what he had told her the previous evening, and she did not broach the subject. He would talk to her again, she thought, but only when he felt ready to do so, when he had adjusted to the fact that his colleague would not recover.

She told him, though, of her intention to go with Grace to the lecture by the Danish parapsychologist. Would he care to accompany them? Cat had recently suggested she might babysit and Isabel wanted to take her up on the offer. It would help to cement her niece's relationship with Charlie, which was not as close as Isabel might have wished. She could not force Charlie on Cat, but she could make it possible for her to unbend a bit and forgive her tiny cousin for being her ex-boyfriend's child.

Jamie looked doubtful. 'I'm not interested in all those . . . those spirits,' he said. 'Is it a good idea? If people survive death, why bother them? It's like running after people you've said goodbye to and trying to start the conversation all over again.'

'I'm rather inclined to agree with you,' said Isabel. 'But I think that Grace secretly appreciates our taking an interest in these meetings of hers.'

'Maybe,' said Jamie. 'But I'm not sure I want to get mixed up in it. Mind you . . .'

'Yes?'

He began to smile. 'You went once, didn't you?'

'I did.'

He remembered her telling him about the meeting she had attended with Grace. Messages had been received, she said, for named people in the room, and received with enthusiasm. He wondered whether this would happen again; if it did, perhaps it would be interesting to see it, even if the messages did not really come from the other side, as he had heard Grace calling it.

'Maybe I'll come.'

She encouraged him, and it was agreed. 'But you must keep a straight face,' she warned. 'It wouldn't be right to go in the wrong spirit.'

It was an unfortunate choice of words, and they both smiled at it, wryly. Isabel felt disloyal to be doing or saying anything that could be considered to be making fun of Grace. There was a simple rule, she thought, holding that we should only say of people that which we are prepared to say to their face. But it was a rule that was almost impossible to follow – at least for those who fell short of sainthood. 'I'm serious,' Isabel continued. 'It would offend Grace if you burst out laughing.'

'I know,' said Jamie. 'I'll dig a fingernail into my palm. Or count backwards from one hundred – in French. That's what I used to do when I was a choirboy. We all found it very difficult not to laugh. We found the Old Testament screamingly funny at that age. All that smiting.'

'And begetting,' said Isabel. 'Boys must find talk of begetting very amusing.'

Jamie looked up, summoning lines from distant memory. '*Goliath of Gath*,' he lisped, '*with his helmet of brath / One day he that down upon the green grath / When up thlipped young David, the servant of Thaul / Who thaid, "I will thmite thee although I'm tho thmall."*'

Isabel imagined Jamie in his choirboy's cassock, holding a candle perhaps, and struggling against laughter. But then her mind wandered and she thought of the folklorists Iona and Peter Opie and their combing the streets for the rhymes and sayings of childhood, those little scraps of nonsense, like Jamie's verse about Goliath and Saul with its flattened vowels and its lisped sibilants. Would Charlie hear any of this in the playground? Would these things be passed on to him?

'I don't remember that one about Goliath,' she mused. 'But what about Skinny Malinky Long-legs, Big Banana Feet? Did you hear about his misfortunes?'

Jamie remembered. 'Of course. *He went tae the pictures*, didn't he? *And couldnae find a seat.*'

'Poor man,' mused Isabel. 'Imagine him – a lanky, rather socially inadequate figure, going to one of those old-fashioned Glasgow cinemas all by himself because he has no friend to go with him. And then that business with the seat, and people laughing at him.'

'He probably had Asperger's,' said Jamie.

Isabel nodded. 'Possibly. I suspect many of the victims of nursery rhymes had Asperger's, or something similar. There was a lot of pathology in nursery rhymes. Georgie Porgie, for instance, who kissed the girls and made them cry but who ran away when the boys came out to play. He obviously couldn't maintain mature relationships with women.' She paused; she was remembering the old copy of *Struwwelpeter* that she still kept somewhere in the attic but that she had decided she would not show to Charlie. The old German children's book had been written in an age when it was considered quite permissible to scare small children with threatening and admonitory tales.

'Augustus and his soup,' she said. 'Remember: we talked about this before. *Augustus was a chubby lad / Fat, ruddy cheeks Augustus had*. But then I'm afraid he developed an eating disorder. *"Take, O take that soup away / I won't eat any soup today!"*'

'And died?' asked Jamie.

'Yes,' said Isabel. 'Wasted away. And Belloc took a similar line, come to think of it. Remember his *Cautionary Tales*? Matilda, who called the fire brigade out without reason and was not believed when the house really did go up in flames? *For every time she shouted "Fire!" / They only answered "Little Liar!"* Or Henry King? *The chief defect of Henry King / Was chewing little bits of string*. And the consequence? Intestinal blockage. Which is another great thing to give children to worry about.'

'What other defects do you think Henry King had?' asked Jamie. 'If eating string was his chief defect, it suggests that there were others, doesn't it?'

'I have no idea,' said Isabel.

'Cross-dressing, perhaps,' suggested Jamie. 'Wearing women's jewellery. *The other defect of Henry King / Was dressing up in female bling*.'

They both laughed. 'How did we get to this?' asked Isabel.

'By thinking,' said Jamie, leaning forward to kiss her lightly on the cheek. He loved the way that Isabel's mind could pursue such odd lines of enquiry. She was unpredictable; she was clever. He loved her so much for both of these qualities, and for being who she was. I could not love anybody else, he thought; not after her, not after Isabel. *Really?* enquired an unsettling internal voice. *Are you sure about that?*

Cat agreed to babysit Charlie the following evening, when they were due to accompany Grace to the Danish parapsychologist's lecture.

'Of course,' she said when Isabel phoned her. And then, after a moment's hesitation, she asked, 'It'll be all right, will it, if I bring somebody with me?'

Isabel had not expected this, but tried not to show her surprise. Since the disappearance of Bruno, Cat's singularly unsuitable last boyfriend, there had been no talk of anybody else. And yet the post was vacant, as Jamie had put it, and judging by Cat's previous behaviour it would not be long before it was filled.

'Of course. That's absolutely fine. I'll leave something out for the two of you. A couple of salmon steaks? You could . . .'

'Not fish, please,' said Cat. 'He doesn't like fish.'

*He*, thought Isabel.

'All right. A stew. How about a venison stew – I've got some in the freezer. And some . . .' She was still thinking of Cat's boyfriend, trying to picture him – on the basis of no evidence at all. He could not be worse than Bruno; nobody could be worse than Bruno, with his elevator heels and his habit of leering. 'Puy lentils.' It was the first thing she thought of, and she was not sure whether she had any. But Puy lentils went with everything, she believed, and she had yet to come across any-body who said, 'No Puy lentils, please.'

'Not venison, I'm afraid,' said Cat. 'I'm not so keen on eating venison. Bambi's mother, and all that. No, he . . .'

Isabel interrupted her. 'Who is he?' she asked. 'I can't really just call him *him.'*

Cat seemed to ignore her question, at least at first. 'I'll just make an omelette,' she said. 'Gordon likes that. I'll bring mush-rooms – if you could leave out some eggs, that'll be fine.'

Gordon. Isabel savoured the name. A Gordon would be utterly reliable; a bit solid, perhaps, in an old-fashioned Scottish way, the product of any number of possible homes in the hin-terland of Edinburgh – Peebles, perhaps, or somewhere like Kelso, one of those Border towns that produced such reliable rugby players, bank managers, engineers.

'Gordon,' she said. 'Have I met him?'

'No, I don't think you have.'

'Ah.'

There was a silence. Then Isabel spoke again. 'Have you been . . . Have you known him long?'

A defensive note crept into Cat's voice. 'Not all that long. A couple of months. He's from just outside Kelso originally.'

*I knew it! I knew it!* It was difficult for Isabel not to feel a cer-tain pleasure at having guessed so accurately the origins of Cat's new boyfriend. We like predictability, she thought, and we are always satisfied when people behave as we think they will. It makes us feel . . . well, powerful; the world is not as complex a place as some might think – at least it is not complex for *us*. She stopped herself. Nemesis stalked those who became pleased with themselves, and it was wrong, anyway, to indulge in self-congratulation. The line between having an adequate view of oneself and smugness was a thin one, and those who walked too close to it usually fell over the edge. So she simply said, 'Kelso?' And Cat, equally simply, answered, 'Yes, Kelso.'

'And what does he do?' This was a more difficult question, and she realised that Cat might resent it. After the rise and (not only metaphorical) fall of Bruno – who had been a tightrope walker – the issue of the occupation of Cat's boyfriends had become potentially awkward. She would not want Cat to think that she was going to draw any conclusions as to suitability based on what they did.

The answer surprised her. 'He's a teacher,' said Cat.

'Oh. Where?'

Cat hesitated. 'He's always taught in boys' schools. It's Firth College.' She named a school with a particularly good reputation and a headmaster whom Isabel had met on several occasions and liked.

Isabel nodded. She knew the school, which was only a mile or two away, on the brow of a hill that looked down across the city towards the Firth of Forth and the hills of Fife beyond. Her father's cousin had been there, as had his two sons, who had just left, and she had dutifully been to see them in the school's production of *The Pirates of Penzance*, put on with the help of girls imported from St George's School for Girls.

'You remember Cousin Fraser's two boys?' she said. 'They were there. They enjoyed it. A very good school. Nice staff.'

'Gordon likes working there,' said Cat. 'The boys are all sons of prosperous farmers and so on, I'm afraid. They play a lot of rugby. There are no discipline problems.' There was a slight note of sarcasm in her voice.

Isabel considered this. There was nothing wrong with playing rugby. There was nothing wrong with being the son of a prosperous farmer. There was nothing wrong with being the son of *anybody*, she felt. And yet Cat had made it sound like an apology. So was she apologising for Gordon being middle class; for working in a conventional institution with conventional values? 'I don't see anything wrong with that,' she said.

'Maybe,' said Cat. 'It's just that this city is so bourgeois. It really is. Everybody's so respectable.'

Again Isabel thought: what was wrong with being respectable? And what, she wondered, was the opposite of respectability? It became important to answer that if Cat was suggesting that one should not be respectable. Bohemian? Dissolute? Unconventional? The problem with that was that if everybody was unconventional, then they became conventional. So wild, bohemian, laid-back places, filled with free spirits, would have conventions of their own, which would soon make conventionalists of their inhabitants.

She began to feel irritated. 'But Cat, you yourself are bourgeois,' she said. 'Sorry to have to say this, but it's the truth. You're ineluctably bourgeois. You own a business. You employ Eddie. You don't even have a mortgage on your flat. Doesn't that make you bourgeois?'

There was a silence at the other end of the line, and Isabel quickly continued, 'Of course, I mustn't throw the first stone. I'm bourgeois myself, I suppose – and frankly I don't see anything wrong with that. I'm very fortunate in this life, I know that, I know that . . . and I try to help . . .' She trailed off. One should *never* boast about what one gave away – and Isabel gave a lot. Yet, Cat's assumption of superiority had irked her, and she almost felt like asking her niece what she gave, which she did not think was very much. And come to think of it, Isabel said to herself, am I all that bourgeois, when I live with a younger

69

man, I don't engage in trade, when philosophy is my job? This was not the normal pattern of a bourgeois life, whatever that might be.

She decided to move away from the subject. 'Those two boys I mentioned,' she said. 'Fraser's boys. Gavin and . . .'

'Steve.'

'Yes, Gavin and Steve. They went off to university, didn't they? They must be almost finished by now. Gavin was the older one, wasn't he? He went off for a gap year in Argentina, didn't he? He got a job as a gaucho, I think. You must remember that. One knows so few gauchos, I find.'

'Gauchos?' said Cat. 'I don't know any. And what have they got to do with it?'

Isabel laughed. 'Don't make the mistake of underestimating gauchos,' she said.

Jamie would have liked that; Cat did not. 'I have to go,' she said. 'I'll see you tomorrow.'

They discussed the time when she and Jamie would have to leave for Grace's Psychic Centre, and then rang off. Isabel walked from her study, where she had taken the call, to the kitchen, where she was going to make a cup of tea. As she did so, the thought that had been hovering around at the edge of her mind, crystallised: *yes, yes.*

She returned to her desk and picked up the envelope she had received from Jillian. She took out one of the papers – the front page of one of the curricula vitarum. She hardly had to read it, as she knew what it would say. *Gordon Leafers.* Place of birth: *Kelso.* Current position: *Senior Mathematics Teacher.*

She put down the piece of paper and then picked it up again. She looked at the date of birth. He would be thirty-eight. She smiled. Cat was in her late twenties, which made a gap of about ten years between them. There was nothing unusual in that, but what was interesting here was that Gordon was younger than the other two candidates. And thirty-eight was on the young side for appointment as a principal, which suggested that Gordon was a high-flyer in career terms. That interested her: Cat had chosen respectability.

She went to the window and stared out. She wondered whether she should be astonished at the coincidence, but she realised that she felt no real surprise. As she and Guy had decided over lunch, Scotland was a village, and a very small one at that. She looked up at the sky, and felt appalled. She had been asked, and had agreed, to look at these three candidates, and it transpired that one of them was Cat's new boyfriend. She now had an interest in the matter and would have to declare it. She could not start investigating somebody who was the boyfriend of a relative, which would go against all the rules, if there were any. But that, of course, was the problem with life. We were often unsure what the rules were or where one found them, even if we knew that they existed. It would be so useful to have a large book that one could put on the table – a book entitled, quite unambiguously, *The Rules*. Life would be so simple if that were the case; but it never was, and even when one paged through *The Rules* one would find areas of ambiguity and doubt, and one's uncertainty would return. That's why, she thought, we have judges and lawyers and courts – in other words, as a Freudian might perhaps suggest, that's why we have *father*. But what if father went away, or said that he really didn't know about the rules and did not want to start enforcing them? The loss of good authority, she thought; that's what happened then.

\*

Jamie looked at Isabel and smiled. 'You're behaving as if you're going on a first date,' he said. 'Calm down. It's just another of Cat's boyfriends, after all.'

She was aware of being nervous, and when she was nervous she felt fidgety. 'You're right,' she said. 'I just have a feeling about this one. I think that somehow he's going to be different from the others.' She blushed, and corrected herself. As a former boyfriend of Cat, Jamie was one of the others himself. 'By that, I mean people like Bruno.'

He reached out and touched her arm gently. 'I know you don't mean me. Don't worry.'

'I didn't. You were different. Although I must say that I'm glad that things didn't work out between you and Cat. Otherwise – no me, no Charlie.'

'I'm glad too.'

There was something else she wanted to ask him, and she decided that this was the time. 'How do you feel about her now? Is there still any awkwardness . . . any difficulty?'

He took time to weigh his reply. 'I don't think so.' He hesitated. 'There used to be, yes. Not now.'

'So in your eyes she's just like anybody else?' Isabel was interested in this. She was not sure that she understood how people could feel indifferent to former lovers. She understood lingering love for somebody who had rejected one, intense love perhaps; reproach; she could even understand hate and detestation; she did not understand indifference.

'Yes,' said Jamie. 'She's just like anybody else now.' He paused. 'Mostly, that is. If I start thinking about her, then . . . Well, then I get all confused, I suppose.' He looked at Isabel almost apologetically. 'That's the way it is. I'm sorry – it just is. So I don't think about her in that way. I just don't.'

'You put the past out of your mind?'

'Yes, I suppose I do.'

Her gaze dwelled upon him, upon the face that seemed to her so perfect. How was it, she wondered, that character could reveal itself so clearly in the structure of human flesh and bone? Jamie looked kind, and intelligent, and gentle, and that was what he was. Could it be otherwise? Could the faces of the wicked look like this, have this light behind them? Perhaps there could be a book of photographs exploring face and character. Goebbels and Mussolini – they could be there to illustrate the proposition at the beginning; Goebbels with his pinched, rat-like features; Mussolini with his thuggish bully's face; both perfect illustrations of the proposition that character shines through. And from the other end of the spectrum? She wondered about that. Nelson Mandela, perhaps, would be a good candidate; his face was suffused with kindness, with a sort of joy that was unmistakable; or Mother Teresa of Calcutta, whose lined, careworn features were so trans-formed when she smiled. She could look severe, sometimes, but that was the effect of suffering and the day-to-day toll of caring for those for whom nobody else would care. And then there were the politicians, some of whom so neatly illustrated pride, ambition and cunning; the various types of bullies; soldiers whose faces often seemed trained into hard, wooden expressions; sleek bankers to remind us of the face of human greed; gentle doctors . . . It would be a book of clichés, she decided, demonstrating that stereotypes – for all that they be derided – are so often true. *The eye is the window to the soul.* Of course it was.

'Isabel?'

'Sorry, I was thinking.'

And then the bell sounded and Jamie raised an eyebrow. 'Do you want me to let them in?'

'No,' she said. 'I'll do that.'

She walked to the front door and opened it. The self-closing lock was stiff – it behaved like that in certain weathers – and she had to tug. But then it swung open and she saw Cat standing in front of her with Gordon a pace behind on the front step. Cat had half turned when Isabel opened the door and was addressing a remark to Gordon. What is said about ourselves on our own doorsteps, thought Isabel, is probably as revealing a judgement as we are likely to hear.

'Well,' said Isabel. 'Here you are.'

Cat moved to one side to effect the introduction. 'I don't think you've met Gordon.'

Gordon stepped forward and offered his hand. Isabel glanced at him quickly and then back at Cat. She's reverted to type, she thought. Bruno, with his elevator shoes, was an exception: Gordon was tall, with the easy confidence of the good-looking. She resisted the temptation to look at his legs – Cat had views on men's legs, she was sure of it. In fact, Cat herself in an unguarded moment had said something about how important legs were. She liked legs to be strong; Toby, the skier, several boyfriends ago, had well-muscled legs, Isabel seemed to remember. Stop it, she told herself. Don't think this way. Stop it.

She invited them into the house, feeling as she did so a stab of guilt over the advantage she enjoyed. This was their first meeting, and yet she knew Gordon's age from the documents in the study, and the university where he had done his first degree: Aberdeen. President of the Students' Union. Scottish Universities' rugby team (captain, tour of South America). In respect of all of this he looked the part; but there was something else – something that she had noticed immediately. Presence.

Jamie was in the kitchen, and she took them there. I feel like a spy, she thought. I feel like one of those people who does the positive vetting of applicants for posts in the secret services; who know everything about the people they meet because they have pored through their records beforehand; absorbed the intimate secrets of a life, stripping away the armour that privacy affords; rendering the other naked.

'We've left the eggs out for your supper,' said Isabel. 'Jamie and I were thinking of going out for a bite to eat after this talk we're going to. Would that be all right?'

Cat glanced at Gordon, as if for confirmation. 'Fine,' she said. 'Take as long as you like.'

Isabel wondered what they would do. Babysitters usually watched television, or that is what householders assumed. But when they came in pairs . . . She recalled reading somewhere about a babysitter who was found taking a bath when the parents returned. Why not? Student flats, in which many babysitters lived, had uncomfortable baths and not enough hot water. Visiting a house with a good supply of hot water and clean towels might be just too much of a temptation. And yet there was an element of trust involved; one did not imagine that a person left in one's house would open drawers, for example, or read one's correspondence, or even run a bath. That was what the story of Goldilocks and the three bears was all about: breach of trust.

She would have to look at this for the *Review*. What were the limits of trust in everyday life? What liberties could we legitimately take when we were entrusted with the property of

75

others? Could you read a book you were looking after for somebody? Yes, she thought you could. Drink from their bottle of water? No. Germs dictated that. Take fruit from a bowl? No. A nut from a dish of nuts? Yes. Sit in their chairs? Of course: chairs are public and one only needs to seek permission to sit in another's chair if the owner of the room is present; once you were by yourself, any chair was fair game. Except the chairs of really important people – one should not sit on a throne when left unattended in a monarch's throne room, that really was going too far. And yet who would miss such an opportunity? There could surely be little doubt but that visitors to Her Majesty sat down on the nearest throne when Her Majesty went out to fetch something. And, indeed, polite American presidents actually engineered excuses to leave the Oval Office for a few moments so that their guests could run round and sit in the President's chair for a few seconds. The only occasion when this had led to embarrassment was when President de Gaulle had visited the White House and had momentarily dropped off to sleep while seated in the President's chair.

Isabel smiled. Cat glanced at her suspiciously.

'Parapsychology,' said Gordon. 'Cat tells me that you're going to a lecture on parapsychology.'

Isabel laughed. 'I know that sounds a bit odd,' she said. 'It's rather complicated. My housekeeper, you see, is a great enthusiast for these things and keen that we should go. I'm not a believer in parapsychology myself. But . . .' She knew that she was telling only half the truth. The full truth, she thought, is that I'm trying to find out about three people, of whom you, Gordon, are one.

'Well, plenty of people take it seriously enough,' said

Gordon. 'And isn't there evidence for the existence of telepathy?'

'No,' said Isabel. 'Not as far as I know.'

'I knew you were going to say that,' said Jamie, and laughed.

Cat looked at him sideways. What was so funny?

Isabel changed the subject, asking him about the school he was currently teaching at, Firth College.

Gordon nodded. 'I've been there for five years now. I like the place.' He paused. 'Although I'm currently in for another job.'

Isabel found herself warming to him. He need not have said that – a more . . . more closed person would have said nothing. She looked at his face; his expression was frank.

'A promotion?' she asked.

'Yes. A headship.' He looked at Cat, and at that moment Isabel realised that as far as Gordon was concerned, his plans included her niece.

'Well, good luck,' said Isabel. 'I have the luxury, I suppose, of being self-employed. But I know what it's like to apply for jobs.'

She thought of the last time she had applied for a job, which involved being interviewed by Professor Lettuce for the position of editor of the *Review*. The interview panel had consisted of three people: Lettuce, who had been in the chair; a woman from King's College, London, who had gazed out of the window throughout the interview; and a slight, rather thin-faced man, who had been a fellow of a Cambridge college but who had looked, in Isabel's view, like a bookmaker from Newmarket Racecourse. Lettuce had barely bothered to look up from the table when Isabel had come in, and the nature of their subsequent relationship had been dictated from that morning. Yet she had been given the job, presumably because nobody else had been prepared to do it for the salary offered, which was virtually nothing.

'Thanks,' said Gordon. 'But I really don't think that I stand much of a chance.'

Don't assume anything, said Isabel under her breath. She wanted him to get the job now – and that complicated matters immensely; how could she be objective in her enquiry if she started off wanting one of the candidates to emerge unsullied and *papabilis*? Life's goalposts, and hurdles too, are never in the right place, she told herself; and they have the unfortunate habit of shifting within seconds. One sees them, and then suddenly they are no longer there, where they should be, but somewhere altogether elsewhere.

# 6

After the Danish lecture, Isabel and Jamie said goodbye to Grace, who was going to have tea with a fellow member of her spiritualist circle in Stockbridge. They had seen this woman at the lecture, and had both noticed her eyes, which were grey and cloudy, as if in the advanced stages of some occluding condition, cataracts perhaps. But no, explained Grace, she saw perfectly well: 'She sees more than we do – far more, I assure you.' Isabel had avoided catching Jamie's eye when this was said, but she saw him discreetly mouth the word, 'Strange!' She shook her head in warning; this was not meant to be funny, and he was not to laugh. 'Don't even think of laughing,' she whispered, as they walked away up the street. 'These people have ways of telling.'

They had reserved a table at the Café St Honoré in Thistle Street Lane, a restaurant that they had been going to for some years now. It was Paris transplanted, but without the falsity that sometimes goes with transplantation. Jamie, in particular, disliked Irish pubs outside Ireland. 'All these O'Connor's Taverns and McGinty's Bars and so on are completely bogus,' he had

79

complained to Isabel. 'I went into one with the band the other day and it was full of old Guinness signs. I looked closely at one of them and saw that it was made in China. And the barman, who had a name badge which said Paddy, was Russian, or sounded like it.'

'People have their dreams,' said Isabel. 'And it's harmless enough. We go to French bistros and Italian restaurants. What's the difference between them and Irish pubs? The intention in each case is to provide you with an illusion. Don't look out of the windows and you could be in Paris or Naples. That's what people want.'

Jamie was not convinced. 'It's a Disneyland culture,' he said. 'Insincere. Infantilised.'

She looked at him sideways. 'I'm not sure about insincerity. Disneyland may not be to your taste, but I don't think it's insincere. They *mean* to be syrupy.'

'Mickey Mouse,' said Jamie dismissively.

She raised an eyebrow. 'Mickey Mouse? I don't see anything wrong with Mickey.' She paused; one did not associate Auden with Disney characters but she recalled an interview in the *Paris Review* in which the interviewer had asked the poet, for some reason, what he thought of Mickey Mouse. And Auden had replied, 'He's all right.' She mentioned this to Jamie, who said, enigmatically, 'Is he?'

'Yes, he is. Mickey's decent. He represents the little person.'

None of this stopped them from enjoying the French atmosphere of Café St Honoré, nor from ordering coquilles St Jacques and a bottle of Chablis.

'Well,' said Isabel. 'Danish psychics?'

Jamie shrugged. 'I'd like to see proof. Proof that stands up in the labs.'

Isabel thought about this. She understood why Jamie should insist on sound evidence for any conclusion, and part of her agreed with that. But she often acted on hunches, on the prompting of her feelings, or on simple intuition. And labs were not always the answer, she felt: there were things that were invisible and undetectable by any physical means but that were none the less real: sorrow, pain, hope, for instance; or an atmosphere of tension or distrust in a room. 'It may be that labs have an inhibiting effect,' she said. 'Have you thought of that?'

Jamie reached for a piece of bread and dipped it into a small bowl of olive oil. The wine had arrived and was now being poured. 'No. I hadn't.' And she could be right, he decided. He had a friend who could not have his blood pressure taken accurately; every time the rubber cuff was placed around his arm, his heart began to thump and a misleadingly high reading resulted. Could it be the same with telepathy? Perhaps it worked only when the people present were in a receptive mood, in the same way that a composer or an artist may need peace and quiet before the Muse will speak.

'Who was that woman you were talking to?' he asked. 'Before the lecture – the woman with the ginger hair?'

Isabel reached for her glass. 'It's to do with this school business.' She watched his reaction; she had not told him about her ulterior motive in accompanying Grace to the lecture. It was not that she wanted to mislead him; she just had not thought to do so. Some couples live in each other's pockets, sharing every bit of their lives, every bit of information. That might suit some, but it was not what she – nor Jamie for that matter – wanted. They both wanted room to lead independent lives, and that is why she did not tell him about everything that happened to do with the *Review* or with . . . this other side of her life. She could not bring herself to describe it as *enquiries*: that sounded far too arch, and *investigations* sounded downright hyperbolic. Isabel did not investigate things; she *considered* them.

'These principals?'

'Yes, or would-be principals.'

He waited.

'The woman with the ginger hair,' she continued, 'is called Cathy. She's the cousin of one of the candidates. Grace told me.'

Jamie reached for another bit of bread. 'The trouble with this French bread,' he said, 'is that it's too tasty. You could fill up on it before anything else arrived.' He dipped the bread into the olive oil, allowing a small drop to fall back into the bowl. 'So? Did you find out anything?'

'Yes,' she said. 'I did. I managed to bring up her cousin's name. I said, "Aren't you John Fraser's cousin?" and before she had the chance to ask me whether I knew him, I said, "I haven't seen him recently." That was absolutely true. I might have said, "I've never seen him," but at least I didn't lie.'

Jamie looked at her. He smiled. 'You didn't lie? No, I suppose you didn't. Not technically.'

'I didn't lie,' she repeated firmly.

'All right. And what did she say then?'

Isabel told him that she had asked about John's climbing. Did he climb as much in the summer as in the winter? Was he planning to go abroad?

'She was clearly very proud of him,' Isabel said. 'Just as Grace had told me. But then, just after she said something about how he had been talking for years about climbing in the Andes, her face clouded over. You know how that sometimes happens? It's

82

as if a dark shadow has come over somebody. She stopped mid-sentence, as if she'd remembered something.'

Jamie was silent. They were sitting off to the side, away from the light, and for a moment it was as if they were completely alone in the room, rather than in a restaurant in which there other diners, movement, warmth.

Isabel continued. 'Then she said something very strange. She said that he was troubled in spirit. Those were her exact words. Troubled in spirit. I asked her why this was, but she didn't answer me. She said that he wanted to come to one of the meetings, but hadn't got round to it. She said that it was a pity because it helped to talk to the one on the other side. Again, those were her actual words. The one on the other side.'

Jamie took a sip of his wine. 'He's lost somebody? Lots of the people at that meeting had lost somebody, I think. That's why they go there.'

Isabel nodded. She had seen it at the previous meeting. 'But who? Somebody he's wronged, do you think?'

'Maybe.'

Isabel looked over Jamie's shoulder. The waiter was approaching their table, plates balanced expertly in either hand. 'If you had let somebody down badly and then . . . before you made your peace, they *crossed over* to the other side, as Grace would say, wouldn't you want to speak to him?'

The waiter put the plates before them. The scallops, fresh and firm, had been arranged to make a peninsula across a shallow lake of sauce. Isabel sniffed at the steam rising from the plate. 'If I had to give up everything,' she said, 'seafood would be the last thing to go. I'd have a final scallop and say, "That's it, that's eating over." And then I'd cross over happy.'

Jamie laughed. He raised his glass to Isabel. 'May that never be necessary.'

She had not been serious, of course, but the absurd, the fanciful may bring grave thoughts in its wake. She and Jamie would not be together for eternity; one day one of them would leave or die – those were the only two certainties – and the other would be on his or her own. It was a thought that crossed the mind of everybody who ever entered into a relationship with another. It applied as much to friends as to lovers and spouses: one day somebody would see the other for the last time, and probably not know it. And there would be things left unsaid, little gestures – kindnesses – left undone; as there are in every part of life.

Jamie tackled a scallop, and then dabbed at his mouth with the starched table napkin. Isabel watched him. *Napery*, she thought: the word for table linen. *Napery* – the word had such a solid ring to it, suggesting houses that had drawers and trunks full of tablecloths and the like, neatly pressed and folded away, like old memories; napery and silver and *plenishings* – words that lawyers used when itemising the household effects of clients who had died and left such things behind them.

'What are you thinking of?' asked Jamie, putting down the napkin.

'Household effects,' she said. 'That table napkin . . .' She pointed, and he looked at it in puzzlement.

'Nothing wrong with it.'

'No, of course not. I was just thinking of how we fill our houses with things. Rather too many things, in most cases.'

Jamie shrugged. 'I don't. My flat's uncluttered. Or was . . . when I last visited it.'

She caught his smile, and returned it. Jamie only used his flat now to teach in, his pupils hauling their bassoon cases up the stone staircase to tug at his antiquated brass bell-pull and wipe their feet on the coir doormat with its *Welcome* legend and ingrained mud. He still used one room there as a bedroom, in the sense that there was a made-up bed in it, but he never stayed there now, and the flat had a cold, rather desolate feel to it. Charlie did not like it, and had fidgeted and fretted when Jamie had last taken him there.

'Your flat . . .' Isabel began, but did not finish the sentence. *Space*, she reminded herself.

'Yes? My flat?'

Isabel waved a hand in the air, carelessly. 'Your flat is your flat,' she said. 'You like it – that's all that matters.'

Jamie frowned. 'But I don't *really* like it,' he said.

She was surprised; he had never said this before. She wondered whether he wanted to get rid of it; he could teach just as easily in the music room in her house, and they were engaged, after all, and would be getting married in due course.

'Is there any point in keeping it then? Do you want to sell it?'

Jamie looked away. She saw how the light accentuated his high cheekbones. She wanted to reach out and touch him; to put her hand against his cheek, which felt so smooth, and which she had become accustomed to touching, briefly, when she awoke and he was there beside her, his head on the pillow. How long would this beauty last? Five more years? Ten? Or was it more fleeting than that, as human beauty inevitably is?

She asked him again. 'How about selling it? Wouldn't you feel less . . . tied down?'

'I might,' said Jamie thoughtfully. 'Do you think I should?'

She hesitated. 'When we're married, do we need it?' *Space*, she thought again.

'No, I don't see why we should keep it.' He looked back at her. 'Can we get married soon? I mean, really soon.'

She felt her heart beating within her. She closed her eyes, involuntarily. 'Yes. I think we should.'

'In two or three weeks' time?'

She felt her breath leave her; she had to force herself to breathe. 'I think so.'

'I don't want a great big wedding,' he said. 'Do you mind? Something more or less private. You, me, Charlie.'

'If that's what you want. Are you sure?'

He nodded, and reached across the table to take her hand. 'Yes, it is.'

They had much to talk about. They would go to Old St Paul's, an Episcopal church where Isabel knew one of the clergy. There was a side chapel there – a tiny place – that would be suitable for a small wedding. The choir, though, might be asked to sing. Would Jamie object to that? He would love it, he said. They would be off to one side, out of sight, but it would be lovely hearing them in the background.

'You choose the music,' said Isabel. 'Naturally.'

He agreed, but said that he wanted her to be happy with his choice.

'No,' she said. 'You're the musician.'

'Ireland,' he said. 'Definitely Ireland, then. "Greater Love Hath No Man". Remember it?'

She did. '*Many waters cannot quench love,*' she said.

He sung, in response, barely above a whisper, '*Neither can the floods drown it.*'

'And what else?'

'Oh, I'll think. We've got at least four centuries of music to choose from.'

Towards the end of the meal, when they were drinking coffee, Isabel said, 'You know, I have an awful feeling about John Fraser. I know it's ridiculous, but I can't get it out of my mind.'

He looked at her with interest. 'What do you feel?'

She knew that she had no grounds for saying what she was about to say. It was ridiculous – a complete whimsy. But the thought had occurred to her and it would not go away. 'That he's killed somebody.' She regretted the words even as she uttered them. It was an accusation – a gross defamation, even if the victim would never hear what was said of him. You can defame people, she thought, even if you speak the words into a void, to be heard by nobody. The wrong in such cases was not that you lowered them in the eyes of others – you did not do this, because nobody heard what you said – but simply that you had *thought* it. It was a wrong done to truth and the cause of truth. And it was *dirtying*; one felt grubby after thinking unkind, uncharitable, or even lascivious thoughts – why? Because for a few moments one imagined that the thought was deed.

She watched his reaction. At first he looked blank, and then he shook his head. 'Surely not.'

'I know, I know. I shouldn't think that of him, but that's what I feel. I know I haven't a shred of evidence, other than that his cousin, who may well be over-imaginative—'

Jamie interrupted her. 'Over-imaginative? She believes in ghosts and . . . and spirits and all the rest. Of course she's over-imaginative.'

'Even so, she thinks that he wants to talk to somebody – through a medium. And if that's true, then it's possible that he's killed somebody and wants forgiveness.'

Jamie was silent as he thought about this. 'Do you really think,' he said, 'that murderers *want* to talk to their victims? Surely it's exactly the opposite: they have no desire to hear from them again.'

Isabel weighed this for a moment. It was probably true that most murderers had no desire to hear from their victims, but there were two objections to Jamie's statement. One was that people could be killed by accident as much as intentionally: so not all of those who took another's life were murderers. And secondly, not everybody who even intentionally caused the death of another would be without all conscience; people had their regrets, and lots of them.

She was on the point of telling Jamie this when he leaned across the table and said to her, very slowly and clearly, 'Isabel, listen to me. This is Edinburgh. *Edinburgh.* We haven't got any murderers here. We just haven't. At the most, people have little failings. That small.' He held up a hand, with barely a chink of light between his thumb and forefinger. 'Mere quirks. So think of something else. Please.'

She laughed. She knew that he did not mean this: Edinburgh was the same as anywhere else, and had the same range of people as others did: the good, the bad, the morally indifferent. They had their quirks, of course; Jamie was right about that. But even their quirks were charming – at least in the eyes of a lover, who would forgive her city anything.

They decided to walk back from the Café St Honoré because the night was a fine one and even at ten there was still light in the sky. Being as far north as Moscow, and only three degrees south of St Petersburg, Edinburgh had summer nights almost as white as those of Russia. Soon the dying day would slip into half-darkness and that curious Scottish half-light, the gloaming, would mantle the city; for now, though, every architectural detail, every branch moving gently in the breeze from the west, was clearly visible.

They walked up through Charlotte Square, past the well-appointed offices of the financiers. 'Money,' said Isabel, 'likes to clothe itself in respectability, doesn't it? And yet why should we kowtow to financiers? All that these people do is lend money to people who actually do things.' She gestured towards the well-set façades of the classical square before continuing, 'But they – these people in these offices – end up having far greater status than those who actually do things with that money. Odd, isn't it?'

Jamie agreed. He had no interest in money. 'We should be more like the Germans,' he said. 'They show more respect for engineers than they do for accountants.'

Isabel said that she was not sure that respect should be based on a person's job alone. A good and conscientious emptier of rubbish bins, she suggested, was better in moral terms, surely, than a self-serving accountant. Yet a job might say something about a person's character: a nurse was likely to be more sympathetic than a futures trader, although not inevitably so.

What she had said clearly interested Jamie, who now made a remark about musicians and their position in society. 'And nobody really respects musicians all that much,' he said. 'We're very far down the pecking order.'

They were now within sight of the Caledonian Hotel, that great red-stone edifice at the end of Princes Street, a battleship made of gingerbread, Isabel thought. She remembered seeing a crowd outside the hotel one day when some rock star had been staying in the hotel and word had got out to the fans. Were musicians all that low in the pecking order? Did people wait outside hotels for accountants, or engineers, or architects?

'Are you sure?' He half turned to her. There was a piper outside the Caledonian, welcoming somebody or sending them off; or possibly just standing there, playing the pipes. Isabel recognised the tune, 'Mist-covered Mountains', a tune that she always found evocative – of what? Of Morven, she thought, or Ardnamurchan, those wild, mountainous parts of western Scotland on the edge of the Atlantic, the last land before the Hebrides and beyond them the cloud banks, the green cliffs of Newfoundland.

She remembered how she had once been in the Old Town of Edinburgh, near the Canongate, when she had heard from somewhere in the vicinity, echoing through the small wynds and closes, the muffled thumping of a great drum. And she had turned the corner to find herself face to face with a pipe band, the pipers draped in dark-green tartan, on the point of striking up 'Mist-covered Mountains'. And she had stood on the pavement, close to the wall to allow the band to get by, and watched them as they slow-marched past her. She had noticed the white spats that each kilted piper wore; she had seen the faces of the young men in the ranks of the band, clean-shaven, smartly turned out, like boy-soldiers. Which is what they were, she learned from a woman standing beside her on the pavement. 'Just laddies,' said the woman, shaking her head as she spoke. 'Just laddies. And now they're away to the ermy.' She pronounced army in the Scots way, as mothers had done for generations, watching their sons going away.

A couple emerged from the hotel, followed by a gaggle of guests. The couple got into a car, and a young man from the group of friends sat on the bonnet of the car, preventing it from driving away. 'Newlyweds,' said Isabel. 'That explains the piper.'

The piper had struck up a different tune, a quicker one; a woman reached out to drag the young man off the car. There were cries of mirth and then applause as the car began to move off towards Rutland Square.

They walked on. Jamie reached for her hand. 'Like us,' he said. 'Soon.'

'Yes.' She paused. 'Are you sure that you want to go ahead . . . so quickly?'

He did not hesitate. 'Of course I'm sure.' He looked at her. His expression was anxious. 'Why do you ask? Are you having doubts?'

She said that she was not. 'It's just that I've become more or less accustomed to how things are at the moment. I haven't really thought about the next stage.'

'But we agreed to get married. Remember?'

She asked him how she could forget.

'Then why the surprise?'

She did not want him to feel that she had become lukewarm. Of course she wanted to marry Jamie; of course she wanted to be with him for the rest of her life. Of course she did.

She squeezed his hand. 'Fine,' she said. 'It's fine. I'm just so happy that it's going to happen. I wanted to know that you were absolutely sure, and now I do. I'm ready. Marry me. Go ahead, marry me.'

He laughed. 'Marriage is not something you *do* to somebody.'

'With, then. You do it together. You do it *with* them.'

'Exactly.'

They were now halfway up Lothian Road. They had passed

the Usher Hall and were walking past a line of dubious bars and cheap restaurants. Two bouncers stood on duty at the entrance to one of the bars; black-clad figures with wires disappearing into tiny receivers in their ears.

'Mesomorphs,' whispered Isabel.

'What?'

'Those types – the bouncers. Mesomorphs. There are ecto-morphs, mesomorphs, and endomorphs. Ectomorphs are thin, lanky people; mesomorphs are large-boned and muscular; and endomorphs are rounder, chubbier, I suppose. Those men back there are mesomorphs.'

'What am I?' asked Jamie.

Isabel looked at him, as if seeing him for the first time. 'Ecto-mesomorph,' she said. 'Which is just perfect.'

She thought for a moment. 'Professor Lettuce – remember him? A large endomorph. Flabby.'

The thought of Lettuce reminded her of his review of Christopher Dove's new book. She had not put him off; she had not written to tell him that she would not have room to publish it, and now she was more or less barred by inaction. And that, she thought, was how people became trapped; they let things slip, they put things off, and then the landscape around them changed and they found themselves in a cul-de-sac from which there was no easy escape; and the cul-de-sac could so easily become a redoubt. They . . . Not *they*, she corrected herself; *we* do that, which includes *me*. The thought depressed her. Life was complicated enough without Lettuce adding to its difficulties.

'But let's not talk about him,' she said.

'I wasn't,' said Jamie.

They continued their walk in silence. Then Isabel said, 'Our honeymoon.'

'Yes?'

'Do you want one?'

He nodded vigorously. 'Of course.'

'So where shall we go? Somewhere exotic? Bhutan? Kerala?'

'Would you mind very much if we had it in Scotland?'

She was surprised, but said that she did not mind; Scotland would be fine.

'It's just that I love the islands,' said Jamie. 'We've been to Jura, so we need to go somewhere different. We could go to the Outer Hebrides. Harris. South Uist. Somewhere like that.'

'Perfect,' said Isabel.

Jamie reeled off a litany of island names. 'Coll, Tiree, Rhum, Colonsay. They're full of poetry, aren't they?'

She thought of Michael Longley, and of his poem to the blues singer, Bessie Smith. The lines were haunting, and came back to her whenever she heard somebody mention the Hebrides: *I think of Tra-na-Rossan, Inisheer / Of Harris drenched by horizontal rain.* She was not sure where Tra-na-Rossan and Inisheer were; Ireland, she assumed. And they had enough rain of their own there, not to be drawing attention to the rain that fell on Scotland. But yes, the poet was right: Harris and the other islands were often drenched by rain, even if not always horizontal. It was more a drifting rain, she thought, a curtain, a veil that came in from the Atlantic, white and smoky as an attenuated cloud.

'Yes. And the Treshnish Islands,' said Isabel. 'I've always loved the sound of the Treshnish Islands.'

'Uninhabited,' said Jamie.

'Therefore ideal for a honeymoon.'

'I'd like to take you on a slow boat somewhere,' said Jamie.

She smiled. 'Would you?'

'Yes. Isn't that what everybody wants to do with the person they really love?'

She opened her mouth to reply, but said nothing. He had uttered a declaration of love that was indirect, but was all the more powerful for that. She did not want to spoil the moment. It was perfect. This young man, this perfect man, had said that she was the one that he really loved. She closed her eyes for moment, and saw herself in a cabin on what must be, she assumed, a slow boat to China. It was hot, and they were half-unclothed, wearing only underwear, for the heat. Through the porthole there was an oily sea stretching out to a hazy horizon, a languid swell. She looked in his eyes; she held his hand; he leaned forward and kissed her. She felt his lips, the warmth of his breath.

When she opened her eyes she wanted to kiss him back immediately, to embrace, unheeding of the people in the street, of the passing traffic. But she saw where they now were, on the pavement outside a large office building at Tollcross. It was the block in which her lawyers had their offices, and that fact alone seemed to inhibit her. But she smiled at the thought. Why should the idea of one's lawyers prevent one from kissing any-body? Could one kiss with enthusiasm if one was thinking of . . . Who would have the maximum inhibiting effect? The answer came to her immediately, and she smiled again. It was a public figure she pictured; a man whom she had seen inter-viewed on the television the previous night, labouring a political point with his interviewer. *He* was very inhibiting. Very. Poor man. Did anybody ever kiss *him*?

Jamie looked at her and again bent to kiss her on the lips. 'There,' he said.

# 7

The next morning Charlie woke at exactly the hour at which he always awoke, and drew himself to their attention by kicking the high sides of his cot. Rattling the bars of his cage, as Jamie put it; which made Isabel think how like imprisonment was the world of the small child. There were barriers everywhere; meals at set times; watchful eyes; long periods of restriction and restraint; supervised exercise. *The prison of childhood.*

She left Jamie to lie in while she attended to Charlie. He was a sunny child, particularly in the morning, when his delight at the world brimmed over into peals of laughter at the smallest thing. She usually carried him to the window so that they could look out together over the garden, and she did that now, standing with him in her arms, watching the morning sun struggle up over the high wall that separated their house from their neighbour's. Occasionally, if they were lucky, they saw Brother Fox trotting along the top of the garden wall, his raised highway, or sneaking into the clump of rhododendrons that was his refuge, his low bower.

'Fo,' exclaimed Charlie, pointing wildly into the garden; *x* defeated him. *He's algebraically challenged*, Isabel had remarked to Jamie, who looked puzzled; *Our son has no x's*, she explained.

'No fo,' she said to Charlie. 'Not today, at least.' Words have power for you, Charlie, she thought; the uttering of a word will make something come to you. And it was the same for adults; what was prayer but that?

She took Charlie into the kitchen and prepared his breakfast. She turned on the radio and listened to the news and the beginning of the morning current affairs programme. The world had not improved from yesterday; there was conflict and disagreement, selfishness, the varying types of hatred, and, to top it all, accelerating ecological disaster. People now talked about saving the planet and nobody batted an eyelid. Only a few years ago such language would have been deemed to be wildly alarmist, even risible. But now there was a real threat and people spoke about it in the same tones as they spoke about the old, well-established threats of drought and floods and the like. Locusts . . . how friendly a threat they now seemed; but presumably the locusts themselves were suffering and found it difficult to plague people in quite the same way as they had in the past.

She looked at Charlie, whom she had placed in his high chair, ready for his breakfast of porridge and strips of bread on which she would spread runny boiled egg, his soldiers. Was this the first time, she wondered, that parents might think, with good reason, that the world would run out on their children; that it might not see out their natural span? She only had to think for a moment before she realised that it was not the first time; there had been many points at which people had thought that their world was ending, and some of these not very long ago. In the sixties and seventies many people thought just that as they watched two bristling super-powers staring one another down, fingers on the triggers of vast nuclear arsenals. One of Isabel's aunts had told her about those days during the Cuban Missile Crisis when she had thought that nuclear war was inevitable. She had found herself feeling oddly calm, and had been determined to spend what she imagined were their last days in peace. 'I sat and looked at pictures,' she said. 'Photographs of college friends. Of our old family house in Mobile. Pictures of the world. I took out our old copies of *National Geographic* and paged through them, just looking at the world in all its variety; saying goodbye to it, I suppose.'

'And you weren't frightened?' Isabel had asked.

'Oddly, no. I should have been, perhaps, but I wasn't. I thought that it would be so quick, you see, and that we wouldn't really have time to feel the pain. And if there's no pain, then what is there to fear? I felt regret, yes, but no fear.'

Returning his mother's stare, Charlie broke into a grin. 'Solds,' he demanded.

She reassured him. The egg was ready for spreading on the fingers of bread. 'Here. Soldiers. You see – patience is rewarded.'

She helped him with the food. There was no point in thinking about what sort of future Charlie would have because there was nothing she could do to protect him from it. She could do her best, of course, not to add to the burden we placed on the earth, but she suspected that this would never be enough. Humanity, it seemed, was too irresolute, too greedy to save itself from destruction.

Charlie opened his mouth to laugh, showering crumbs over his mother. She laughed too. Children had a way of reminding us of the immediate, and that, she felt, was exactly what she needed. She abandoned her morbid thoughts and concentrated on breakfast. Grub first, then ethics. Brecht? Which in her case meant breakfast first, then the *Review of Applied Ethics*.

Jamie came downstairs and into the kitchen. His hair was uncombed, tousled from the night, and he was still rubbing the sleep from his eyes.

'You could have stayed in bed,' she said.

Charlie looked up from his breakfast, shrieked with pleasure, and waved his arms about. It pleased Isabel to see her son's love for his father, every bit as much as it pleased her to see Jamie's love for Charlie.

'I'm *de trop*,' she said, offering Jamie the plate with its two remaining boiled-egg soldiers. 'Here you go.'

Jamie took the plate. 'He loves you just as much. It's just that . . .'

'A boy loves his father,' said Isabel. 'Naturally.'

Jamie bent down and kissed Charlie on the top of his head. The little boy gave another squeal of delight.

'You go and have a shower,' said Jamie. 'I'll take over.' He looked at the clock on the wall. He had nothing to do, he explained, until noon and would look after Charlie until then if Isabel wanted him to.

Isabel sighed. 'I've got a whole pile of things on my desk. Grace said that she wanted to take him to the Botanics this afternoon. I could get my work out of the way . . .'

'You do that,' said Jamie. 'Go on.'

She nodded. I could give up working, she thought. I could spend all my time with Charlie, which is what I would love to do. But would I be any happier? And would it make much difference to Charlie? She looked at her son, who was now tackling one of the soldiers given him by Jamie. Being a parent was such a gift, and everybody said that it was a fleeting one. *So precious, those years, hang on to them, Isabel.* That had been Cousin Mimi from Dallas. They had been talking about what it meant to have children and Mimi had warned her of how quickly the childhood years went past – not for the child, but for the parent.

It was true. Already she found it hard to remember what Charlie was like as a tiny baby. Again that was something that people had warned her about: *Take photographs and look at them regularly, just to remind yourself.* There was a popular song, was there not? She turned to Jamie; he knew about these things and could reel off the lines of the most obscure songs. *How do you do it?* I don't know, I just do. I remember songs. I forget lots of other things – the capital of Paraguay, for example – but I remember songs.

She asked him, 'Isn't there a song about it?'

He looked up, and smiled. 'About what? Boiled egg?'

'About how children grow up so quickly.'

He thought for a moment. '*Fiddler on the Roof.* I think the song's called "Sunrise, Sunset". It asks how it all happened so quickly, how they grow up, become so tall, while nobody's watching.'

She remembered. 'It's true, I think.'

Jamie shrugged. 'I suppose so. But I don't think we should worry about it. We've got years ahead of us. He's not all that tall just yet, are you?' He pinched Charlie gently on the cheek and the little boy burst out laughing, as if sharing in some vastly amusing joke.

'*The years shall run like rabbits,*' she said, remembering what

Auden had said, but refraining from telling Jamie, who sometimes sighed when she mentioned WHA.

'Like rabbits?'

Charlie chuckled. 'Abbits,' he spluttered.

Hearing this, Isabel thought of its crossword potential. Cockney customs? Abbits. Senior members of monasteries? Abbits. Not the right thing to do? Bad abbits.

She smiled. 'What's the joke?' asked Jamie.

'The loss of a letter changes everything,' she said.

Jamie reflected. The years did run like rabbits, he supposed. Rabbits ran quickly, shot off, and then disappeared, which is what the years did. He dealt with a final piece of egg-smeared bread and then looked up to see that Isabel herself had disappeared . . .

. . . into her study. She had a number of letters to deal with, some opened, some still in their envelopes, lying accusingly on her desk. The postman tended to the apologetic, particularly in respect of large parcels, which he knew contained manuscripts or books for review – work, in other words. He had arrived very early that day and had said, 'This one's really heavy,' as he passed her a large padded envelope franked in Utah. He glanced at the customs declaration stuck on the front of the package. 'A book,' he said. And then, rather quickly, 'I'm sorry, we're not meant to read anything but the address. It's just that . . .'

'Willy,' she said, 'you're the model of discretion. I couldn't do your job. I'd die of curiosity as to what was in the letters I was delivering.'

Willy looked sheepish. 'Yes, it's tempting, isn't it? I never look at letters, even if the envelope has been torn and some of the inside is showing. I look the other way.'

'And postcards?' asked Isabel, innocently.

He blushed. 'You can't help but see,' he said. 'You have to read the name and address and the message is right there – sometimes just a few words. How can you not see them?'

'You can't,' agreed Isabel. 'And that's fine. If people write things that are meant to be confidential on a postcard, then it's their own fault if somebody else reads it. *Caveat scriptor* – let the writer beware.'

Willy handed her a sheaf of other letters from his bag. 'I've seen some pretty odd postcards,' he said.

Isabel's curiosity was piqued. 'Such as?'

Willy hesitated. 'You won't tell anybody?'

'Of course not. Except Jamie. Do you mind if I tell Jamie?'

'That's all right,' said Willy. 'Well, I had to deliver this postcard, see. I won't tell you where. Not far from here – not your street though. Anyway, it was a plain postcard – no picture – and on the message bit the sender had written, clear as day, "I didn't do it – you've got to believe me. It was Tom. I saw him. And he knows I know. So if anything happens to me, make sure to tell Freddie that Tom's the one they should blame."'

Isabel smiled. 'Well, well! So now we know too. Except . . .'

'Except we don't know who Tom is.'

'Yes,' she said. 'How frustrating. He could be getting away with . . . with murder, I suppose. It could be, you know.'

Willy nodded. 'I thought of that. But what could I do? It could all be about something very ordinary. Something like cheating.'

Isabel considered this. There was an obvious inference that it was not something inconsequential; one did not fear for one's safety if one knew about something minor. So it had to be something that Tom would go to some lengths to conceal, even

101

to the extent of removing the writer of the message. She pointed this out to Willy, who thought about it for a few moments, and then said that he agreed.

'There is something you could do,' she said. 'Do you know the person to whom you delivered the postcard?'

'Of course. I've been delivering his mail for years.'

Isabel looked away. She liked Willy, who was an old-fashioned postman: she had nothing to teach him about life, she thought, nor about the obligations we encounter along the way. And yet she was a philosopher, and philosophers should not feel awkward about telling people what to do.

'You could have a word with him,' she ventured. 'You could say something about not being able to help but see what was written on that card. You could say that you had been losing sleep over it and could he set your mind at rest.'

Willy started to shake his head even before she had finished speaking. 'Sorry,' he said. 'Sorry, but no.'

Isabel raised an eyebrow. 'It wouldn't cost you anything.'

Willy's head started to shake again. 'Dangerous,' he said. 'He would then know that I know. And what if he told Tom? Then something could happen to me.'

Isabel thought this rather fanciful. 'Come on, Willy. This is Edinburgh, not . . .' She waved a hand in a vaguely south-easterly direction. 'Not Palermo.'

'I mean it,' said Willy. 'I could be in real danger.'

'Surely not. This person – the person to whom the card was delivered, surely he's perfectly respectable . . .' It sounded odd: what was respectability these days? But what other expression was there? she wondered. Law-abiding? That said what she wanted to say, but somehow sounded equally old-fashioned.

Willy smiled. 'He's not, you know. He's . . . he's a criminal.'

At first, Isabel did not know what to say. But then she wondered how Willy knew. One had to have proof to make that sort of allegation, and what proof would he have? She looked at his bag. He carried secrets; he carried people's lives about in his bag. He knew.

'See?' said Willy. 'So I can't really do anything. Not where I live.'

Isabel understood, and the thought depressed her. She had often speculated on what it must be like to live in a rotten state, where those in power and authority were corrupt and evil. Stalinist Russia must have been like that; the Third Reich; and countless lesser examples of tinpot dictatorships. How trapped one must feel; how dispirited that there was nobody to assert the good. There were courts and investigative journalists and public-spirited politicians who could be turned to, but what if one were powerless or without much of a voice? One needed grammar, and volume, to be heard. What if one lived in an area where the writ that ran in the streets was that of a local gang leader? Or where, if one incurred the disfavour of somebody powerful, a nod could arrange a nasty accident? For many people, that was a reality: the police, the state, could not give them real protection.

'We can't put everything right,' she said. It was a shameful admission, and contrary to much of what she believed. But it was true, at least for Willy, who sighed and said yes, she was right. We could not put right even a tiny part of what was wrong.

'Compromise,' he said, making ready to leave.

Isabel watched him walk down the path. He was right about compromise; and who amongst us, she thought, did not make

103

compromises, all the time? The answer came without prompting: Charlie. He lived in a world of absolutes, but would learn to compromise soon enough so that he could live in a world that was far, very far, from the peaceable kingdom of our aspiration, of our imagining. Nor had Charlie yet learned to lie; what he said was what he thought. And yet at some stage he would learn to lie and at that point, Isabel thought, would his moral life really begin. The struggle with lies was for many of us the first, most difficult, and most long-lasting battle of our lives. It was not surprising, perhaps, that so many people gave in at an early stage. Only Kant, with his categorical imperative, and George Washington, with his chopped-down and possibly apocryphal cherry tree, and a few others, formed the company of those who were constitutionally incapable of telling a lie. The rest of humanity was, she feared, fairly mendacious.

She imagined, for a moment, Charlie, a few years hence and able to wield an axe, even if a tiny one, cutting down her cherry tree – and there was a small cherry tree in her garden – and then saying, 'Didn't.' That's what children said: *didn't*. They knew it was not true, and that in most cases they should have said *did*. But no turkey, when asked the time of year, if speech were possible for turkeys, would say *Late November* or *December 24.*

She started to tackle the mail, beginning with the package from Utah. She knew who would have sent it: Mike Vause, a professor at a university there, had corresponded with her over the last few years since she published an article of his on the subject of mountaineering ethics. From time to time he sent her articles and books that he thought she might like, even though she had never met him. It was typical of Midwestern generosity, she thought; that direct, helpful attitude that made her proud of her half-American ancestry. Her *sainted American mother* had had that quality too, she reflected; and I love her so much, although her memory is fading. *Don't leave me altogether; don't leave me.*

Isabel took the book out of the package and saw on it a picture of a high mountain ridge, with climbers strung out along it, tiny figures like ants. Tucked into the jacket flap was a note from Mike:

Isabel – I mentioned this book to you once. Now I've found a copy that I'd like you to have. This author really saw some of the things we talked about – it's unbelievable. Or rather, it's very believable. People can be pretty wicked, can't they? Are you still disinclined to climb? One of these days I'll come over to Scotland and show you how to climb Ben Nevis. You can do it, you know. Anybody can. And you never know: you might find that you have a good head for heights after all!

Mike.

She looked at the description of the book. The author had decided to climb Everest. He had looked forward to an expedition in the company of high-minded people; instead he had found a mountain riddled with all sorts of unattractive characters: thieves, charlatans, ruthless exploiters of would-be summiteers. She frowned, remembering again her conversation with Willy. He had suggested that a criminal lived a few streets away – which should be no great surprise, as criminals, large and small, had to live somewhere, and that had to be next door to somebody; but should criminals infest Everest, of all places? Everest, like any mountain, should be a place of purity, of high driven snow, of clean – if somewhat thin – air.

Isabel sat down in her chair and began to read. The rest of the mail remained ignored and unopened. An hour later, Jamie came in with a cup of coffee.

'I didn't want to disturb you,' he said. Glancing at the book, he asked whether she was reviewing it.

'No.' She put the book down. 'Tell me Jamie, if you were climbing Everest . . .'

He laughed. 'Yes. Easily imagined. So I'm climbing Everest . . .'

'And high up – not in the Death Zone yet, but still pretty high . . .'

He asked her what the Death Zone was. 'Where there's so little oxygen that you're likely to die quite quickly.'

Jamie shuddered. 'It must be like drowning,' he said. 'Drowning in air, like fish taken out of the water.'

'I suppose so. Anyway, there you are, making your way up the mountain and you see another climber collapsed in the snow. What would you do?'

Jamie shrugged. 'I'd stop and ask him how he was.'

'And then?'

'Give him a hand.'

She had not expected anything else. 'Help him down the mountain?'

Jamie answer naturally. 'If that was what was necessary. I suppose it wouldn't be practical for me to go and get help, would it?'

Isabel did not think it would.

'In that case,' said Jamie, 'I'd help him down to . . . base camp, isn't it? There'd be a doctor there, no doubt.'

Along with the thieves and extortionists, thought Isabel. 'Yes, there'd probably be a doctor. But you'd probably be alone if you tried to help him, you know.'

Jamie looked at her for explanation. 'But I thought that Everest was quite busy. Aren't there always several hundred people on the mountain – if you include the base camp – all the hangers-on?'

Isabel put down the book. 'Yes, so I gather. But very few of them sign up to the old ethic of mountaineering.'

'Which was?'

'One of fellow feeling for other mountaineers. If you came across somebody in need of help, you helped them.'

Jamie was thoughtful. 'Like the custom of the sea.'

'I suppose so.'

He remembered a yachtsman friend who had told him that one could not count on that any more. He had mentioned that there had been cases where ships ran down yachts and were suspected of not stopping. 'It's survival of the fittest,' he had said. 'These large ships have places to get to and can't be bothered to lose the time.'

Jamie had been appalled, and Isabel too, as he told her. 'So it's like that on Everest?'

Isabel gestured to the book. 'So we are told. It's a different sport today. Look.' She opened the book to show Jamie a photograph of a mountaineering expedition in the thirties. A group of three men stood on an ice field, roped together. They were wearing tweed jackets, with waistcoats and ties. 'Ties!' exclaimed Jamie.

Isabel smiled. 'Yes. And plus fours. Look.'

She turned to another picture, this time showing a mountaineer equipped for an assault on Everest. It was difficult to make out his features under the goggles and the breathing apparatus. In his hand he carried a satellite phone. *In touch with headquarters six thousand miles away*, said the caption. She turned the page to find another photograph, which she showed to Jamie. 'That's him,' she said. 'That's the young mountaineer who was passed by forty other climbers as he lay dying. Nobody helped him.'

Jamie looked at the face. The photograph had been taken at the beginning of the expedition; the man was smiling, looked optimistic. It was the face of a healthy sportsman, but it had the poignancy of being the last photograph, or almost the last photograph. The camera catches somebody in the fullness of life but the subject's fate is already decided.

'He could have been saved?'

'It seems so. Or, at least given a chance. But that would have meant that the rescuers would have lost their chance of getting to the top.' She reached out to touch the photograph; to put a finger on the mountaineer's cheek. *Live in high places, die in high places.*

She stopped. She did not know where that expression had come from. Had she made it up, or had she heard it somewhere? It was difficult to tell; was it just a reworking of *Live by the sword, die by the sword*?

She touched the photograph again. Jamie was watching.

'Why are you doing that?'

She answered softly. 'Because he's dead.'

Jamie moved to the window. 'Those flowers,' he said. 'The ones by the wall. What did you call them again?'

She told him, giving the Scots vernacular name as well as the botanical one. But her mind was elsewhere. Guilt. *He walked past somebody*, she whispered.

Jamie turned round. 'Who did?'

She closed the book. 'I think I know what's troubling John Fraser,' she said. 'He walked past another climber, who was dying. He didn't help him.'

Jamie looked at her in astonishment. 'Isabel! How do you know that? You haven't got a shred — not a shred — of evidence.'

She just felt it, and told him so. She did not need evidence for hunches — that was what hunches were all about.

He shook his head. 'You're doing it again. Inventing things. Whole stories now. Making them up.'

She got to her feet. 'But that's what the world is all about, Jamie. Stories. Stories explain everything, bring everything together.'

Jamie walked towards the door. 'How do you know that John Fraser ever went to Everest?'

'I don't.'

'Well, it would have had to be somewhere like that,' he pointed out. 'It wouldn't be so dramatic in Scotland. If you left somebody, the mountain rescue people would be there within a couple of hours. Our mountains don't have Death Zones, Isabel.'

'Yet people die on them,' she pointed out. 'Every year. One or two — sometimes more.'

'That's because they slip.' He paused. He was thinking of a boy he had known at school, a boy called Andrew — and he could not remember his surname. But he could picture him, and saw him now, with his untidy fair hair and his permanent smile. He had been a climber and had died in the Cairngorms when he tumbled headlong into a gully that had been disguised by a fall of snow.

She noticed his expression; he had told her about this. 'Your friend? You were thinking about him?'

'Yes.'

'How often do you think about him?' she asked.

He looked surprised. 'Why do you ask?'

Because she was interested, she said. Death was such a strange event – simple enough in its essentials, of course, and final enough for the person who dies; but human personality had its echoes. *Non omnis moriar*, said Horace's *Odes* – I shall not wholly die. Yes, and he was right. As long as people remembered, then death was not complete. Only if there were nobody at all left to remember would death be complete.

'I sometimes think of him,' said Jamie. 'We were quite close. In fact, we were very close.'

He stopped. She reached out for his hand.

'I think of him a lot,' said Jamie.

Isabel squeezed his hand. 'Loved him?'

Jamie nodded. 'I suppose so. You know how it is with boys. Those intense friendships you have when you're young.'

'I think so.'

'I went to the place,' said Jamie. 'I climbed up there a year or so later. Just by myself – in summer. It wasn't a hard climb at all – more of a walk, even if the gully itself was quite deep. I looked over the edge and imagined what he had seen as he fell – he must have seen something, unless he was knocked out straight away, which they thought had not happened. And then I just cried and cried. I went down the hill, cried all the way down.'

She pressed his hand. 'Of course.'

'I think I understand why mountaineering involves such . . . such passion. Climbers do get passionate, you know. They're very spiritual people.'

Isabel glanced at the Everest book. 'Some of them. Maybe not so much now. I think our world has become harder, you know.'

She did not want that to be true, but she thought it probably was. What had happened? Had the human soul shrunk in some way, become meaner, like a garment that has been in the wash too long and become smaller, more constraining?

# 8

'Have you ever climbed anything, Charlie?'

It was at a party, a rather noisy one, in the Scotch Malt Whisky Society in Queen Street that Isabel was address-ing Charlie Maclean, Master of the Quaich, and Scotland's greatest expert on whisky. Charlie wore his learning lightly, but everybody in the room knew that if there was one man who could identify a glass of anonymous amber liquid and attribute it to any one of the country's distilleries, name the man who blended it, and talk at length about the history of the glen from which it came, then it was Charlie.

They were standing at the window of one of the upstairs rooms, and beyond them, swaying in the summer-evening breeze, were the tops of the trees lining Queen Street Gardens. That wind was mild, and had on its breath the scent of the Firth, the river, and of the hills beyond. And of newly cut grass, too, for the gardens had been attended to that day and the smell of the grass was strong.

While Isabel was talking to Charlie, a well-built man in a

linen suit and sporting the only monocle still known to be worn in Scotland, Jamie was on the other side of the room, engaged in conversation with a tall man whom Isabel knew well. This was Roddy Martine, a well-liked recorder of social events who kept society, and its doings, in his head. Roddy knew who did what, with whom, and when. He knew, too, who knew what about whom, and why.

Charlie raised his glass to his lips and looked at Isabel across the rim. 'Climbed?' he said. 'When I was very young I was at school in Dumfriesshire. Until about eleven. Pretty odd place. They used to take us climbing the hills down there – Kirkudbrightshire and so on. Nothing very big. And I climbed a bit when I was at St Andrews. The occasional Munro. And you?'

'Not really,' said Isabel.

Charlie remembered something about the school. 'Funny, I never really think about that place. It's closed now. It was a pretty dubious institution. One of the masters . . .'

Isabel imagined that she was about to hear some awful story of cruelty, of the sort that had been surfacing so much – ancient traumas exposed and scratched at, like sores. But no, Charlie's memories were benign.

'He was called Mr MacDavid,' Charlie went on. 'He was the most unusual teacher. All he ever taught us – for years – was the Boer War. He knew a lot about that. So by the time I was eleven, I knew everything there was to know about the Boer War, but was pretty ignorant about everything else.'

Isabel laughed. 'The relief of Ladysmith,' she said. 'The siege of Mafeking.'

'Don't start on that,' said Charlie. 'But why did you ask me about climbing?'

Isabel took a sip of her wine. A waiter approached; their host had ordered trays of elaborate canapés and not enough guests were eating them. 'Please take something,' pleaded the waiter. 'These are very nice.' He indicated a row of miniature haggis pies.

Isabel picked one out; Charlie took two in one hand, popping another one into his mouth. Isabel thanked the waiter before she answered Charlie's question. 'I thought you might know about it. I've been reading a book about Everest. I had no idea.'

Charlie, swallowing another tiny haggis, looked interested. 'No idea about all those goings-on?'

'Yes.'

'Well I do,' said Charlie, licking his fingers. 'I know somebody who went there a couple of years ago. I met him through Pete Burgess. He went up Everest, but didn't get to the top. Something went wrong. They're always dying – once you get past a certain point. Apparently the mountain has got hundreds of bodies on it – they can't get them down.'

Isabel was thinking. Edinburgh was not a large city. How many people living there would have climbed Everest? One or two, if that. 'I think I may know him,' she said. 'Or rather, I don't actually know him, but I know who he is. John Fraser.' And then she added, 'I think.'

Charlie was looking across the room as Isabel spoke. She thought at first that he had not heard her, as he started to say something about a woman who stood in the doorway. 'I've seen her somewhere,' he said. 'She's an actress, I think, and the trouble with actresses is that you think you know them because you've seen them . . .' And then he stopped. 'Fraser? Yes. John Fraser. Tall chap. He's a teacher, I think.'

Isabel felt her heart beat faster. 'You said that something went wrong. What?'

'One of them fell. They weren't all that far up, I gather. This chap fell. I think he was . . .' He looked away again. The actress was talking to a small, rather neat man; she was taller than him by at least a head.

'Who was he – the one who fell?'

Charlie looked at Isabel again. She found herself studying his moustache – a handlebar affair that seemed to suit him so well. It must have taken years, she thought, to reach that stage of perfection; a generous act, undertaken for the benefit of others, as any act of personal enhancement was, since one did not see it very much oneself.

'I don't know,' he said. 'But I do know that he played rugby for Scotland. They had a minute's silence for him at Murrayfield Stadium. He was one of the wings.' Then he remembered. 'Chris Alexander. That was his name. I recall it now because his father was a director of a distillery I had dealings with. Nice chap. I met him. He was also a good amateur nose. He sometimes nosed for one of the distilleries on Islay. I forget which one. '

Isabel had heard Charlie refer to 'noses' before. They were the people who remembered just how to achieve the taste of a particular whisky. He was a nose himself.

'Are you interested in all this?' Charlie said. 'You've never talked about it before.'

She could not tell him, of course, and so she changed the subject. What she had heard confirmed her conviction that something had happened on the mountain to torment John Fraser. And she was already beginning to imagine what it was: Chris Alexander had fallen and John Fraser had left him to die.

That was what John Fraser sought to expunge from his conscience, and that, she imagined, was what the anonymous
letter-writer had somehow found out. This was quite possible,
even if she had not a shred of evidence to support it. But
would this hypothesis – for that was all it was – be enough to
justify going to the chairman of the board of governors of
Bishop Forbes and suggesting that this was what lay in one of
the candidates' past? He might say – and he would be justified
in doing so – that she had jumped to conclusions. But if he did
not, and if he proved to be willing to listen, then what did all
this reveal? Simple cowardice – or something worse than that?
Was it murder to leave somebody to die? No, it was not, but
it could still be criminal, if you had an obligation to do something to help somebody and you did not. That was called
culpable homicide, she believed, and it was not what one
would expect to find in the background of the principal of a
school.

So if all this proved to be true, then John Fraser was out
of the running for the post, and that meant that Cat's new boyfriend, Gordon, would have a much higher chance of appointment, particularly if Isabel found something questionable in
the background of the third candidate. And that, she reflected,
was exactly the way she should *not* be thinking. If you play a
part in a competition for a public job – and a principal's post
was a public job – you should not favour your friends, or the
friends of your friends, or the friend of your niece. That was
what she reminded herself, but then it occurred to her: why
not? The overwhelming majority of people would without
question favour a friend or a relative, if they had the chance,
and not think twice about it. Were all these people wrong? Yes,
thought Isabel; but then she thought, no. Morality could not be

a matter of counting heads; but counting heads was sometimes a useful way of seeing whether a system of morality suited human nature as it actually was. Moral rules should not be devised for saints, but should be within the grasp of ordinary people; and ordinary people preferred those they knew to those they did not know; everyone knew that, but most of all, ordinary people knew it.

The next morning, Isabel took Charlie out in his pram to go shopping in Bruntsfield. It was an outing that he particularly enjoyed as it inevitably culminated in a visit to Cat's delicatessen, where Cat would give him a marzipan pig from a small box she kept on a shelf behind the counter. He knew exactly what lay in store and would shout 'Pig! Pig!' as they entered. Then, with the treat grasped firmly in his hands, he would bite off the pig's head, watched in astonishment by Eddie and Cat.

'It's almost indecent,' said Cat. 'He has no sympathy for the pig.'

Isabel felt that she had to defend her son. 'But it's just sugar to him. It's not a living pig.'

'Does he like bacon?' asked Eddie. 'Would he eat it if he knew?'

Isabel sighed. It was the right question. If he knew that bacon had once been a pig, then he would probably not eat it. There were pigs in a book she read him; three of them, two feckless and one wise, and he clearly loved them. Yet how different were we humans from the wolf who persecuted the three pigs?

*Pigs give us bacon.* This was the way it had been put to her in a book she had herself possessed as a child: *Farmer John.* Farmer John, a bucolic character in blue overalls, took the reader round

117

the farmyard and explained what was what. *Hens give us eggs* – we steal them, thought Isabel. *Cows give us milk* – ditto. And then, in an act of astonishing self-sacrifice, *Pigs give us bacon.*

Eddie was good with Charlie, and Charlie seemed fascinated with the young man, who lifted him high in the air and then pretended to drop him, to squeals of excitement. While this was going on, Cat made coffee for herself and Isabel and carried the cups across to one of the tables.

They talked briefly about the delicatessen. The mozzarella cheese was late, Cat complained; she was thinking of changing their supplier. And the Parmesan too, although that was never delayed for more than a few days. Isabel listened politely; she wanted to hear about Gordon. Had he heard anything further about the job? she wanted to ask, but it was difficult with Cat going on about mozzarella and Parmesan.

Cat paused, and Isabel seized her chance. 'I like him a lot, you know.'

'Who?'

'Your new boyfriend, Gordon.'

Cat was cagey. 'So do I.'

'But of course you do,' said Isabel quickly. 'One would not dislike a boyfriend, surely.' As she spoke, she thought of Bruno, the stunt man with elevator shoes. Had Cat actually *liked* him, or had Bruno been more of a perverse fashion statement? A boyfriend or girlfriend could easily be thought of in those terms, she realised. Or Cat might be making another point altogether, showing that she was her own person; sometimes people needed to find somebody the diametrical opposite of their parents just to make a point about independence. That happened often. A boy with dreadlocks, or a hard rock musician, a member – in good standing – of a biker gang perhaps;

a girl with multiple piercings in the nose and tongue; how easy with such a choice to remind parents that one's tastes, one's attitude, and one's voting intentions were not to be taken for granted.

Cat tensed. 'Of course not.' She hesitated, but then, relaxing, said, 'Gordon is very popular.'

Isabel said that she was pleased to hear that. There was always some reason for popularity.

'Oh yes?'

'Yes,' said Isabel. 'Have you ever met somebody who's popular but unpleasant?'

Cat thought about this. 'No, not really.'

'Well, there you are.' She took a sip of her coffee. 'So he has no faults – as far as you know?'

Cat shrugged. 'Everybody has faults.'

'So they do,' said Isabel. 'We all have our quirks.'

Cat looked at her with interest. 'And yours are? Your faults, I mean: what are they?'

'We don't always see our own faults with *crystal* clarity,' said Isabel. 'But since you put me on the spot, I suppose I would have to say that I tend to over-complicate matters – it's my training. And I can be nosy – so Jamie tells me.' She noticed that Cat was nodding in agreement, and felt slightly irritated. What she wanted was for Cat to say, "*You* over-complicate things? *You* nosy? Surely not."'

Isabel was about to ask Cat about her own faults, but Cat suddenly said, 'He's too generous with his time. That's one of his faults. It can be misinterpreted.'

Isabel was careful not to appear too interested in this. 'A nice fault to have,' she said. 'And it's better, surely, than being grudging with one's time.'

'He'll listen to anybody,' said Cat. 'He lets them go on about things, and then they think that he's more interested in them than he really is.'

Isabel said that she saw how this could be awkward: expectations could be raised; hopes dashed. While she said this, her heart sank. Gordon was not going to prove to be the flawless candidate she had hoped. Affairs: that was what Cat was alluding to.

'Tell me,' she said. 'Was he . . . with somebody before you met him?'

Cat took the spoon from her saucer and retrieved a residue of milky foam from the bottom of her cup. 'There was somebody.' She paused, as if uncertain whether to go on. 'Not that it amounted to anything on his side. One of these one-sided things.'

Isabel looked out of the window. A one-sided thing. She saw a man waiting at the bus stop on the other side of the road; a young woman passed by and his head turned. She thought he said something; the woman stopped, half turned, and then walked on. A one-sided thing.

'You mean somebody fell for him, but not the other way round?'

Cat nodded.

'Well, that can be difficult,' said Isabel. 'Yes, I see that. But all that needs to be done, presumably, is to indicate that it's not on.'

'She was rather unstable,' said Cat. 'And married.'

'Oh.'

'It's not a big thing,' said Cat. 'Women get infatuated. Remember what's-her-name? Madame . . .'

'Bovary.' Isabel sighed. 'Married. And there was a betrayed husband, I suppose.'

Cat's answer was spirited. 'It wasn't his idea. I've been trying to tell you that. It was her.'

'How far did it go?' asked Isabel. The question seemed prurient and she was not sure whether she wanted to know; but it was too late now. Cat looked at her angrily. 'It didn't go anywhere. I told you that.'

Perhaps it was not as bad as Isabel had feared. 'Well, so no harm was done.' She wanted to change the subject because she did not want Cat to begin to ask why she was so interested. She looked over to the other side of the room, where Eddie was feeding Charlie small pieces of black olive. 'He must be the only child in Scotland who likes olives,' she said.

Cat rose from the table. 'I must get on with things.'

Isabel reached out. 'I meant what I said. I really like him.'

Cat softened. 'Well, thank you. I'm glad about that.'

She wants to share him, thought Isabel. It was a lover's pride. A lover wants others to see the beloved in exactly the same light as she does. And that was true of how Isabel felt about Jamie; she assumed that others would see him as she saw him. Yet she knew that this was an illusion: the light that surrounds the one we love is not always as bright to others. Indeed, they were often unaware that it was there at all.


Isabel finished the last of her coffee and then crossed the room to relieve Eddie of Charlie. The marzipan pig, slightly bigger than usual this time, had been produced and was being flourished enthusiastically by Charlie. 'Pig! Pig!' he shouted. And then, exactly as anticipated, he bit off its head.

Eddie laughed. 'Olives and pigs. His two big things.'

'And the fox in our garden,' said Isabel. 'He loves him.'

Eddie bent down and ruffled Charlie's hair. 'Their hair is

always so soft,' he said. 'Like an owl's feathers. Have you ever felt an owl's feathers, Isabel?'

Isabel said that she had not.

'I have,' said Eddie. 'There was a guy who had a little barn owl on a sort of string. The string was tied around its leg. He was a falconer, and he brought it to the Meadows Festival.'

Isabel smiled encouragingly. Increasingly, Eddie spoke of things he remembered, whereas in the past he had been largely silent about his life outside the delicatessen. It seemed to her that he was reclaiming something, piece by piece, assembling a life.

'He let me stroke the feathers on the top of its head,' he continued. 'I had never felt anything so soft. It was like . . . like Charlie's hair. Even softer maybe.'

Eddie touched Charlie's hair again, and the little boy looked up appreciatively.

'He likes you,' said Isabel. 'I think you're one of his favourite people.'

The compliment had a marked effect, and it seemed to Isabel that Eddie grew in stature before her, swelling with pride. He straightened up; his head moved back. Like a soldier on parade, thought Isabel; but how strange that mere words should do that to people – inflate them, deflate them too.

Eddie looked at his watch. 'I'd better get on with things,' he said. 'I have to slice some Parma ham and people will be coming in soon. It's always busy around lunchtime – as you know.'

Isabel picked up Charlie to put him back in his pushchair. 'Of course. And Charlie will need his sleep, won't you, darling?'

'Pig,' said Charlie, examining the marzipan animal.

'Insults won't help,' said Isabel.

Eddie laughed. 'He said pig and you thought . . .' He looked at his watch again. Then he seemed to remember something, and turned to Isabel. 'Did you enjoy the film?'

Isabel looked blank. She had not been to the cinema in two months, and she could not remember what it was that she and Jamie had seen last − something at the Dominion, she thought. But what was it? It had not been memorable. 'What film?'

'That Italian film,' said Eddie, reaching for a large Parma ham. 'The Parma ham made me think of it. Remember that scene where . . .'

Isabel frowned. 'Italian film?' She could not remember when she had last seen an Italian film.

'*La Famiglia*,' said Eddie. 'Remember? Last Wednesday. I saw Jamie when I went out to get something to drink. Weren't you there too?'

Isabel was fastening the straps that held Charlie in the pushchair. She did so very slowly, listening carefully to what Eddie was saying. His voice seemed to echo, for some reason. It was loud in her ears.

'Where was it?' she asked. 'The Dominion?'

'Never go there,' said Eddie. 'No, it was at the Film House in Lothian Road. I love going there. My friend used to work there. He sometimes gave me tickets. Maybe he shouldn't have − I don't know.'

Isabel would normally have said that he should not, but her mind was preoccupied. Eddie had seen Jamie at the cinema. Jamie had not said anything about seeing a film. Why?

'Are you sure it was Jamie?'

'Yes. Of course. It's not as if I don't know Jamie.' He paused.

'We said hello. He said "Hello, Eddie" and then he went back in.'

'Oh . . . Oh. Well.'

She finished securing Charlie and turned to go. She said goodbye to Eddie, and he made a cheerful remark about keeping another marzipan pig for Charlie. 'It's not that I want to ruin his teeth. It's just that . . .'

Isabel did not hear the rest of the remark. She had pushed Charlie out on to the pavement and now, for a moment, she had no idea which way to turn. Was she going to walk back to the house – in which case she would turn left – or was she going to go back into Bruntsfield – in which case she would turn right? She felt completely lost. She felt empty, scoured out; as if somebody had taken a great knife and hollowed her.

She turned left, and began to walk back along Merchiston Crescent. A woman was approaching her on the pavement, going the other way. It was a woman she recognised but did not know – one of those nodding acquaintances that one builds up in a city even if in many cases one never finds out who they are or where they live. She was a small, bird-like woman who wore a scarf over her head, like an old-fashioned French farmer's wife. Isabel did know a little bit about her. She lived in a flat in Merchiston Crescent and Grace, who knew her too, had been told that she was a singing teacher. 'I saw somebody going to her place,' Grace once said. 'He was standing outside her front door, about to ring the bell. A very round man with slicked-down hair and highly polished shoes. He must be learning to sing.'

The singing teacher drew level with Isabel, and, seeing Charlie, slowed her pace.

'Such a beautiful little boy,' she said. 'Do you mind my asking: what's he called?'

This was the first time that Isabel had heard her voice; it was high, with a West Highland lilt to it.

'Charlie.'

'Bonnie Charlie,' said the woman, bending down to examine Charlie more closely.

Isabel took a deep breath. I am not going to cry, she told herself. I am not. But when the woman looked up, she saw the tears in Isabel's eyes.

'My dear . . .'

Isabel reached in her pocket for a handkerchief. 'It's nothing. I'm all right.' She realised, as she spoke, how trite the words were. People said things like that without thinking, but it helped neither them nor the people trying to comfort them.

The woman placed a hand on Isabel's arm. 'It's hard being a mother, isn't it? There are so many things.'

Isabel nodded. 'Thank you. Thank you.'

'If I can do anything to help?'

Isabel shook her head. 'Thanks. I'll be all right. I must get Charlie back for his sleep.'

They parted, although the singing teacher looked over her shoulder a few yards on. She saw Isabel continue her journey, walking more swiftly now, head down, as if to fight a wind that was not there, on this calm day, with its clear sky and darting birds.

# 9

There had been painful days in Isabel's life, as there are in the lives of all of us. There had been days during her brief marriage to John Liamor when she had felt a blanket of despair about her – a dark, enveloping blanket that prevented her from doing anything, from thinking about anything other than her distress. And it brought with it self-pity, for which she had a particular distaste when she saw it in others, but which she nevertheless understood perfectly well. *I shall not*, she said to herself as she returned to the house. *I shall not. No.* But what was it that she would not do? Think Jamie capable of deception, of . . . ? She could hardly bring herself to think the word, let alone mutter it to herself; but now she said it, the word escaping her lips in an almost inaudible whisper: *Unfaithfulness.* And then, the word still hanging in the air, she muttered: *Affair.*

She passed the photograph of her sainted American mother in its place on the hall table; her sainted American mother who, as she had subsequently discovered, had had an affair. She had learned this from a conversation with her mother's cousin, Mimi

McKnight, who had tried to protect her from the knowledge but who had had it drawn out of her. Mimi had put it as tactfully as she could, and had wanted Isabel to forgive her mother, which she had done, of course; forgiveness, Mimi pointed out, can be as powerful when it is posthumous as when it is given in life; perhaps even more so. This had intrigued Isabel, and she had realised that it was quite true: forgiveness of others allows us to adjust our feelings towards the past, assuages our anger. Our parents may disappoint us in so many ways: they could have done more, they made us neurotic, they should have insisted we learn the piano – and now it is too late; they were too strict, in big things or small; they were too poor, too ignorant, too rich and possessive. There are so many grudges we can hold against the past and for the love and approval that we did not get from it. But if we forgive, then the past can lose its power to hurt.

She looked at her mother. The photograph had been taken on a trip that she had made to Venice with a college friend whose name Isabel had now forgotten. The friend was in the background, clutching at a straw hat she was wearing; there was a breeze and there were flags fluttering in the background; St Mark's Square, and the outside of the Caffè Florian, which had been such a favourite with Proust, and had been portrayed in a glorious Scottish Colourist painting. She looked at her mother's face; she was smiling, and now it seemed to Isabel that the smile meant, *My dear, life is like this; there are so many disappointments; so many . . .*

Isabel turned away. Charlie, whom she had taken out of his pushchair in the outer hall, was niggling. He was tired and would settle quickly, but now nothing would satisfy him. She picked him up as Grace came out of the kitchen, a tea towel in her hand.

'I heard you come in. I've just made tea. Would you like a cup?'

'He's so tired,' said Isabel. 'Tea? No thank you.'

Grace approached Charlie and picked him up. 'Little darling. Tired? Tired now and ready for a nap?'

Charlie made a fist and struck Grace across the chin.

'No!' Isabel's voice was harsh, and Charlie looked at her in wide-eyed astonishment.

'That's all right,' said Grace. 'Didn't hurt.'

'It's not all right,' said Isabel testily. 'Don't tell him it's all right to hit people. Just don't!'

Grace looked at Isabel, registering much the same surprise as did Charlie. 'He didn't mean it.'

Isabel half turned away. 'He did. He hit you.' She turned back and looked at Charlie. 'You mustn't hit people, Charlie. Wrong. Bad.' She thought, inconsequentially and absurdly: *I speak as the editor of the* Review of Applied Ethics, *not just as your mother. Wrong. Bad.*

Grace was stroking Charlie's cheek, and the little boy was smiling in response. 'Grace put you to bed?' said Grace. 'Grace tuck you up?' She looked to Isabel for confirmation.

'Yes,' said Isabel. 'If you wouldn't mind. I have . . .' She gestured towards the study door. 'I have work to do . . . Or rather I have to . . .'

'If you need to go out,' said Grace, 'I'll look after our wee friend here. I've done all the ironing – it's all stacked away. I could take him to Blackford Pond later on.'

'Ducks,' shouted Charlie.

'You see,' exclaimed Grace. 'Clever boy. Clever, clever boy! There are indeed ducks in Blackford Pond.'

'On it,' muttered Isabel.

'What?'

'On the pond. There are ducks *on* the pond. There are fish *in* it.' Even as she spoke, Isabel had no idea why she was being so pedantic, and she looked at Grace apologetically. But Grace, perhaps not noticing the correction, in her turn simply corrected Isabel. 'There are no fish left,' she said. 'The ducks have eaten them all.'

'I don't think ducks eat fish,' said Isabel, her testiness returning. 'They eat weed and things like that. Bits of . . . of sludge.'

Grace was tight-lipped. 'I'll take him upstairs.'

'Thank you,' said Isabel. 'And look, I'm sorry. I'm upset about something.'

Grace looked at her with concern. 'Is everything . . .'

'It's fine,' said Isabel. 'I'm just trying to deal with something that's worrying me.'

'What is it?'

Isabel shook her head. 'A private thing. You know how we all have worries – silly things. But they worry us.'

'And they usually are silly,' said Grace. 'Aren't they?'

Isabel nodded silently. Not this one, she thought. This is not silly.

'Go shopping,' said Grace. 'Treat yourself. Go to Jenners. Buy something.'

Isabel smiled weakly. 'Retail therapy?'

'Precisely. It always works.'

Isabel shook her head. 'Not for me. It makes me feel guilty.'

Grace started to leave the room, carrying Charlie, who was waving a small hand at his mother. 'You feel guilty about far too much,' came her parting shot. 'It's all that philosophy. How guilty they must all have felt, those people. Plato. Old what's-his-name. And the other one, the one who couldn't.'

She left. Isabel pondered: which was the one who couldn't? It occurred to her a few moments later. Kant. But she could not smile at the thought, as she normally would have done. She couldn't.

The gate of West Grange House was open. Isabel, who had walked over from her house, looked up the gravelled drive and saw that Peter Stevenson's car was parked at the front door. But as she began to walk up the drive, Susie came out of the house holding a plastic shopping bag. She had clearly not been expecting a visitor, and gave a momentary start before she recognised Isabel.

'You're going out,' said Isabel. 'Sorry – I should have phoned.'

Susie went forward to meet her. 'Not at all. I was just nipping out to the supermarket and I can do that any time. No, I mean it. Come in.'

Reassured, Isabel followed her back into the house. Susie said that she would make coffee and they should both go into the kitchen. 'Peter's in there. He'll be pleased to see you.'

'I'm sure you've both got things to do,' said Isabel.

'We haven't.' They were making their way down the corridor that led to the kitchen, and Susie suddenly stopped. Lowering her voice, she asked Isabel if everything was all right. 'Is there anything . . .'

'Yes,' said Isabel. 'There is.'

'I could tell,' said Susie. 'There was something in the way you looked.' She gestured towards the door that led into the drawing room. 'Would you prefer to be in there?'

Isabel hesitated. It was, in a sense, woman's business, but she wanted to talk to Peter too. She shook her head. 'Both of you,' she said. 'I wanted to talk to both of you. Do you mind?'

'Of course not.' She took Isabel's arm, gently. 'Come on.'

Peter was surprised to see her, but immediately realised from Susie's manner that something was wrong. He had been sitting at the kitchen table filling in a form of some sort, and he rose to his feet as Susie and Isabel entered. 'An unexpected pleasure,' he said, folding the form and slipping it into a plain manila file on the table. 'Bureaucracy. Forms. There are forms for absolutely everything these days. Permission-to-breathe forms.'

'Don't jest,' said Susie. 'There's probably some official drafting one right now.'

Isabel made an effort to smile. 'I suppose that having so many bureaucrats, we need to find something for them to do.'

Peter agreed. 'Work expands to fill the time of the people you employ to do it. It's ever thus. Coffee, Isabel?'

Isabel sat down at the table. She was aware that both Peter and Susie were looking at her in a solicitous manner. For a few moments, nothing was said. Susie took the kettle and filled it under the tap; Peter moved the file on the table so that it lined up with a crack between two planks.

It was Peter who broke the silence, clearing his throat and then, hesitantly, asking whether there was anything wrong. He did not want to pry, but he wondered . . .

Isabel looked down at her hands. 'Yes, I'm afraid there is.' She looked up and felt a sudden flood of gratitude to her two friends. In the lives of most of us there are a few people to whom one can go at any time, in any state of mind, and expect complete, unconditional sympathy. Peter and Susie were such for her.

She started to tell them. She explained how Eddie had made

the comment in an offhand, incidental way. 'He was absolutely certain that it was Jamie,' she said. 'And I'm equally certain that Jamie said that he was rehearsing that night. I remember it very clearly because I asked him what they were playing and he said it was a dreadful programme that he couldn't stand and he didn't want to be there.'

Peter listened carefully. In the background, Susie measured coffee grounds into the pot; her head half turned from her task in order to catch what Isabel was saying.

'So you're saying that he said that he would be at a rehearsal and wasn't. Is that all?'

Isabel frowned. 'All? He was at the cinema with some-body . . .'

Peter held up a hand. 'Hold on. Hold on. All you know is that he was at Film House, or wherever, and that he saw an Italian film. That's all that Eddie said.'

Isabel replied that people did not go to the cinema by them-selves – or not very often. 'Why would he? And if he did – if for some reason he decided on impulse to go – then surely he'd tell me. And he didn't.'

Susie, pouring boiling water into the pot, spoke over her shoulder. 'Not necessarily. Married couples – and you're virtu-ally that – don't give each other every detail of their day-to-day lives. Didn't you tell me once – I'm sure you did – that you and Jamie both give each other room for a personal life? You did say something like that, didn't you?'

Isabel had, and she admitted it. 'But not something like this. I wouldn't go off to a film with somebody and not tell Jamie.'

'With somebody?' interjected Peter. 'You don't know that, Isabel. You don't know for sure that he was with somebody else.

'And what if it was just a friend – a male friend? Somebody from the orchestra.'

'Men don't do that,' said Isabel flatly. 'They don't go off to the cinema with their male friends. Women do. Men don't.'

Peter did not contradict her. She was right, he thought. But it seemed to him that this was a misunderstanding rather than a deception, and he put this to Isabel. She listened, but as he spoke she started to shake her head.

'I just have a feeling about this,' she said. 'I just feel that there's something wrong.'

'Then talk to him,' said Peter flatly. 'Ask him.'

She shook her head. It would not be possible; she simply could not do it. What would it be, anyway? An accusation. *Where were you last Wednesday? Somebody saw you, you know!*

Peter listened. When Isabel stopped, they looked at one another across a gulf of disagreement. Peter glanced at Susie, exchanging a look that Isabel knew meant that they had discussed something before. They must have talked about me, she thought; about my problems.

Peter shifted in his seat. 'Come on, Isabel. This could just be a simple misunderstanding. The rehearsal might have been cancelled, and Jamie might well have gone to the cinema on his own or with an orchestra friend, although it is a little odd he didn't tell you afterwards.'

She listened, but as he went on she started to shake her head. 'I just have a feeling about this,' she said. 'I just feel that there's something wrong.'

'Then talk to him,' Peter repeated quietly. 'Say that you heard from Eddie that they had met at the cinema, and let the facts unfold gently. There may well be a simple and unexciting explanation.'

Again she shook her head. No. She could not talk to him about it.

Peter seemed to hesitate, and Isabel could see that he was considering carefully what to say next 'Listen,' he said. 'This isn't perhaps about something completely different, is it?

Isabel stared at him. 'What do you mean?'

'Well, we like Jamie very much and we think it's wonderful that you are so happy together . . . but we have asked ourselves occasionally . . .' He looked at her cautiously, gauging her reaction. 'Occasionally we've asked ourselves if the real threat to your relationship might not be Jamie falling for a younger woman, but your finding out that aside from physical attraction, Jamie did not bring enough to the relationship to keep you interested.' He paused. 'Is that what this is really about? Are you finding yourself drifting apart from Jamie?'

She felt herself blushing. He was wrong, and he should not have said it; there were boundaries in friendship and one of those, she felt, had just been crossed. 'No, not at all,' she said. 'And, frankly, that's not what one expects even a close friend to say.'

'Close friends,' replied Peter, 'are there to risk saying these things, if only to get them out of the way. So you're quite clear you want your relationship with Jamie to continue? You definitely want to marry him?'

'Yes, of course I do. Jamie and Charlie are . . . well, everything, as far as I'm concerned.'

Peter nodded. 'All right, but let's get our feet firmly back on the ground. You firstly have to find a way of speaking to Jamie about the visit to the cinema. You can't let it fester in your mind. If he is having an affair, which I think unlikely, you and

134

Jamie need to discuss what it says about Jamie's feelings for you, and what Jamie is going to do about it.'

She started to speak, but he continued. 'Then, if you establish that it is the misunderstanding I suspect it is, you really are going to have to try to be more at ease with the relationship which you have with Jamie. How often have we talked about this?'

He answered his own question. 'You've constantly spoken and agonised about the age gap, haven't you? And what has everybody said to you – us included? Don't make such a big thing of it. Relax and enjoy your good fortune.'

He glanced at Susie for confirmation, and she nodded. 'But it's continued to eat away at you. And you'll remember that on many occasions I've told you to loosen up, and to stop thinking about it so much. But you've gone on seeing yourself as a foolish older woman who has taken up with a toy boy. You're going to have to come to terms with fact that it's an unusual relationship, but one which seems to work.'

He stopped, and looked at her, as if assessing whether she could take any more. He decided she could. 'I'm sure there'll be stresses and strains as you both get older. It could be that his youthfulness will become an issue – I don't know. It might not. But you'll manage, I think.'

Susie pointed to Isabel's cup. 'More?'

Isabel shook her head. She looked out of the window. Halfway across the lawn a large cedar tree bore its spreading branches with dignity. The morning light on the foliage revealed green beyond green. She had heard from her friends exactly what she imagined she would hear, and what they said was, of course, completely right. We need others to say what we really think. We need them to do that, she thought, because

135

we often cannot utter the words that in their blindingly obvious nature do just that: blind us.

Peter offered to drive her back to the house, but she said no, she wanted to walk. She chose her route back along Church Hill, past the furniture shop and the shop where the photographer used to have his premises. J. Wilson Groat, the business used to be called; and she remembered having her first passport photograph taken there, by Mr J. Wilson Groat himself, who had peered from behind a cumbersome-looking camera and enquired after the teachers at her school, whom he had photographed, he explained, over the years, going back . . . oh, a long time, of course, when Edinburgh had so many photographers to make a record of the life of the city. J. Wilson Groat was such a marvellous name, Isabel thought, not unlike the name of the fish merchant who used to call at her parents' house in his van with a picture of fish on the side and his name in large letters: J. Croan Bee. The slogan beneath the name had been simple and memorable: *From the sea to your tea, with J. Croan Bee.*

She thought about this as she crossed the road and made her way up Albert Terrace, on the brow of the hill that fell away sharply to the south, down into deep Morningside, with the Pentlands beyond, veiled now in a drifting mist that had not yet quite reached Edinburgh itself. It was a terrace of well-set Victorian houses on the roof of which, at either end, a large stone heron was perched. She and Jamie used to walk that way when they took Charlie to the supermarket and she used to point out the herons to Charlie, who looked up but saw only clouds, she suspected . . . She stopped. She felt too raw to think about that. *Used to*; what if that became the tenor of all her memories of Jamie, as it must do to all who have been deserted by somebody? *Used to.* I used to be happy, she thought. I used to have a lover who was mine and mine alone. I used to think that . . . Unbidden, the line of Auden returned to her. It was from 'Funeral Blues', that poem of his that had become so well known after being declaimed in a popular film: *I thought that love would last forever: I was wrong.*

# 10

Grace met her at the front door. 'He's fast asleep,' she said, nodding in the direction of upstairs. 'Exhausted. Out for the count.' She rolled her eyes heavenwards. 'I wish I could sleep like that. The benefits of a clear conscience, perhaps.'

'Or no conscience,' said Isabel.

Grace, who had started to go back into the kitchen, stopped sharply and turned round to face Isabel. 'Why do you say that?'

Isabel did not feel like engaging in a discussion; she felt weary and defeated. But she had to explain herself, and so she told Grace that in her view Charlie did not yet understand right and wrong, and that she very much doubted whether he would be plagued by conscience, were he to do something wrong. 'Or not just yet,' she added. 'A child that small doesn't really understand the feelings of others. Charlie can't see the world from our point of view.'

Grace listened with what seemed to be growing impatience as Isabel trailed off with a half-hearted reference to the Swiss psychologist Piaget and his theories of moral development in children.

'Charlie understands more than you think,' she said grimly.

Isabel shrugged. 'It's not really about understanding things. It's about empathy.'

Grace was not to be put off. 'I'll give you an example,' she said. 'When I took him to see the ducks at Blackford Pond once, there was a horrible little boy there. He was five or so; bigger than Charlie. A horrible, *vulgar* little boy. And he picked up a rock and threw it at one of the ducks. Do you know what Charlie did?'

Isabel noted the use of the word *vulgar*. Grace could get away with saying such things; she could not. She shook her head. 'What did he do?'

'He screamed with rage and then . . .' Grace paused. 'And then he shouted *Mine, mine!*'

'Well . . .' Isabel began.

'So he was cross because that other boy had done something to *his* duck. Charlie knew it was wrong, you see, and he protested.'

Isabel was lost in thought. She thought of Jamie, and then she dragged herself back to where she was: standing in the hall discussing ducks and conscience with Grace.

'I'm not sure if he knew that it was wrong,' she said. 'Charlie shouts *Mine* when other children touch his toys. I think he was cross because the other child was doing what he would have liked to do, had it occurred to him.' She looked at Grace half apologetically, aware of how disloyal it must sound to be attributing to her own son so base a motive. 'I'm afraid that Charlie would love to throw a stone at a duck.'

There was an audible intake of breath from Grace. 'No. You're wrong.'

Isabel shrugged. 'I don't think we need to get ourselves all het up over it. All I'm saying is that very small children don't really know what's right or wrong. He'll learn, but not just yet.'

Grace moved off towards the kitchen. 'And by the way, ducks do eat fish. I looked it up on the internet. It said that the diet of ducks includes weed *and* fish.'

Jamie returned to the house shortly after one, carrying his bassoon case. Isabel was in her study when she heard the front door open, and the sound made her heart lurch. She rose to her feet, and then sat down again. She had tried to work since she had returned from her visit to Peter and Susie, but she realised that she had done very little other than read through a few pages of the proofs of the new issue of the *Review*. She kept losing her place as her mind wandered, and had read and re-read the same bit of text several times. It was not an interesting article, she decided, and she wondered why she had accepted it for publication. 'Citizenship and the Duty to Vote': should criminal law be used to ensure that everybody who could vote did in fact do so? It was a potentially interesting subject, but the author, she felt, rendered it ineffably dull: *Rights, as the classic Hohfeldian analysis of jurisprudence reminds us, exist in a close relationship with corresponding duties, one of which is to do that which gives the right its basis* . . . She had checked up the spelling of Hohfeld; did it have a second *h*? And did the author need quite so large a footnote – twelve lines – to explain who Hohfeld was when his relevance to the main thrust of the paper was so tangential? And what exactly was the main thrust of the paper anyway? That you should vote and could be obliged to do so? But was that not intolerant of those who might not like the choice available at a particular election?

Should the ballot paper provide *None of the Above* as an option for the reluctant voter?

She pushed the proofs to one side and waited. She could hear Jamie outside in the hall, and then the door of her study opened and he came in. She held her breath. She suddenly felt that she hated him; she hated this man coming into her study. It was so easy, so very easy.

He smiled at her. 'Busy?'

How dare you smile? she thought. *How dare you?* She looked away.

'Isabel?' He sounded anxious.

'Yes.'

He immediately picked up the coldness of her tone. 'Is something wrong?'

She opened her mouth intending to say that nothing was wrong, but that was not what came out. Instead, she said, 'Did you enjoy that film?'

He looked puzzled. 'What film?'

'That Italian film.' Her voice faltered.

The effect was immediate, and dramatic. 'Oh God . . .' He moved quickly towards her, and then stopped. He had been carrying an envelope that he had picked up off the hall table, and now he dropped it. He did not bend down to pick it up. He said, 'Oh God . . .'

He was now standing close to her. He reached out, but she avoided his touch.

'Eddie told you,' he said simply.

She looked up at him. It was true; there was no innocent explanation. If there had been one, he would not look like this: drained, guilty. *The onset of conscience,* she thought. *Throwing a stone at a duck.*

'I didn't want you to know,' he admitted.

She turned on him angrily. 'Evidently not.'

'Because I felt so awkward about the whole thing.'

Awkward? She shook her head in disbelief. 'As one might,' she said. And then, almost under her breath, but audible none the less, she continued: 'I hate you, you know.' The words were flat, were ugly, and she regretted saying them the moment she uttered them; she did not hate Jamie, she loved him, but she hated him too, wanted to harm him, to strike him, push him away from her. She closed her eyes. *This isn't happening. I don't know what I'm thinking or doing. Go away.*

Her eyes were still closed, but she felt his hands upon her shoulders. She tensed: it was not a lover's touch, would never again be such.

'Isabel,' he whispered. 'It's not what you think. It really isn't. Prue invited me there. The rehearsal finished early and she asked me to go to the cinema with her.' He paused. She heard his breathing; she felt his breath against her cheek. 'What could I do? You know about her. She's the one who's ill. Dying.'

She opened her eyes. She looked at him; there were the beginnings of tears in his eyes.

'I only went with her because . . . because I couldn't say no. She has nobody.'

She reached out and took his hand. Her relief made her feel almost dizzy. 'Oh, Jamie . . .'

'And there's something more,' said Jamie. 'I wanted to talk to you about it, but I didn't know how to.'

'I'm sorry,' said Isabel. 'I thought . . .' She did not know how to say what she had thought. How could she tell him that she had not trusted him?

'It doesn't matter,' he said. 'I don't blame you for feeling as you did.'

She shook her head. 'What's this other thing?'

He looked away. 'It's very difficult to know how to put it. Prue asked me to go back to her flat with her after the film.'

Isabel was quite still. She felt her hand in his, but she did not press it as she normally would. 'And?'

'Well, of course I said no. But I didn't say to her what I should have said.'

'Which was?'

'That I can't. She knows about you, but she behaves as if it made no difference. She's pretending that you don't exist.'

Isabel tried to smile. 'I do.'

'I don't want to hurt her. She's only got a few months to live.'

'Of course you mustn't hurt her. Of course not.'

She felt a sudden tenderness; a return of tenderness really. He was so kind; he could never hurt anybody, even a persistent girl who needed, however gently, to be told that what she wanted could not be.

Jamie seemed to be preparing to say something more. Was there anything more? Suddenly it occurred to her that he might already have been unfaithful, and that the cinema outing was nothing important; a sequel rather than a prequel to something else. She felt herself tensing again.

'She said something to me,' said Jamie, his voice lowered. 'She said that she had never had a proper boyfriend. Then she said that she did not want to die without ever having had a lover. That's what she said. The implication was . . . well, I could hardly misread it.'

Isabel drew in her breath. 'Oh . . .'

'What could I say? So I didn't say anything. I called her a taxi and came home. But I felt . . . well, so awful about it.'

Isabel rose to her feet. Now she felt angry. 'I don't know what to say either. What can one say? This is . . . well, it's blackmail, moral blackmail — if there's such a thing. It's terrible. She's trying to get you to sleep with her because you feel sorry for her — and who wouldn't feel sorry for somebody in her position. But it's an awful thing to do to anybody.'

Jamie nodded his head miserably. 'Yes, it is. I should have felt angry with her, but . . .' He shrugged. 'How could I? How can you feel angry with somebody in her position.'

Isabel looked out of the window. What Jamie said was right: you could not be — *should* not be — angry with somebody who was dying; or . . . or could you? The fact that somebody was suffering from an incurable disease did not give them licence to behave as they wished; that was absurd. And presumably there were people who knew that they were dying who did things for which they could quite properly be censured. One might feel sympathy for them; one might exempt them from punishment, but one could still be angry with them and tell them that their actions were unacceptable.

She turned round to face Jamie again. He was sitting on the edge of her desk now, looking at his hands. 'I'm afraid you're going to have to talk to her.'

He answered bluntly, 'What should I say?'

She felt slightly irritated that he had asked this question. Everybody should know how to let a would-be lover down gently. Did she have to spell it out for him?

'Say that your relationship can be a friendship, but nothing more. Tell her that you're fond of her, but that's as far as it can go.'

He nodded. 'Yes, you're right.'

'So when will you do it?'

He looked away. 'Some time. I don't know.'

'But you will do it?'

He looked hounded. 'It's not going to be easy . . .'

She felt a growing sense of frustration. 'Of course not. But life isn't necessarily easy, Jamie. It's messy.' A further possibility occurred to her; not an obvious one, and she barely thought about it before she expressed it. 'Unless I do it myself.'

He did not think this a good idea. 'You can't do that,' he protested. 'I don't want her to know that I've spoken to you about this. And anyway, why should you do my dirty work for me?'

'Because I'm not sure that you're going to do it,' Isabel challenged. She did not see why Prue should not know that they had discussed what had happened. Engaged people shared secrets with their fiancés; did Prue not know that? Perhaps not: Jamie had said that she had never had a proper boyfriend, and it could be that she simply did not understand the emotional intimacy of such relationships.

'I suppose I'm just putting it off,' said Jamie.

He was, she thought, but only because he had no desire to hurt. 'Kindness is holding you back. You don't want to hurt her, but I'm afraid she has to be hurt here – even if only a little.' She paused. Perhaps it was not such a bad idea for her to take this matter in hand. 'And it might be easier if I were to do it, rather than you. That way she may still be able to idealise you – she won't blame you; she won't think that you've turned against her.'

It was not his fault. Some people attracted others to them through flirtation, implying availability even when they were not. She had encountered that type before, and they were dangerous.

There had been somebody like that in her undergraduate philosophy class, a girl who timed her entrances into the lecture theatre with calculated precision, so that the men were already mostly seated and she could brush past them on her way to her place, smiling coyly, invitingly. And there was another such person she had met in Cambridge, a good-looking young man from Yorkshire, avowedly heterosexual, who had nevertheless picked up at his expensive boys' boarding school the habit of fluttering his eyelids at other males without understanding the confusion that this could cause. These people asked for a particular sort of attention – and got it. Jamie, with his matinée-idol looks, turned eyes – and heads – but did not contrive to do that and never encouraged it. No, it was not his fault that this unfortunate girl had been drawn to him, moth-like; and while a flirt who got what he asked for might reasonably be expected to dig himself out of a self-created hole, that did not apply to an innocent victim like Jamie.

She seemed to be convincing herself, even if Jamie's expression betrayed his continued doubts. If she spoke to Prue – gently, of course – she could make it quite clear to her that Jamie was unavailable. Not only that; she could go further and tell her that she, Isabel, had asked Jamie not to see her, other than in a professional context. Isabel would come across as the ogress, the possessive woman, and the poor girl could continue to harbour whatever romantic notions she liked of Jamie, keeping him unsullied. And that, thought Isabel, was surely kinder. Prue would spend her last days in the knowledge that there had been somebody, and he had been fond of her, but another woman prevented him from showing just how fond he was. It was an easier version of the truth; a better conclusion to a life.

They left it unresolved between them, although in Isabel's mind, at least, it was clear that she would save Jamie the discomfort of a showdown with Prue. What was an awkward half-hour or so tactfully explaining to a much younger woman the boundaries over which she should not cross? Nothing; and she would do it soon.

But first she had to make it up to Jamie. She had said that she had hated him, and while it did not seem to her that he was taking her words seriously, they had to be withdrawn.

She put her arms about him. 'I didn't mean what I said.' She kissed him. 'I wasn't thinking.'

He smiled at her, touching her cheek gently. He had a way of doing that, as if he was confirming the reality of something he could not quite believe. It was a flattering gesture, and one that made her weak with pleasure. 'I didn't hear you,' he said. 'What did you say?'

She thought quickly. An apology for something forgotten or not heard was not always helpful. 'Oh, I said something silly.'

He smiled again. 'You? Something silly? I don't believe that. Anyway, what was it?'

'I was cross with you. It made me . . .'

'I know you were cross. But I wasn't listening. You didn't say that you hated me or anything like that?' He laughed: the very thought.

'You did hear,' said Isabel reproachfully.

Her hands on his shoulders, she felt him stiffen. It was almost imperceptible, but he had reacted.

'I don't know what I was thinking,' she continued. 'I was all over the place, and I feel awful that I could even have thought that you would allow somebody to come between us.'

He was gentle. 'Let's not give it any more attention. It's over.

147

Remember: we're going to get married soon. Just think of that.'

She hugged him to her. 'I know. I know.' They had not talked about it much since that evening when the decision had been taken. There were dates to discuss. Was one month too short a period for preparations? What exactly had to be prepared if one was going to have a small, virtually private wedding? And there was the next issue of the *Review of Applied Ethics* to consider; or should one not take notice of such things when one was getting ready to be married?

'Misunderstandings occur,' said Jamie.

She moved her hands up to the back of his neck; his skin was so smooth, like a piece of silk. 'They do, don't they?'

'And then they go away. Just like that. And the sun comes out again.'

She smiled at the words. 'That sounds very poetic.'

He slipped a hand round the back of her blouse, the inside. 'Do you remember that funny little poem you made up about the tattooed man? Remember it?'

She did – even if she had not given it a second thought after the telling of it. Something about a tattooed man who had a tattooed wife and was proud of his child, the tattooed baby; it was a snippet of nonsense; a haiku-like bit of nothing. It was surprising that he remembered it, she thought, but he sometimes tucked her words away and came up with them later.

'Make up something about the sun coming out again.'

'Do you really want me to?'

He said that he did. 'It will show that you forgive me.'

She thought for a moment. Then she whispered to him, '*Gentle as love itself is Scottish rain / Before the healing sun will shine again.*'

Jamie said nothing at first, and then asked why the rain was gentle as love.

'It just is,' Isabel said.

They stood together, arms about one another, quite still. She wondered, what do I have to forgive him for? For being too kind? Or for something else? *Undisclosed failings*, she thought; that great weight we all carry around with us, some of us for all our lives, unable to speak about them, unable – involuntary Atlases all – to share the burden.

# 11

It was a raw feeling – that feeling of emptiness, of bruising that sometimes descends after the witnessing of an act of human cruelty or folly. But even if Isabel felt this way after confronting Jamie, it was not to last: a vacuum in the soul, like an area of low pressure on the weather map, attracts repairing winds: and these came.

They made it up, in the way in which a couple may make it up: tenderness, expressions of concern for the feelings of the other, solicitude, acts of gentle touching. If unforgivable things had been said, then these words seemed soon to be forgotten. Charlie distracted them, of course, and reminded them that they were bound together not just by love and affection but also by the life of this small boy. So Isabel tried to put out of her mind what she had said, even if she could not help but ask herself how she could have said it. And what, she wondered, if Jamie had taken her seriously: would he have repaid her with the same coin? The tendons of love could snap very easily and when they did they frequently failed to heal. Falling out of love, after all, was just that: a fall.

It would not happen again, thought Isabel; she would never again distrust Jamie. And even thinking this made her blush with shame that she could have suspected him of an affair, like some insecure teenager worrying about an errant boyfriend. That would not happen again; ever.

They were both busy: Isabel continued with the final preparations of the next issue of the *Review* and with sending out the piles of books that publishers hoped would be mentioned in the *Books Received* column. There were reviewers to be contacted, some of whom required something perilously close to flattery, or even cajoling, before they agreed to write the reviews. There were ambitions and enmities to be considered: she had once sent a book out to a reviewer in Australia who had rapidly accepted the commission – too rapidly, perhaps, as she later discovered that the author under review had seduced the reviewer's wife, a scandal that was well known in Australian philosophical circles; the seduction had taken place at a weekend conference of the Australasian Association of Philosophy, on, as it happened, loyalty – but there was no way in which she could have been aware of that. The reviewer, now spending a lonely retirement in an echoing house in the Blue Mountains, must have fallen upon her request to write a review as one coming upon manna in the desert. 'I shall be delighted to do this for you,' he wrote back. 'Do not bother to send the book: I have recently purchased the work and will work with my own copy, so I can start immediately. Thank you again.'

She should have been warned by the effusiveness of the response, but she was not. And when the review came in – there was nothing to make her suspicious, except perhaps the final sentence. This read: *The author needs to reflect on what he has done*. The general tone of the review was highly critical, with reference being made to 'egregious errors' and 'sloppy scholarship'. But such remarks, although discourteous, were within the range of what might be expected in the cut and thrust of academic debate. A few weeks after publication, though, when the background was pointed out to Isabel, she had read the final sentence, and indeed the entire review, in a very different light. It was an act of revenge.

While Isabel worked on the *Review*, Jamie had a week of rehearsals in Glasgow; he was standing in for a woman bassoonist who had gone off to have twins and would be away for at least six months. It was regular work and he liked the conductor; he was happy. He knew most of the orchestral players already and he enjoyed playing for opera, especially for the Italian repertoire that Scottish Opera was working on. 'It always makes me want to cry,' he said. '"*Una furtiva lagrima*", in fact. Donizetti does that to me. Brings out the furtive tears.'

'But of course music should do that,' she said. 'I'm never dry-eyed when I hear "*Soave sia il vento*". I can't help myself.'

'Mimi's death did it for me,' said Jamie. 'I first saw *Bohème* when I was thirteen. We went to the Theatre Royal in Glasgow, with the school, and her death scene had me in floods. I didn't want the other boys to see, and so I looked down at the floor, which meant that I really didn't see much of her actual demise. But I think the others noticed and one of them kicked me on the shin.'

'Boys,' said Isabel. They were always hitting each other, kicking things; that lay ahead with Charlie, who was gentle, like his father, but who would no doubt go through the phase of testing the fragility of the world. Yesterday he had thrown a toy wooden train at a door and been thrilled by the experience; there would be more to come.

Jamie inclined his head in agreement. 'Yes, boys. But then years later I saw *Bohème* done in a modern setting – an artist's warehouse in New York rather than a garret in Paris. Everything on the stage was very minimalist; acres of white, even minimalist white, if that's a colour. Mimi was still dying of consumption, though, and it suddenly occurred to me that there was a real problem here. If it was meant to be contemporary New York, then Mimi wouldn't have died. She would have been given antibiotics . . .'

Isabel burst out laughing. 'I'm not sure that antibiotics help opera,' she said. 'They could change so much.'

'And they would have meant so much more Mozart,' mused Jamie, for whom the death of Mozart had been the big tragedy. He had once said to Isabel: 'Mozart's dying so young, Isabel: was that, do you think, a bigger loss for the world than the wiping out of the dinosaurs?' She had been about to say: 'A silly question, Jamie' but had realised that it was not so silly at all; in fact it was profound, whichever way one looked at it. Was a refined statement of truth and beauty – some great artistic creation, perhaps – better in its essence than a destructive and brutish life form? Better for whom? And if the dinosaurs had continued to exist, would we – or Mozart – have come into existence? Perhaps we had progressed enough in our understanding of the world to abandon our claims to being *that* special. If the choice were between dinosaurs and *Homo sapiens*, then did it really matter one way or the other, except to the species involved? Ultimately, of course, if we were the ones passing the judgement, then it was infinitely better that it was people rather than dinosaurs. But that was a conclusion simply begging for objections because it meant that we could despoil the world at will, as long as we judged what we did to be in our best interests. The dinosaurs had gone: next might be the tigers, if we wanted their forests or if we thought that they might eat a few too many of us; or the whales, if *we* wanted to eat *them*, or make them into watch oil or some other product. No, the moment one began to deny any value other than that conferred by humans, the moral game was up. There could be no morality beyond the limited world of what we did to each other.

But now Jamie continued: 'Just think, if Mozart had been given another thirty-five years. Just imagine.'

Isabel wondered whether the composer had said everything he wanted to say by the time he died, as had happened with Auden, who had said less and less in his later years, and much of it rather cantankerous. Perhaps there was a time for an artist to die, or at least to become silent, before he said something that contradicted everything he had said before. She had thought this recently when a distinguished philosopher – a long-professed atheist – began in his final years to write articles that took a different view. Those who had applauded his earlier works were dismayed and put the change of view down to senility. She had mentioned this to Jamie – read it out from a letter published in the newspaper – and he had said, 'Yes, but he still believed what he said when he wrote those articles. He may have been losing the place, but he still believed what he said.'

'Undoubtedly. But the belief might have been based on a physical change in the brain.'

Jamie looked unimpressed. 'But still *his* brain.'

'His brain at . . . whatever age he was. Let's say eighty-something.'

'But a man aged twenty is the same person as the same man at eighty-something, isn't he?'

She said that the answer to this was yes and no. 'The same physical person, yes, but we can be quite different persons in other respects.' She looked at him thoughtfully. How would *he* change? she wondered. 'And perhaps we shouldn't judge people in the same way throughout their lifetimes. We can become different people, don't you think?'

He looked doubtful, and so she carried on: 'All we need to do is to make it clear that we're talking about people at a particular point in their lives. Look at those people who were communists in the thirties and then changed their minds when they saw what communism could do. What do we say of them when we sum them up at the end of their lives? That they were communists? That they condoned the Gulag?'

Jamie shook his head. 'No. We look at what they became. That's their . . .' He paused, searching for the right expression.

'Their final position?'

'Yes. That's what counts.'

She considered this charitable – and she approved of that. There was not enough charity. There was plenty of readiness to blame and to punish; there was never enough generosity of spirit.

She thought: we do not need to look for reasons for love – it is simply there; it comes upon us without invitation, without reason sometimes; it surprises us when we are least expecting it, when we thought that our hearts were closed or that we were not ready, or we imagined it would never happen to us because it had not happened before. But if I were to ask myself why I love you, or perhaps try to find what is the main cause of my being in love with you, perhaps it is because you

155

are generous of spirit. It is not because you are beautiful; not because I see perfection in your features, in your smile, in your litheness – all of which I do, of course I do, and have done since the moment I first met you. It is because you are generous in spirit; and may I be like that; may I become like you – which unrealistic wish, to *become* the other, is such a true and revealing symptom of love, its most obvious clue, its unmistakable calling card.

The energetic substitution of one task for another, more awkward task may make one forget for a while, but only for a while. Isabel knew that, and even as she buried herself over the next few days in performing the admittedly pressing work of putting the *Review* to bed – delicious term, she thought – at the back of her mind was the knowledge that there were other things she should be doing: thinking of how to deal with Professor Lettuce and his unsolicited review; speaking to Prue; finding out more about the candidates for the Principal's post; and, of course, getting married. That made her smile; an impending marriage should occupy one's mind almost entirely, but here she was merely adding it to a list of things to do. There were people, she knew, who simply never got round to getting married; they might have decided to marry, but for some reason the timing might never seem quite right, or sheer inertia might take over. She had read of one engagement in the Highlands of Scotland that had lasted for twenty-eight years before the couple got round to holding a wedding. The groom had bought a wedding suit that had remained in the cupboard during all that time, as had the bride's dress; the spread of middle age had made both too small.

Of course Isabel knew that things moved more slowly in the

remote communities of the Scottish Highlands, where there is no need to rush things; and as she thought this, she remembered that suits became too small there for other reasons. In her student days, on a camping trip with friends, Isabel had passed a small farmhouse – a croft – in Wester Ross and seen a man's suit hanging out to dry on a line. People did not wash men's suits, but they did here, where there was no alternative; and there it was, hanging on the line, dark against the green grass, gesticulating in gusts that came in from the sea, arms filled with wind. The picture remained in her mind, so vivid after all these years that she could smell again the grass and the iodine scent of the drying kelp on the seashore and the wind that came in from the rolling Atlantic.

They would talk about marriage again, and soon. She would suggest that they give themselves a little more time – a few months – to make their plans. If they were to go away on honeymoon, then there would be the *Review* to think about: one could not simply leave a philosophical journal to look after itself. And there were Jamie's commitments to consider: his programme of rehearsals and short-notice session work meant that he would have to make arrangements too. And then there was Charlie: he would come with them, of course, but that would rule out some of the places that Jamie had said he would like to visit. One could not easily take a small child to uninhabited islands off the coast of Scotland, for example.

Isabel had agreed to a Scottish honeymoon, but, had she been given a completely free choice, she would have chosen something like trekking in the Himalayas. But such a choice was definitely not a good one for a child under two. Himalayan tracks were steep enough for an adult; for a toddler they might as well be vertical, unless, of course, Charlie were to be carried all the way, perhaps by one of the Sherpas who hired themselves out as porters. Charlie could be well wrapped up and strapped to one of those impossibly large packs of luggage the Sherpas shouldered; but what fun would such a honeymoon be for him? And there were those narrow mountain paths where one false step might send one sliding hundreds of feet down a side of scree or over some dizzy precipice. No, a better honeymoon from Charlie's point of view would be somewhere with a beach and a friendly, barely tidal sea at just the right temperature. That sort of place was, of course, hardly romantic, but then a honeymoon with a small child could not be expected to be a conventional honeymoon.

She would sit Jamie down and talk to him about all this. They would identify a date and plan accordingly, but for now they would get on with the immediate tasks of life, one of which, for Isabel, was to attend a dinner party. She would be going by herself, as Jamie was playing in a concert in Dundee that night; and her attendance would bring back into focus at least one of the matters that she had been shelving: the shortlist.

'People in Edinburgh forget about us,' said Jillian Mackinlay, as they looked out over the lawns at Abbotsford.

Isabel took the glass of wine that a young man offered her on a small silver tray. He was dressed in the uniform of a waiter or steward – black trousers and white shirt – but she could tell from his hands that he was really a gardener, or tractor man perhaps, inveigled into household duties. She thanked him, and he broke into a broad smile. 'You work here?' she asked.

'No. I'm a shepherd.' He nodded towards a man standing at the other end of the room. 'His shepherd.'

Isabel took a sip of her wine as the young man moved away. 'An Ettrick shepherd,' she muttered.

Jillian looked puzzled.

'James Hogg,' said Isabel. 'The Ettrick Shepherd. The essayist.'

Jillian looked flustered. 'Of course.'

'You were saying that people in Edinburgh forget something . . .'

Jillian returned to her theme. 'Us. They forget us. They think everything of any consequence happens in Edinburgh. They think that nothing happens down here, out in the country. They really do. Take this place. They forget that this is the greatest literary shrine in Scotland – Sir Walter Scott's house, no less, and we've had terrible trouble interesting them in it.'

'Oh, but I think they are interested,' said Isabel. 'I am. I love Scott. And I think he's still pretty widely read, isn't he?'

'I'm not sure how many people still read him,' Jillian said. '*Rob Roy*, perhaps, but beyond that, well . . .'

Isabel thought that the problem was time. Who had time for the great historical novels? 'Some of it might seem a little . . . heavy these days. People have so many claims on their time.'

'Well, they'll come in their droves once the trustees sort this place out,' said Jillian, looking up at the ceiling. 'This gorgeous ceiling, for example, and all this . . . all this stuff.' She gestured at the collection of ancient weapons adorning the wall. It was a romantic's dream.

'Scott must have been a bit of a magpie,' said Isabel. 'So many *things*.'

'He was fascinated by the past. His life was a great big jumble of romantic history. Mists, glens, castles and so on. He suited his time absolutely perfectly. And just think – this is where he actually lived, where he wrote. We can take a look at his writing room after dinner. His desk is still there.'

The dinner at Abbotsford was Jillian's husband's idea. As a supporter of the project to restore Scott's house, he had invited a group of likely donors for dinner and Jillian had suggested that Isabel join them. 'I'd like you to meet Alex,' she explained. 'And we're *not* asking *you* for money. You're here as . . .'

Isabel waited.

'As a friend,' Jillian continued. 'And you'll have the chance to meet Harold and Christine. He's the outgoing head of Bishop Forbes. I wanted you to meet them socially rather than formally.' She lowered her voice conspiratorially. 'He doesn't know that you're looking into this whole thing for us. But it could be useful for you to meet them.'

Isabel wondered why. The outgoing Principal, she had been told, had nothing to do with the appointment of his successor, and so it was difficult to see what difference it could make for her to meet him. But she was keen to see Abbotsford again after so many years, having visited it last as a schoolgirl when the sisters were still in residence. These sisters, direct descendants of Scott, had kept the house going as best they could, but a roof so large and walls so rambling had eventually defeated their resources. Living in Scotland was like that: a battle against the elements; against the rain that would eventually wash away even the hardest stone; against wind that could lift the heaviest slate and curl the thickest roofing lead; against cold that would shrink the snuggest mortar.

Jillian now led Isabel to the other side of the room. Her husband, a tall man with aquiline features, emanated an energy that impressed itself immediately. *Committee man*, thought Isabel; *a natural chairman*.

Alex met her gaze as they shook hands. She noticed his eyes, which were pale blue, filled, it seemed, with an intense light. It was curious how it happened, and she had sometimes wondered about it: some eyes appeared to have the light within them rather than without. And yet eyes should reflect rather than emit light.

He drew her aside, leading her to one of the large windows that looked out over Scott's grounds.

'We obviously won't have the opportunity to talk very much,' he said quietly. 'Not with this mob.'

A mob of donors, she thought. That could be the collective noun. Or should it be a *prospect* of donors? Or a *wealth* of donors? The latter – clearly.

'Jillian has filled me in,' he continued. 'So I understand you – how shall I put it? – look into certain matters for people. Delicate matters. Jillian has convinced us that one of those firms, you know, who look into fraud and such things, would be less discreet, and all this could somehow get out.' He paused. 'So we need somebody tactful. Like you.'

She looked down at her glass. He saw her do this.

'That sounds a bit like parody,' he said. 'Sorry. But then parody often makes exactly the point one wants to make.'

She realised that she had misjudged him. Alex Mackinlay was not a typical bluff businessman, full of clichés and superficialities; there was a subtle intelligence at play.

'I understand,' she said. 'And I'm happy to help.'

He looked at her appreciatively. 'I'm very grateful. Although I must say that it crossed my mind to ask you why.'

It was a well-tried technique. If there was something that one wanted to know but did not want to ask directly, then the simplest thing was to announce that this was a question that one had no intention of asking. It always paid off; just as it worked when politicians said that the one thing they were not going to raise about a candidate was his past. That put every-body on notice to look for scandal.

'I do this sort of thing because I can't find it in myself to refuse,' said Isabel. 'That is my weakness. I freely admit it.'

Alex smiled. 'Well at least that's honest. I'm not sure I would own up to my weaknesses quite so freely.'

Isabel raised an eyebrow. 'Really? Of course I shall resist the temptation to ask you what those weaknesses are.' It was his service returned.

He did not answer. 'Those three names,' he said. 'As Jillian will have told you, we fear that one of them is not quite what he claims to be. Or is otherwise unsuitable for appointment. But we don't know which one it is.'

Isabel thought about this. If he was as shrewd as she thought he was, then surely he would have his views on who the rotten apple might be. If the apple *was* rotten, of course.

She asked him directly. 'Who do you think it is? You must have your suspicions.'

He thought for a moment. 'I'm very reluctant to say.'

'Because you're unsure?'

He nodded. 'Yes. That doesn't mean that I don't have a view, but I'm afraid I've learned not to trust my own judgement when it comes to people.'

This surprised her. 'But how can you not? You're a busi-nessman, I believe; you must have to form an opinion of people every day of the week. You must trust your own judgement.'

He was adamant. 'Not people. Facts and figures – yes, espe-cially balance sheets. But when it comes to people – I'm just not sure. I used to think I could tell, but not any more.'

'You'll have to tell me why,' Isabel said. 'You can't leave it at that.'

He hesitated, but then he decided. 'All right. I'll tell you. I used to be chairman of a company based in Glasgow. We had a problem with embezzlement – money went missing. We didn't want to get the police involved, and so we tried to sort it out ourselves. I asked the manager to give me his views on who was doing it. I had a high opinion of him and I thought that he would probably have a fairly good idea of his staff and what was going on. So he gave me a name, and I called this chap in. I looked at him and I decided that he *looked* dishonest. So I asked him outright if he knew anything at all about the missing funds. He was all over the place. He mumbled. He looked up at the ceiling. He avoided eye contact.'

'You decided it was him?'

'Yes. I did.'

'So what did you do?'

Alex looked down at the floor. He was himself avoiding eye contact, thought Isabel. 'I had no proof, and so I just warned him and said we were watching him. I didn't say anything more than that – I couldn't, and so I left it there. He left the room, and that was it.'

'And?' asked Isabel.

'And he went away that night and threw himself off the Erskine Bridge. That was it. Left three children, and one on the way.'

Isabel winced. 'These tragedies happen,' she said. 'Guilt can be very powerful.'

'Except he wasn't guilty,' said Alex, looking back at her again. There was no light in his eyes now. 'He was completely innocent. I'd made a huge error of judgement, hadn't even realised that he was suffering from very serious depression. I mishandled it totally. A few weeks later the manager was caught more or less red-handed. I'd misjudged him too – as well as that poor man who jumped off the bridge.' He paused. 'There you have it.'

She was silent for a while. It was an appalling story, and she could not ask him again to give his views. But now he did. 'Tom Simpson,' he said. 'The third name on that list of yours. There's something about him that makes me suspicious.'

Isabel thought: a guilty look? Wrong colour of tie?

'Stupid,' said Alex. 'He's stupid, that man. Nobody else at the interview thought so – nor did his referees. But I think he's not very bright.'

'But he could be a good administrator,' suggested Isabel. Did principals of schools have to be intellectuals? Surely what counted was the ability to motivate staff and students – and keep the parents happy. None of that relied entirely on intellectual ability.

Alex smiled. 'Yes. They used to have school heads like that, but not any more. It's changed a lot since our day. No, what worries me is that he claims to have a first-class honours degree – and a master's with distinction. I somehow feel that's just not possible.'

'You could check,' said Isabel. It would be a simple business to get in touch with the universities in question and ask.

'I have,' said Alex. 'I took it upon myself to contact the registry of the University of Bristol. They said that he'd been there, but they wouldn't reveal the class of his degree – something to do with data protection. You know how people won't tell you what time of day it is because of data protection.'

Isabel laughed. 'I heard of somebody who refused to give his name when asked. He said it was on the grounds of privacy.'

'Some people are strange,' said Alex.

'Very.' She paused. 'And the others? Gordon Leafers and John Fraser?'

Alex shrugged. 'I met them at the interview. John Fraser I knew slightly anyway. We had a couple of mutual friends.'

'That's useful, isn't it?' said Isabel. 'What do they say about him?'

'They admire him. But they say that he's rather gloomy. That was the word they used: gloomy.'

As well he might be, thought Isabel; with the life of that other climber on his conscience, he might well be gloomy.

'And Gordon?'

Alex's answer came quickly. Gordon, in his view, was above reproach. 'Everybody likes him,' he said. 'An immensely attractive character.'

Yes, thought Isabel. Too attractive, perhaps? Or too attractive to married women?

A woman came into the room from a side door and signalled to Alex. 'That's dinner ready,' he said. 'I believe Jillian has put you next to the current head. Harold Slade. You'll like him.'

They filed through to the dining room and took their places. When everybody was seated, Alex tapped his knife against a wine glass and stood up to speak. He was grateful to them all for coming, he said, and he hoped they would enjoy what they saw of Abbotsford. Scott would come back into fashion, he thought, and claim the imagination of a new generation. He was pleased to play a small part in this, and they could too.

Isabel frowned involuntarily; would an electronic generation, brought up on a diet of quick-fire humour and pyrotechnic cinematic effects, embrace somebody like Scott, whose stories could be weighed in pounds? And yet writers who wrote long books still survived: people still read Dickens and Stevenson; they still read Proust, for that matter, or *claimed* that they did.

'As long as people are interested in Scottish history,' said Alex, staring down the table as if to challenge those who were not, 'then Scott will have his public.'

There were nods of agreement, and Isabel found herself joining in. The year before there had been a gathering of the clans in Scotland and people had flocked from every corner of the globe to join in. These were people who lived in distant modern cities, in the Cincinnatis and the Canberras of this world, but who felt the pull of Scottish ancestry, even now; they had come to Edinburgh and watched Highland dancing and displays of every sort of Scotticism, lapping up the riot of tartan. And why not? People felt the need to come from somewhere, even if it was a long time ago and they were not sure exactly where it was and when. Blood links, she thought; that was what it was about. However tenuous such links were, people regarded them as standing between themselves and the void of human impermanence. For ultimately we were all insignificant tenants of this earth, temporary bearers of a genetic message that could so easily disappear. We had not always been here, and there was no reason to suppose that we always would be. And yet we found such thoughts uncomfortable, and did not like to think them. So we clung to the straws of identity; these, at least, made us feel a little more permanent.

Scott was part of that; this wonderful house, with all its reminders of the Scottish past, was part of it. *Keep me from the pain of nothingness*. The words came to her mind from somewhere, but she was not sure where: *Timor nihil conturbat me*, a play on that line of Robert Henryson. It was not becoming nothing – death – that we must fear but *being* nothing.

This line of thought distracted her, and she did not hear Alex's final observations before he sat down. Something further about Scott, and his feeling for Abbotsford. The speech over, in the outbreak of conversation that followed she turned to Harold Slade, seated beside her. They shook hands, and he announced that she had been pointed out to him by Alex Mackinlay as somebody who might come to the school one day and talk to the boys about doing a degree in philosophy. 'If you think that's a good idea, of course,' he said. 'One of the interesting things that I have found in the past is that people don't necessarily believe in what they do.'

Isabel laughed. 'Oh, I believe in philosophy, Mr Slade.'

'Harry, please.'

'Philosophy is something that you have to believe in,' she continued. 'The moment you begin to think, you engage with it.' She paused. She was sounding pedantic, and did not want to. 'I'd be happy to talk to the boys, Harry.'

He inclined his head. 'Thank you. Perhaps you could manage it before I hand over. I'm going, you see.'

'I'd heard that. Singapore, isn't it?'

He nodded.

She looked at him, taking in the details; the lines around the eyes, the strong chin, the slight fraying of what must be a favourite, over-used shirt. He was an imposing-looking man, and she could imagine him encouraging the rugby team on the touchline; there was a certain unabashed masculinity, a simplicity of spirit, that one found in people who spent their lives in boys' schools. But that apparent simplicity, she thought, was probably misleading. His charm, she suddenly decided, was dangerous.

'And are you looking forward to the change?'

'I shall be doing much the same thing, I imagine. But in a rather different place.' He smiled at her. 'I like Singapore. It's very well-ordered. We're becoming so slipshod and chaotic here; they aren't.'

She agreed that there was something to be said for social order. 'Who amongst us likes nastiness, brutality and shortness?' she said.

'Indeed.' He paused for a moment, breaking a small bread roll that had been placed on his side plate. 'They're very well-mannered in Singapore, you know. Courteous. You never see public drunkenness or fighting.'

They were, she said, but she wondered whether the atmosphere could become a bit . . . Order could be taken too far perhaps . . . She did not finish what she was saying. 'My wife thinks that,' he said, looking down the table. 'She's not too keen to go, I'm afraid. But I've persuaded her to give it a try. We're prepared to run separate establishments for a few years if push comes to shove. She could stay back here.'

'People do that,' said Isabel.

'It must be said that she's not keen, though,' he said. 'I feel a bit bad about it.'

He looked down the table again. Following his gaze, Isabel glanced at the thin, rather bony-looking woman who was sitting several places away from her. The woman looked up and, as their eyes met, Isabel saw something unsettling: jealousy. For a few moments she was uncertain what to make of it. What woman would resent her husband sitting next to another woman at a dinner? Only one who felt insecure in the man's affections. *A possessive wife*, Isabel thought. But then she stopped. I know nothing about her, she said to herself. All that I know is that she does not want to leave Scotland; that she wants to stay where she is. But then she realised: with that small bit of information, I know everything.

She looked down the table again. Christine Slade was staring into the bowl of soup that had been placed in front of her by the same young man who had served drinks before dinner, the shepherd. She looked miserable, and Isabel felt a sudden surge of sympathy for her. How many wives were there, she wondered, whose lives were ruined by the career ambitions of their husbands? Who lived in their shadows and never complained? Who endured the loss of friends and family because they were obliged to move from pillar to post? And might one say the same thing about husbands in a similar position, who sacrificed themselves to their wives' careers? One might, except for one major difference: one did not have to say it very often because there were so few of them.

She turned to Harold. 'Perhaps you should think of staying in Scotland if your wife is so unhappy about moving.'

He looked at her in surprise. 'But she'll get used to it,' he said. 'I'm not worried about her.' And then he added, 'People adjust, you know. They get used to anything.'

Isabel mulled over his words. *I'm not worried about her.* No, she thought, you aren't; you take her for granted. And then she thought: this is a ladies' man, used to the affection and interest of women.

She looked across the table. Jillian, who was seated directly opposite, was staring at Harold. Isabel saw the other woman's lips move, mouthing a word. She snatched a glance at Harold;

he had intercepted the unspoken word and was smiling back at Jillian. Isabel felt uncomfortable, as an unwitting stranger must feel on stumbling upon something, some intimate exchange between friends.

After dinner they drank coffee in the drawing room, and Isabel was able to make her way over to where she saw Christine Slade standing. She reached her just as she was about to strike up a conversation with a man who was paying close attention to a painting on the wall. Isabel introduced herself. 'I enjoyed your husband's company at dinner,' she said. 'He was telling me about Singapore.'

The woman smiled, but her smile seemed weary. Her eyes moved over Isabel without interest. 'Yes,' she said. 'Singapore.'

Isabel sipped at her coffee. It was cold. 'These international schools must be fascinating,' she said. 'All those different nationalities.'

'This one is very British. Cricket. Prefects. All that.'

Christine's tone bordered on the dismissive: there were ways of pronouncing *cricket* that indicated disapproval.

Isabel smiled. 'Such an odd game. Moments of great excitement and then hours in which nothing happens. Like life, perhaps.'

Christine looked at her vaguely, as if conscious of the fact that something witty had been said, but not quite sure what it was. 'Maybe.'

Isabel searched for something to say. 'Will you live in a house or a flat?' Even as she asked the question, its dullness struck her. What earthly interest did she have in knowing whether these people, whom she had just met, would live in a house or a flat? Most people in Singapore lived in flats, she imagined, although some would live in houses. But what did it matter?

The question, though, seemed to spark some interest. 'A house. There's one that goes with the job. A house with a maid.'

'Ah.' Isabel racked her brains for something else to say. What would the maid be like? Would there be a drive to the house; somewhere to park the car? Would there be a car?

'It gets very hot,' said Christine suddenly. 'It's more or less the same temperature most of the year, but that's quite hot.'

Isabel nodded. It was hot in Singapore. Yes, she had heard that.

'You're not keen to go?' It was a direct question but she wanted to get the conversation past its abysmal small-talk stage.

Christine threw a glance across the room to where her husband was standing, deep in conversation with Alex and another man. 'I don't mind,' she said flatly. 'It's what Harry wants. That's the important thing.'

Isabel said nothing. It occurred to her now that the situation was not quite as simple as she had imagined. Harry wanted to go to Singapore because of the job. That was clear, but . . . but what if he wanted to go to Singapore because his wife, this rather dull woman, did *not* want to go there? If one wanted to get away from one's wife, then it made perfect sense to go to a place to which she would be reluctant to follow one. So that ruled out places like Paris or Melbourne or Vancouver, where it was no great burden to live, and ruled in certain places were *nobody* would like to go. Singapore, of course, was not on that list, being a rather attractive place where people led comfortable, secure lives. But some people might not like the heat or the distance from home, and, like Christine, might not wish to follow.

Now if Harry had decided to go somewhere far away to escape what must be a very dull home life, then he would obviously not wish Christine to accompany him. But he would have to be circumspect about it. If he made it clear that he did not want her to come with him, then that would only persuade her that she must at all costs accompany him in order to prevent his going off with somebody else.

Of course she could be dissembling. She might secretly be rather keen to live in Singapore but not wish to give that impression. It might suit her very well for her husband to go off to Singapore and leave her in Scotland . . . with *her lover* . . . The new young sports teacher perhaps. Isabel stopped herself. This was absurd. The situation had no such complexities: this was a straightforward case of a man taking a job in a place where his wife did not wish to live because she was set in her ways and happy where she was. However, she would follow him, and life for them would go on very much as it went on back in Scotland. There was nothing under the surface here; what you saw was what there was. Nothing more than that.

Isabel, who had momentarily turned away, turned round again and saw that Christine was moving off towards other guests. *She* thinks *I* am boring, thought Isabel. But then she had every right to reach this conclusion after that conversation; every right. Isabel finished the last of her cold coffee and put the cup down on a table. Harry and Christine depressed her. There was no happiness there.

She looked at her watch. She was driving back to Edinburgh and she made a quick calculation. She had had one glass of wine before dinner and half a glass during the meal. That quantity, spread over three hours, made it quite safe for her to drive. If she left now, she would be home in not much more than an hour, and Jamie would not be much later. Grace was babysitting and would stay the night.

A few minutes later she was in her green Swedish car and heading back along the road to Edinburgh. The Border country-side could just be made out under a three-quarters moon: wide fields punctuated by dark woods; rolling hills, silhouetted against the night sky, crouching shapes like sleeping bears or humpback whales. This was the landscape of Walter Scott, and she imagined him at Abbotsford, looking out of his library window, at the world he peopled with his characters; a world of desperate doings and heroic quests.

That was not what the world was like now, and she should not allow her imagination to suggest otherwise. There were no hidden dimensions to the world of Harry and Christine. They had nothing to do with the unresolved problem of that shortlist, and in that enquiry she was no further along than she had been before, except, perhaps, she now had the knowledge that Alex distrusted Tom Simpson and wrote him off as being intellectually inferior to the other two can-didates. And a fraud, of course. That changed the picture – if it could be proved. And that should not be too difficult, despite Alex's unsuccessful efforts: one either had the degree one claimed to have or one did not, and there must be some way of ascertaining that. She could try to find out, although she thought that it was probably a waste of time. It was just too unlikely a thing for a candidate to do. No, she would not bother. The real subject of the anonymous letter, she decided, was John Fraser. He was the one who had something serious to hide.

As she came into Edinburgh from the south and saw the lights of the city laid out below her, her thoughts turned to Jamie's friend Prue. Down there, there were so many people she knew, or who knew about her. There were links and associations and relationships; there were all the tissue, the sinews, of human society. And one of these people whose light might still be burning at this hour was that unhappy, frightened girl whom she would have to see; whose heart was presumably already broken by the arbitrariness of her illness, and for whom only disappointment and sorrow lay ahead. Unless . . . the thought that came to her was unexpected, and outrageous. Unless she were to share Jamie – as an act of charity towards a girl who did not have long to live. She had everything, and that young woman had nothing; was it out of the question to allow Jamie to go to her and comfort her, to give her the experience of love before she died? Most women would be appalled by the idea, yes, appalled. But that was not how Isabel felt. She felt ashamed, embarrassed perhaps, but she did not feel appalled. And how would Jamie react if she made the suggestion? She saw him looking at her with that reproachful look that he sometimes adopted. 'Isabel, are you serious? Or are you out of your mind? Perhaps you are. Completely. How could you? How could you?' Or, more likely, he would just stare at her in justified shock.

He would be right: how could she? It might have seemed an act of generosity, of sharing, but it was also an act of insouciance, an implicit statement that she did not care enough to bother if the man to whom she was about to be married had an affair with another woman. Of course she cared; of course she wanted Jamie to the exclusion of all others – what were the precise words of the marriage service, before linguistic meddling had destroyed its poetry? *Forsaking all others?* What a powerful, resonant word was *forsake*. The phrase *forsaking all others* meant so much more, made its point so much more emphatically than its weaker alternatives. And yet the thought had occurred to her. It did not come from nowhere. It had occurred to her, and the things that come into our mind are *ours*. If they are outrageous, then it is because somewhere within ourselves we have an outrageous part; a dark twin in whose mind thoughts of infidelity, carnal excess, selfishness dwell with ease and naturalness.

# 12

Of course she said nothing about it to Jamie. The following morning, over the breakfast table, as Jamie fed Charlie his boiled-egg-and-Marmite soldiers, the thought crossed her mind again but she quickly dismissed it by deliberately thinking of something else. This, she understood, was the technique adopted by the saints, actual and aspiring, for whom impure thoughts were temptations to be put out of mind; they thought of heavenly subjects, choirs of angels and the like, and the unsettling thoughts were elbowed out. Or they flagellated themselves, which was another way of dealing with the errant mind, though not a practice one could easily adopt at the breakfast table. In Isabel's case she thought of Christopher Dove, and imagined him sitting over breakfast, frowning at his bowl of muesli, plotting his next move. To this picture she added Professor Lettuce, sitting on the other side of the table, glancing with admiration at his younger colleague. The thought made her smile, and it worked: *I have stopped dwelling on that dreadful idea of mine.*

Jamie, unaware of Isabel's mental struggle, discussed the day ahead. He was entirely free and wanted to take Charlie to the Botanical Gardens. He had recently discovered the fish that swam languidly in one of the hothouse pools; they would visit them, he said, and look at a few of the more exotic plants. Charlie wanted desperately to touch a cactus, it seemed, and Jamie wondered whether he should be allowed to discover about thorns and spikes for himself. 'That's how they learn, isn't it?' he asked. 'How else?'

Isabel looked fondly at Charlie. There was so much that she wanted to protect him from in life – as every parent does. Cactuses were on that list somewhere, she supposed.

'I don't think so,' she said. 'There'll be time enough to find out about cactuses in the future. Cactuses, alcohol, the breaking of the heart: lots of time to learn about all that.'

She had her own plans for the day. The previous day, before going down to Abbotsford, she had telephoned Charlie Maclean with a request to meet the father of the man who had been lost on Everest. Charlie had mentioned that he knew him, and she wondered whether she could have a word with him. Charlie was obliging, and came up with a telephone number. 'He's retired now,' he said. 'He actually lives not far away from us. He still does some nosing for one or two of the distilleries. He was very good.' He paused. 'Apparently he never really recovered from what happened. He was an only son – the climber. There's a daughter, but she's not quite right, I believe. Unfortunately she's a bit glaikit.' He used the Scots word for mental handicap. It was not a word that many used any more, preferring *learning difficulties*, the modern euphemism. But there was nothing unkind about glaikit, which survived because the policing of language had not extended to the Scots lexicon.

She had telephoned the father and he had said that he was prepared to see her. He asked her what it was about and she explained. 'I want to know more about what happened on that expedition,' she said.

He sounded weary. 'You're writing something?'

'Not exactly.'

'You really want to talk to me?' he asked. 'I wasn't there, you know.'

'If you don't mind.'

There was a short silence. He does mind, she thought, and understandably so. But this is not what he said. 'Very well. If it's important to you.'

He spoke with resignation, but it was not his tone of voice that struck her: it was the phrase *If it's important to you*. That phrase, she observed, was the foundation of so much of our moral dealing with others. We recognise what is important to them; we take it into account. And if we did that, then so much else followed: recognition of rights, the practice of courtesy – everything, really, that made for peaceable relations between people. Gay marriage, she thought: some people might not like the idea, but if they thought *if it's important to you,* the case for their recognising it became so much stronger, so much more obvious. Unless, of course, one applied the same question to the objectors; in which case one was back where one started – trying to reconcile two mutually antipathetic positions, which was about as easy as ensuring that olive oil and balsamic vinegar remain mixed after shaking.

Isabel closed her eyes; one could not construct a moral position based on analogies of balsamic vinegar.

'Are you there?'

The voice on the line brought her back from her philosophical wandering.

'I am. Sorry. I was thinking about something else.' She apologised again and then made the arrangement. He would see
her at his house at ten-thirty. He gave her the address, which
was just outside Edinburgh, near Roslin Chapel, on the edge of
the Pentland Hills. He lived off a road that ran between Roslin
and the village of Temple; a strange slice of landscape, caught
between narrow, twisting glens and the more rolling terrain
that became the Border hills.

'You can't miss our house,' he said. 'It's ochre. You won't see
any other ochre houses. You can't go wrong.'

As he had anticipated, she found the house easily. It was
larger than she had imagined: somewhere between a functional
farmhouse and a house that would in the past have been called
a laird's house – a house that at the time of its building would
not have been grand enough for a family with real aspirations,
but which would have been perfect for one that wanted to be
comfortable.

The house was served by a short drive, on which gravel had
been freshly laid, making a satisfactory crunching noise under
the tyres of her car; a noise like the crashing of waves on the
shore; a *good* sound, she thought. She parked, and then, getting
out of the car, looked at the house before her. It was a fortunate
house, she decided, as it must have been built just before
Georgian became Victorian. The shadow of Victoria was there,
but had not quite fallen on this building, which still had the
scale and pleasing proportions of Georgian architecture. An
easy house. A house that was comfortable in its skin, or mortar
perhaps.

The ochre came from the harling, that roughcast coating of

179

tiny pebbles and lime that was applied to the outside of Scottish houses. This had been painted in the warm shade that one found occasionally in eastern Scotland, brought from somewhere else, from the Netherlands, perhaps, in the days of trade between the Scottish ports and their Dutch neighbours over the North Sea.

He had seen her and opened the front door as she stood before the house, looking up at its façade. 'Miss Dalhousie?'

Iain Alexander looked somewhere in his early seventies, perhaps, but well groomed and with the clear, slightly ruddy skin of the Scottish countryman. Wind and rain were the foundations of that complexion; wind and rain and the cloud-scudded skies.

They shook hands. She gestured to the front wall of the house. 'You're very lucky living here,' she said.

'I know that. Yes, we are fortunate. Ochre is such a warm colour.' He spoke simply, with an accent that was redolent of old-fashioned Edinburgh. 'My late wife was particularly fond of this place.' He pointed vaguely at the grounds. 'She created a marvellous garden, which I'm afraid I've rather let run to seed. But one can't do everything – or anything, sometimes.'

He invited her in, leading her down a book-lined corridor into a large drawing room that faced, unusually, the rear garden. There were paintings on the walls, all of them conventional: landscapes, a study of birds in flight, a small classical study, an old framed map of the county of Midlothian. And there, above the white marble fireplace, was her Raeburn, the one that she had examined with Guy Peploe and that she thought he would be bidding for on her behalf next month. She stood still for a moment, wondering whether she was mistaken. Was it a copy? Or was it another painting altogether, one that looked uncannily like the real Raeburn?

'Is that . . .' She broke off. It *was* her painting; it had to be.

'Raeburn,' said Iain. 'My pride and joy. Or it is at the moment . . .' He, too, trailed off, before adding, 'It has to be consigned to the auction house soon. I shall miss it.'

Isabel moved forward to examine the painting more closely. At the bottom of the frame there was a small gilt lozenge on which she now read the inscription: *Sir Henry Raeburn: Mrs Alexander and her Granddaughter.*

Mine, she thought. My painting of my four-times great-grandmother. She turned to him. 'Why are you selling it?' It was a tactless question, and she realised this immediately after asking it. People sold things because they did not like them or because they needed the money. There were hardly any other explanations. And he liked this painting.

'Needs must,' he said. 'I'm reluctant to part with something that has family associations, but . . .' He shrugged. 'Financial necessity.' He spoke with an air of embarrassment, and she understood: he belonged to a generation that viewed any discussion of money as in bad taste. Indigence was borne with fortitude; solvency with modesty.

She blushed, and thought: I have made him admit to poverty. She looked again at the picture. 'I know about this portrait,' she said.

He did not seem surprised. 'Raeburn is well known.'

She turned to look at him again. 'I know who this woman is.'

'It's on the frame,' he said simply. 'Mrs Alexander. A distant relative of mine.'

'And of mine,' said Isabel softly. 'Except not-so-distant, in my case. My four-times great-grandmother.'

For a few moments he said nothing. They looked at one

another rather sheepishly, both aware that the nature of their encounter had suddenly and subtly changed. They had begun as strangers; now they were relatives, even if distant ones.

He looked out of the window momentarily and then back into the room. 'Is this really why you've come to speak to me? Is it to do with this painting?'

She shook her head. 'No, not at all. I had no idea that you and I were connected.' She paused. 'And I must say I'm delighted to discover a new distant cousin.'

He seemed to relax. 'Extraordinary. But then we're not a large population in Scotland, are we? I read somewhere that the DNA people say that an awful lot of us are related. More than we think.'

'The Alexander connection should have occurred to me when I saw your name. I wasn't thinking.'

Iain gestured to a chair, inviting her to sit down. 'I have a family tree somewhere,' he said. 'We had a cousin from New Zealand who turned up and burrowed away in Register House for months. He came up with this great long chart that he unravelled on the kitchen table. Rather like the Book of Genesis: so-and-so begat so-and-so, unto the $n$th generation. A lot of pretty boring detail.'

She knew what he meant. She understood why people did such things, but she could herself never summon up interest in the details of who had married whom and who had which children; unless of course, there was interesting historical anecdote. She was related, through her mother, to the first man to land an aircraft in Mobile, Alabama, and to a woman who became a nun after being cleared of murdering her lover, the owner of a disreputable nightclub in New Orleans. That was interesting, but only mildly so. The fact that one had landed an early aircraft in Mobile meant that one had an aircraft in a day when very few people did; it also meant that one was brave, perhaps, or foolhardy. And as for the nun . . . She *must* have done it, thought Isabel, and the jury must have reckoned that the man deserved it; juries regularly acquitted the flagrantly guilty as long as they thought the victim was sufficiently deserving of his fate. All owners of nightclubs were disreputable, she thought; it was not a profession that attracted fine, upstanding people. Not generally.

She sat down and there followed a conversation about how she and Iain were connected. It was not complicated, but it was very distant, following lines that had diverged almost two centuries before. And yet it was something – this knowledge of association; it could not be ignored. It was a form of connectedness, the one with the other, that people looked for instinctively when they met somebody. This was why people searched for mutual acquaintances when they were introduced to strangers, trying to find if the other person knew the people they knew. It was as common as conversation about the weather; and as reassuring, in its way. Weather bound us together: remarks about rain, or cold, or whatever the isobars were doing to confound our hopes reminded us that even if we did not know somebody, they felt the same as we did and had to put up with, or, more rarely, to celebrate the same weather as we did.

Isabel glanced again at the painting. 'I'm sorry that you're having to sell her,' she said.

His lips curled into a smile. 'It is better, of course, to sell the grandmother of another than one's own. She is your grandmother – great, great, whatever it is – rather than mine.'

Isabel appreciated the dry humour. Why did we use the

expression *to sell one's own grandmother*? Was that *really* the worst thing one could do?

'I must confess to something,' she said.

He looked at her expectantly.

'I saw the painting in the Christie's catalogue,' she said. 'And I was planning to bid for it.'

If he was surprised by this disclosure, he did not show it. 'Well, I do hope you get it. It would be nice to know that it had gone to an appropriate home. Much better than going abroad – or whatever happens to Raeburns these days.'

She was about to say something about how at least some Raeburns returned to Scotland – she had seen one offered by an Edinburgh gallery, a striking portrait of a Scottish doctor. But she stopped herself, and within not much more than a few seconds she had made her decision; it was an unusual idea, but these were unusual circumstances.

'What if I bought it?' she said.

He raised an eyebrow. 'It will be a public auction. If you want to, then you can bid.' He seemed embarrassed as he continued. 'It won't be cheap, you know.'

'I know that,' she said. 'But what if I bought it from you – directly? You could withdraw it from auction.'

His embarrassment became acute. 'I'm very sorry. I don't want to seem grasping, but I'll get a higher price in the saleroom. And I need the money, I'm afraid. I have a daughter, you see, who has a difficult condition. I need the money for her care.'

Of course, she thought: the daughter whom Charlie Maclean had mentioned.

'I'll offer you as good a price as you can reasonably expect,' she said. 'Above the estimate. And I know what that figure is, as it happens.'

He seemed confused. 'I don't know . . .'

Now she made the offer that she had been thinking about as they spoke. She wanted to put a hand on his shoulder; she wanted to embrace this dignified, courteous man in his pride. 'And there's something else. I'd be quite happy for you to enjoy this picture for, let's say, the next five years. You can keep it. I'll buy it, but you can keep it here. I'm quite happy to wait five years, and it'll give me pleasure to know that you're enjoying it.'

He stared at her. 'Are you serious?'

'Very,' she said.

'But why? Why should you do this astonishingly generous thing for me?' He paused. 'Which I can hardly accept, of course.'

She was dismayed by his rejection. 'But why not? We are, after all, related.' She smiled. 'If only very slightly. But a gift between relatives . . .'

He shook his head. 'You make too much of that.'

'No, I don't. But may I tell you something? Would you mind?'

He frowned. 'If you wish.'

'Doing this will give me pleasure. It will also suit me. I will get a painting I want, and you will have the advantage of being able to keep it for a while. You're giving me something, and I'm giving something to you. I know I don't have to. I could go and buy it at the same price at the auction, but I would like you to keep this painting for a time. Please allow me to do it.'

He was listening carefully, his expression grave. She thought: it sounds as if I'm giving him a lecture. 'Sorry,' she said. 'I don't mean to lecture you.'

He raised a hand. 'No, I'm the one who should apologise. You offered me a gift and I immediately said that I could not accept it. That is churlishness – sheer churlishness.'

'So you accept?'

He shook his head, as if to clear his growing confusion. 'This is really rather strange. You telephoned me and asked to speak to me about Chris's accident. I said yes, although I couldn't imagine what I would have to say about it that would be of interest to you. And then you turn up and claim to be a relative and offer to buy my Raeburn but not really buy it . . .'

She agreed that it all sounded rather odd. 'But life is like that, Mr Alexander. It really is. Odd things – unexpected things – occur all the time. I think we should let them happen.' She crossed the room. He was still seated, and she reached down and took his hand. He was surprised, but allowed her to hold it, and there was created a sudden moment of intimacy between them. It was not embarrassing in any way; it was reassuring.

'I take it that you had a valuation from Christie's?'

He nodded. 'Yes. They gave me a figure.'

'I shall give you that,' she said. 'Withdraw it from the auction. You can explain, quite truthfully, that you want it to remain in the family.'

'The auctioneers might not like it,' he objected. 'They may ask for their premium. They do that, you know, if you sell it privately to somebody who's seen it in their catalogue.'

She was not bothered by this. 'Fair enough. I'll pay their premium. They won't lose anything.'

Iain seemed to be having difficulty in grasping what was on offer. 'And so the painting really will stay here? But you'll be the owner?'

'Yes. But there will be what my father – he was a lawyer – used to call a back letter. It will say that the painting is to

186

remain in your possession for the next five years. Would that be all right with you?'

He laughed. 'How could I possibly object?' Then he added: 'This really is unbelievable.'

Isabel grinned back at him. 'I suppose that it's not the sort of offer you could refuse.'

'You aren't the mafia?' he asked in mock alarm.

'I don't think they allow women,' said Isabel. 'And that's another reason for closing them down.'

He stood up. 'I know it's rather early, but I always have a small sherry before lunch. May I tempt you, or would you prefer something soft? Lime cordial?'

'That would suit me very well,' said Isabel. 'You have your sherry and I'll have a glass of lime. And then, perhaps we could . . .'

'Talk, yes, I know that's what you want to do. We can talk about Chris.'

He left the room and Isabel went to stand once more in front of the Raeburn. Mrs Alexander, her forebear, looked down on her from the other end of almost two centuries, her look one of complete approbation; not that Isabel saw this. Modesty would have prevented her from thinking in such a self-congratulatory way. She had simply done what was right; in most circumstances this is not expensive – the right thing is easily and cheaply done. Sometimes, though, it can be costly, and this was one such an occasion. But it was still the right thing to do, and when Iain returned to the room Isabel showed no regret at all. An Edith Piaf moment, she thought. *Non, je ne regrette rien* – even thirty-six thousand pounds, tied up for five years in a Raeburn that she would own but not possess.

\*

They sat near the window. Outside, the sky was light, with only thin streaks of cloud striated across the cold, empty blue. He said: 'I never liked Chris's mountaineering, but I knew that it was hopeless trying to stop him from doing the one thing that he wanted above all else to do. It was more important to him even than his rugby. Did you know he played for Scotland? Even as a small boy he was always climbing up things, you know. We had to get him down off the roof on more than one occasion, and when we went to Jura one summer he shot up one of the paps without telling us. He was twelve at the time, or thereabouts. We thought that he had gone off to see a friend who was also staying on the island, but he hadn't. He'd gone climbing.'

'I went to Jura,' said Isabel, remembering the visit with Jamie.

Iain nodded. 'Lovely island. Chris likes . . . liked to go there, even recently.'

Isabel noticed the transition from present to past tense and thought that it must be one of the most difficult of all adjustments to make when one loses somebody. Or even when a love affair comes to an end: the present is abolished and at the same time there is no future tense.

'I knew the dangers,' Iain continued. 'But I told myself that there were plenty of other much more dangerous sports. So I tried to persuade myself that Chris was level-headed and very cautious and that it was only people who became impatient or sloppy who got into trouble. But that's not true, is it? Anybody – even the most skilled climber – can make a mistake. Or can simply put his foot in the wrong place and find himself falling into a crevasse. There are hundreds of things that can go wrong without any human error being responsible.'

Isabel waited for him to continue, but he was silent, staring into the small sherry glass that he was now turning in his right hand.

'What exactly happened?' she asked. 'He was climbing with John Fraser, wasn't he?'

Iain nodded. He was still looking down into the sherry glass. 'He and John were on Everest. It was his great dream to go there – I suppose every climber's great dream. They were a day or two away from the summit, just below the final camp, or whatever they call it. They were walking over an ice field and apparently Chris stumbled and fell. John came back for him and they returned to the camp below. He helped Chris all the way – John and the Sherpa did that, taking it in turns to support him. But when he got down to the camp he was delirious and he only lived another couple of hours, apparently. Altitude sickness, complicated by . . . Oh, I forget the exact terms of the medical report.'

Isabel listened, transfixed. In her mind's eye she saw a high ice field, white in brilliant sun, and two men helping a third across a ladder bridge, below them a cavern of blue ice.

'John Fraser was a real hero,' said Iain. 'I gather that there are many climbers these days who wouldn't even bother to take somebody back – they'd just tuck them up in an ice hole somehow and leave a flag to mark the spot in case they were still alive when they came down again. Can you believe that? Can you really? Is this what we've come to?'

Isabel did not answer his question; she was thinking about how wrong her assumptions could be. She was not surprised by her wrongness; she often misunderstood a situation or reached entirely the wrong conclusion.

But then Iain said, 'It's such a pity about the other one, though.'

Isabel became alert. 'What other one? Was there somebody else on that expedition who didn't make it?'

He shook his head. 'No, that other climb. The one in Scotland. Up north.'

Isabel spoke quietly. 'Another tragedy?'

'Yes,' he said. 'Chris told me about it. It happened a few years before they went to Everest.'

She enquired whether Chris had been present, and Iain confirmed that he had. 'He didn't see what happened, but he had a very good idea what took place.'

'Which was?'

'I don't like to pass on rumours,' he said. 'I have no proof. All that I have is hearsay.'

'I shall take that into account,' said Isabel. 'Please tell me.'

He looked pained. She had just been immensely generous to him, and here he was denying her a scrap of information. Well, even if he could not be absolutely sure about it, he could at least pass on what he had heard. 'I've heard it said that John Fraser cut somebody's rope,' he said. 'He was climbing with a man called Cameron, who had been a friend of Chris's, although he was a bit older. Cameron slipped, or fell, or whatever, and John Fraser cut his rope in order to save himself.'

He did not say anything more. He looked ashamed, as if he regretted crossing some imaginary line between simple narration and scandal.

'But if it's a choice between two people,' asked Isabel, 'then surely it's understandable if one prefers oneself. And is there any sense at all in two people rather than one being carried down to their deaths?'

Iain weighed this for a moment. 'I am not suggesting that he should not have done it. And I'm not even saying that he *did* it.

190

All I'm saying is that this is what I was told. He cut a fellow climber's rope in order to save his own skin. That's all.'

Isabel was silent. Would she have cut another's rope? How many people could honestly say that they would not? But then what if Jamie were on the other end of the rope? Or Charlie?

'Where did that take place?' she asked.

Iain seemed sunk in thought. 'I'm not sure. It was in Glencoe, I think. One of those mountains that loom over you as you drive through the pass. One with a lot of gullies.'

The conversation went on for a short time more before Isabel, looking at her watch, said that she had to go.

'Do you still intend to . . .' Iain looked towards the painting.

Isabel reached out to take his hand. 'Enjoy it,' she said. 'It stays exactly where it is. I'll get Simon Mackintosh to write to you. He's my lawyer.'

'I know him,' said Iain. 'I also knew Aeneas, his father.'

'Well there you are,' said Isabel. 'All arranged.'

'Isn't Edinburgh marvellous?' he suddenly remarked. 'That we can do all this on . . . trust.'

Isabel smiled. 'It works very well,' she said. She wondered, as she left the house, whether that sounded smug. It might, she thought, but on the other hand every city had its way of working; every city, no matter how large, relied on the fact that people would know one another and act well towards their fellow citizens. What was wrong with that? Only those who believed in chaos would want it otherwise; or those who believed that we should have no sense of who we are, of where we are placed, and of what we owe to those with whom we have bonds of fellow feeling. There were of course many such people: many who hated the local, who hated the sense of identity that people had, who wanted us all reduced to the servitude of anonymity, living in vast impersonal states, governed from a distance by people whose faces we never saw, whose names we would never find out. They thought this somehow better. Let them think that; she would not. She would not be ashamed of loving her place, her city, and of doing her utmost to ensure that the things that gave it a sense of itself, the small, personal things that bound its people together, would survive. No, she would not.

# 13

The following day, a Saturday, was a delicatessen day. It had been planned some weeks before and although Isabel had other things to do, she did not feel that she could ask Cat to change the arrangement. Cat was going to London for the day, leaving on the six o'clock train from Waverley Station and coming back on Sunday morning. The occasion was a lunch for a school friend who was getting married to an army officer.

They had discussed this couple a few weeks earlier, when Cat had first said that she hoped to go to the wedding. 'He's drop-dead gorgeous,' said Cat. 'He's called Jon, without an aitch.'

'Dropped his aitch?' asked Isabel. 'Or born without one?'

Cat did not think this funny. 'Who cares?'

'I don't,' said Isabel. 'But you did mention it. You said that he didn't have an aitch. Usually Johns do.'

'I think it's sexier not to,' said Cat. 'Jon's a really sexy name.'

Isabel said nothing. John Liamor spelled his name with an *h* and he was . . . well, he was sexy, which was why she had married him. That had been her conclusion; after all that soul-searching and wondering where she had gone wrong, she had come to the conclusion that she had been seduced by his looks.

'I don't think that one should concern oneself with the sexiness – or otherwise – of a person's name,' she said. 'And I don't think that you should marry somebody because they're drop-dead gorgeous.' She paused. Cat was turning red.

'I didn't say—'

Isabel tried to calm her. 'No, I didn't say you did. I'm sure that your friend is marrying Jon for a whole lot of other reasons. All that I'm saying is that in general it's a bad idea. Don't go for a good-looking man just because he's good-looking. Men make that mistake all the time. They go for looks and they end up with a woman they can't stand, or who bores them rigid.'

Cat stared at her. 'And you?' she said.

'What about me?'

'You're hardly one to talk, are you?'

Isabel opened her mouth – wordlessly.

'Well, you aren't, are you?' Cat went on. 'Jamie. Look at him.'

Isabel gasped; Cat, though, was adamant. 'I'm sorry, but you can't criticise others for something you yourself do.'

'Are you suggesting that I have taken up with Jamie because of his looks? Are you really accusing me of that?'

Cat looked down at the floor. 'I'm not accusing you of anything. However . . . forgive me for wondering whether you and Jamie would have got together if he had been . . . well, podgy and shorter than you. Or had halitosis and terminal dandruff. Do you think you would have? Do you really think so?'

'Looks are nothing to do with it.' Isabel spat the words out.

'People tell themselves that. But who *really* believes it?'

'I do. People love others who are not at all prepossessing. Are you saying they don't?'

Cat shook her head. She was not saying that; what she was saying, she explained, was that people made do with what they could get. Of course an unattractive person can be loved, but it is harder and they have to earn it. Whereas an attractive person is loved immediately and by any number of others. It was obvious, she said; obvious. Just look at couples. The beautiful fell for the beautiful, and got them; everybody else made do.

You silly, shallow woman, thought Isabel. You superficial . . . But her anger faded away in seconds; it was not real anger. Isabel would have been more outraged if it had not occurred to her at that moment that Cat was probably right. If Jamie had been as Cat described him, then it was at least possible that she would not have become involved with him; she might as well be honest with herself. But what a bleak conclusion that was: that it was the accident of looks that determined affection. Surely she was above such shallowness.

'Maybe not,' she said.

'Well, there you are,' said Cat.

They had moved on from the topic of looks and Isabel had asked whether Cat's friend was worried about her husband-to-be being sent off on active service. 'We have so many small wars now,' she said. 'The life of an army officer is not what it used to be. They used to play polo and go skiing, now they . . . well, they have to go out and get shot at. I suspect that not all of them appreciate that when they join the Army.'

'She says that she isn't worried,' said Cat. 'But I don't believe her. Maybe these wars will end.'

Isabel doubted that. 'There will always be another one, and

another one after that. There'll be no shortage of wars, I'm afraid. Has there ever been?'

At least these wars seemed increasingly to be fought by volunteers, she reflected, which was some consolation, even if not very great; and it was not a consolation that stood examination, being based on the assumption that they were real volunteers. Poverty and limited options were powerful recruiting sergeants, and neither of those burdens was exactly voluntary.

Cat went off to the wedding in London. Isabel left Charlie with Jamie and made her way to the delicatessen shortly after eight-thirty; that would give her time to grind coffee and make other preparations before she opened the front door at nine. There was always a busy period immediately after opening, during which regulars would snatch a morning cup of coffee. If she and Eddie had everything ready in advance they could dispense coffee at the rate of one cup a minute; she had timed it once, in a time-and-motion mood, and announced the results to Cat, who had seemed unimpressed.

'But if you serve them so quickly,' Cat said, 'then they won't buy anything else. Their eyes will have no time to linger on chocolate and other essentials.'

'We could ask them whether they wanted any chocolate,' suggested Eddie. 'That's what they do in that place round the corner. They say: *Do you want a muffin this morning?* And you shake your head and they look all disappointed.'

'I hate that,' said Isabel. 'I hate people asking me if I want something else. If I wanted it, I would have asked. And quite frankly I think it's wrong in principle to implant muffin ideas in the minds of the public. For one thing, it undoes all the anti-muffin work of the Government. They spend all that money on persuading us to eat healthy food and then along comes somebody asking whether we wouldn't like a muffin.'

'What has the Government got against muffins?' asked Eddie.

The discussion had proved inconclusive; Cat was aware of the fact that Isabel was unpaid for her help in the delicatessen, and you could hardly instruct somebody who was working for nothing, and who was, anyway, your aunt. So Isabel was left to serve coffee at the pace that she determined, and did so.

That morning, Eddie was in talkative mood. He supported a small football team from an obscure town in Fife – an arrangement that was the result of his father having been brought up there. This team, which bumped along the bottom of a secondary league, was of little distinction but could count on the near-fanatical loyalty of its supporters. Now, though, this support was being tested by a scandal that had even made the national papers. The team's goalkeeper had been found to have taken a bribe to allow a goal through. The bribe had been sexual rather than monetary, the understanding being that if he allowed the goal he would be rewarded with the sexual favours of the girlfriend of one of the players in the opposing team. He had accepted this offer, but had not been duly rewarded – the girl in question said that she had never intended to carry out her side of the bargain. This had so out-raged the goalkeeper that he had told his friends that he had been duped and that the young woman in question should feel ashamed of herself.

Isabel listened to this story with fascination. 'He was perhaps a bit naive,' she remarked. 'And talk about shooting yourself in the foot. Presumably that's the end of his goal-keeping career.'

Eddie agreed. 'He wasn't much good, anyway. But he

197

shouldn't have trusted her, should he? He should have made sure that she . . . well, that she carried out her part of the deal before he let the goal through. He was really stupid.'

Isabel, who was grinding coffee, momentarily stopped the machine. 'But, Eddie, he shouldn't have done it in the first place.'

'No, he shouldn't. But since he did, he should have done it differently.' Eddie paused. 'And now everybody's laughing at us. That's what really gets me.'

'I'm very sorry.'

Eddie acknowledged the expression of sympathy. 'It's her fault,' he said. 'No man can be expected to resist an offer like that, can he?'

Isabel shook the ground coffee into a jar. She glanced at Eddie. Was he suggesting that men are incapable of controlling themselves? She frowned: Is that what he really thought?

'Do you mean that?' she asked. 'Do you really think he couldn't have said no?'

He blushed. 'I don't mean that men shouldn't say no to women like that. What I mean is that I blame the woman – I really do.'

Isabel said nothing. Perhaps that was the way Eddie saw the world, with women as temptresses, circling about vulnerable goalkeepers. She looked at her watch and signalled for Eddie to open the door. They could return to the subject later on – or perhaps not. Of course men could control themselves, and did so. Jamie did; the girl, Prue, who had set her sights on him had found that out. Poor girl . . . No, she thought; unfortunate, maybe, but calculating and prepared to steal a married, or almost married man. But then so many people seemed utterly ruthless when it came to getting the person they wanted.

Would she stand back if there were one person she wanted above all else, if she felt that this person was the only person in the world for her? Would she deny herself if it happened that the person she wanted belonged to somebody else? She was not sure. And that realisation depressed her as she served coffee that morning. When it came to those currents of the heart, who amongst us would not be prepared to do virtually anything to achieve what we wanted? People behaved like that all the time; reason, restraint, conscience – these were all small defences against the onslaught of passion, small defences against the tides of raw emotion that we all knew could so easily overwhelm us. And that had always been well understood by human society, which had put up all sorts of barriers against what it saw as destructive forces. Marriage, disapproval, self-denial: all cautionary responses to our human weakness, to the inescapable facts of human biology.

She glanced at Eddie. Eddie was no philosopher, but he understood perfectly well. She, by contrast, was a philosopher, yet she did not think she understood the world any better than he did: she knew the technical terms for life, he knew how life was when you *suffered* from it. And when you considered the views he expressed, it would be easy to pick holes in his remarks, in particular what he had said about blaming the woman. But perhaps he was right. Perhaps it was that young woman's fault. Perhaps Eve was far guiltier than Adam.

No, she could not accept such a conclusion. Eve was framed: everybody knew that by now.

They were particularly busy that morning and it was not until well after two that they were able to take a break. The hour between two and three was usually quiet, and now there were no customers at all. Isabel looked at Eddie and wiped her brow. 'Heavens! That was busy.'

'You can sit down,' said Eddie. 'I've got some stuff to clear up.'

'No,' said Isabel. 'You take a break. Then me. I'll . . .' She was going to clear up for Eddie when the door opened. Her heart sank. They would be on the go until six, when they closed. She would be exhausted.

Eddie nudged her. 'It's him,' he whispered.

Isabel turned to see Gordon Leafers closing the door behind him. For a moment she did not take in who it was, but then Eddie picked up her hesitation, whispering, 'Her man. Him. Cat's man.'

Gordon came up to the counter. 'Is Cat around?' he asked. He had clearly not expected to see Isabel and he looked puzzled. 'I hadn't expected you . . .'

Isabel wiped her hands on her apron. 'A family firm. We all help out.' She gestured to Eddie. 'Eddie and I are a long-established team. He's the boss.'

Eddie looked nervous. 'Not really. She is. I'm just . . .'

Isabel helped him. 'The assistant manager, then. And a very good one. Cat, I'm afraid, is in London.'

Gordon suddenly remembered. 'Of course. There was a wedding. She told me.'

Men never remember, thought Isabel. Women tell them things and they never remember. 'I'll tell her that you dropped in.' And then she added, 'A coffee? Or tea?'

He looked at his watch. He would have time, he said, for a quick cup of coffee. 'I'm meant to be turning up at a cricket match. I'm not all that keen, but it's an important match for the school.'

Isabel gestured to a table. 'I'll join you.' She turned to Eddie. 'Would you mind taking the second break, Eddie?'

He shook his head. 'No. Go ahead.' He looked unhappy, though.

She made two cups of coffee and took them over to the table at which Gordon was sitting, looking at a copy of *The List*, the magazine that set out forthcoming events in Edinburgh and Glasgow. She glanced at the heading of the page he was reading: *Lesbian, Gay, Bi and Transsexual*. There was a boxed advertisement for gay athletic games in Queen Street Gardens. He turned the page quickly. She watched him. Was it possible that he was . . . transsexual? If he were, then would he be attracted to Cat? Surely if he was in the course of becoming a woman then he would, as a woman, in the normal run of things be more attracted to men. Unless he planned that his new identity as a woman would be lesbian, in which case Cat was an entirely appropriate choice, although she, of course, might not be prepared to convert a heterosexual relationship with a man into a lesbian relationship with a former man, now a woman, even if, as a man, he had already been her lover.

She discreetly studied his features as she took a sip of her coffee. Her eyes went to his chin, where there were signs that he needed a shave; perhaps he did not bother on Saturdays. And then she saw his hands, with their thin covering of dark hair; again not a feminine feature.

He must have noticed her staring, as he shifted uncomfortably in his seat.

'Sorry,' said Isabel. 'I was thinking about how we are what we are – biologically – and how difficult it must be to escape that identity.'

He looked at her quizzically. 'Oh? What prompted that?'

She could not tell him. 'I find my mind wanders off at a tangent. I think of something – some odd question or hypothesis – and then my train of thought seems to acquire a direction of its own.'

He relaxed. 'Day-dreaming. Everybody does it. I find I have to fight it in the classroom. Boys start looking out of the window and they're just not there any more. They off somewhere altogether different.'

She met his eyes. 'Do you enjoy your job?' she asked.

He shrugged. 'At times it's tremendously rewarding; at other times . . . well, I could strangle the boys. I really could.'

She thought: *what if he had?* But she said, 'You never would, of course. You can't raise a hand to them any more, can you?'

'Strangling was never exactly encouraged,' said Gordon, smiling.

She changed the subject. 'You told me that you were applying for another job. Have you had any news?'

'No. Not yet. As I said, I probably don't have much chance of getting it, though.'

She lowered her cup. 'And why's that?'

'Because of the competition. I happen to know who else is on the shortlist.'

She touched the side of her cup lightly with a forefinger, tracing a tiny pattern in the crust of milk foam. She spoke very casually. 'Oh? How did you manage that? I imagined that these lists would be confidential. Other candidates . . .'

'Might not want it to be known that they were applying. Yes, they should be confidential. But people talk. You know how they are.'

She raised an eyebrow. 'Really?'

'Yes.'

She thought: the person who wrote the letter knew who was on the list. He knew . . . She put it syllogistically: (1) The writer of the anonymous letter knew the names of the candidates; (2) Gordon knows the name of the candidates; (3) therefore Gordon is the writer of the anonymous letter.

That was fallacious, of course. The major and the minor premises were true, but the conclusion made a massive and unjustifiable leap. What it should have said was: therefore Gordon falls into the category of people who *might* have written the anonymous letter.

She wondered whether he really knew. Information from the rumour mill was not always reliable. 'Who are they?' she asked.

He looked at her teasingly. 'You won't know them.'

'I might. In fact, I've heard . . .'

He cut her short. 'I doubt it.'

'John Fraser,' she said. 'He's one. And Tom Simpson.'

He looked at her in complete astonishment. Isabel laughed. 'Perhaps I listen to rumours too,' she said. I said *perhaps*, she thought; I have not lied to him.

Before he could say anything more, she leaned forward and, dropping her voice, said, 'John Fraser is a keen climber, isn't he?'

Gordon nodded almost imperceptibly.

'And I've heard,' continued Isabel, 'that he was involved in a couple of climbing accidents.'

Gordon was looking at her coolly. 'So they say.'

'On Everest, for instance.'

He was impassive. 'I read about that. They lost a member of their party. It seems to happen a lot.'

'Yes, the Death Zone.'

She waited for him to say something, but he merely watched her silently.

'And then there was Glencoe,' she went on. 'Something happened there.'

His features showed barely a flicker of movement. 'Lots of things happen in our mountains. How many climbers do we lose a year? Half a dozen?'

'I have no idea.'

He picked up his coffee cup and took a final swig. 'I must dash. That cricket match.'

'Of course.'

She watched him leave. Eddie, who had been busying himself with a task behind the counter, came over to her table and joined her.

'I don't like him,' he said. 'I just don't like him. He's worse than Bruno. Far worse.'

'But he's not,' said Isabel. 'He's infinitely better.'

'He never looks at me,' said Eddie. 'He comes in here and looks straight through me. It's as if I don't exist.'

'Are you sure? Perhaps he's shy. And have you greeted him? Have you done anything to show friendly feelings to him?'

Eddie pouted. 'Why should I?'

'Because people who don't show friendliness towards others can hardly complain about others not showing friendliness to them. That's why.'

They left it at that; a couple of customers came in and they needed to attend to them. As Isabel did so, she reflected on what she had just learned. Gordon knew all about John Fraser, and, what was more, he had been cagey about this. It now occurred to Isabel that the solution was staring her in the face. Perhaps Gordon had written the anonymous letter in order to put one of his rivals out of the picture. He had the motive and he had the knowledge. But if he had done that, then why had he not revealed what he knew? He had hinted that one of the candidates had something to hide, but had not said which one it was and what he had done. Would there have been any reason for him to be so indirect, so coy? None, she thought. And yet she said to herself: why shouldn't it be him? And she could think of no reason why it should not.

That meant that there were two conclusions she should now report to the board. The first was that one of the candidates was suspected – suspected, and that was all – of an act of cowardice, and the second was that there was a possibility that one of the other candidates was prepared to write an anonymous letter in order to boost his chances of success. The board of governors could make what they wished of that information, but of one thing she was sure: Tom Simpson, by some accounts the least intellectually distinguished of the three, would get the job – unless, of course, his claim to a master's degree proved to be false.

She felt irritated that the school had imposed on her in this way. And she felt angry with herself for allowing it. I am weak, she thought. I should be more selfish. Like Cat. Like virtually everybody else. And then she thought: I should not think in this uncharitable way; Cat is my niece, and my friend. If I think uncharitable thoughts about her, then what shall I think about Christopher Dove, or – and here she shuddered – Professor Lettuce? The thought of Lettuce brought to mind a field of vegetables, dreary, wilting, devoid of feature. And Lettuce himself, standing glumly looking out over that field, uncertain what to do. No, she would not think about him either. Yet the process of thinking that one should not think about something requires that one think about it. She attempted an experiment. She tried not to think about coffee, and immediately it came to mind: heaps of coffee, coffee unground and then ground, its characteristic smell, so evocative of morning and all its possibilities. Of Paris (for some reason). Of crisp unread newspapers and the morning sun.

# 14

She had to act. Issues were piling up: the school enquiry, with all its complexities and uncertainties; Lettuce's piece on Dove's new book – which would arrive at any moment; a slew of indigestible books that would have to be sent out for review – why were philosophers *so* prolix?; Prue; her wedding even – if it was to take place. She had to act.

She arrived back late from the delicatessen, tired and looking forward to changing out of her clothes and having a long, relaxing bath. Working with food made one smell of food – and by the time she reached home that Saturday evening she had become convinced that she had about her a distinct aroma of strong Italian sausage. Jamie kissed her as she came in the front door and she was sure that she saw his nose wrinkle slightly, as it might if one were called upon actually to kiss a salami or a parcel of ripe French cheese.

'I'm sorry,' she said. 'It's handling all those sausages and French cheeses and things. It rubs off.'

He leaned forward to kiss her again. 'There's nothing wrong with garlic.'

'Maybe not,' she said. 'But I need a bath.'

She listened to him as he told her that Charlie had been exhausted and had been put to bed early. He had dropped off to sleep immediately, Jamie said. She was disappointed; she always had enough energy for Charlie, even when at the end of her tether. But she would not disturb him – and so she went straight to the bathroom off their bedroom and cast off her delicatessen clothes. Was every day like this for Cat? She sympathised if it was. And she *did* smell of salami, or at least of the garlic which infused their particular brand.

Naked, she walked to the bath and felt the temperature of the water. They had an old-fashioned boiler in the house, an arrangement that made Alex, their plumber, smile and make references to museums of industrial technology. 'But it delivers oceans of hot water,' she had protested, and he had refrained from modernising it. Now those oceans were filling the tub and sending up clouds of steam, as in a Turkish bath. The water was soft to the touch – straight from the Pentland Hills. How they would love this water in London, where their own supply was so hard, so laden with calcium and other things. They might have opera and theatre in abundance in London, but when it came to water . . .

She turned off the taps and lowered herself into the tub with its ample, Victorian proportions. They were not mean, the Victorians, at least in bathroom matters, and this bath could easily accommodate . . .

Jamie. He had followed her upstairs and was standing in the bathroom doorway. He was watching her, smiling. 'Would you mind?' He nodded towards the bath.

It suddenly occurred to Isabel that they had never shared a bath. There was no reason why they should not have – no inhibitions, no reserves of prudery – but they had never bathed together.

She gestured towards the other end of the tub. 'There's plenty of room.'

He began to remove his clothes. He was just wearing a tee-shirt and jeans, and in a few moments he was divested of them. She looked up at him and then looked away, back at the water, which, for reasons of light reflected off tiles, was light green. She moved so as to lean against the back of the bath. The enamelled surface was warm to the touch.

He moved forward, the soft light upon his skin. He carried no spare flesh; had never done so. He was lithe; muscled, as in a sculpture by Praxiteles. I, she thought, am soft and pliant; Eve's flesh.

'Jamie,' she said.

'Yes?'

She spoke what she was thinking; private, ridiculous thoughts. 'Please don't ever change.'

He laughed as he lowered himself into the water, facing her, his knees drawn up. 'Everybody changes.'

'Not you. The rules don't apply to you.'

He sent a small splash in her direction. A wisp of steam rose from the point where he had disturbed the water. 'When did you last share a bath?'

She closed her eyes. 'I can't remember. When I was small, I suppose. I had friends to stay over and we used to share baths, I think. I must have been eight or nine.' She opened her eyes. 'And you?'

He looked away. 'I can't remember. It's so long ago.'

She felt he was saying to her that he did not want to talk about it. She sensed that, and stopped. She reached out and touched the side of his leg. She moved her hand against him. They did not speak. He turned on the cold tap, briefly, and let the cooler water mingle with the warm. She closed her eyes. It was a delicious sensation, that drop in temperature followed by a slow warming as he turned the hot tap on again. It took her back, far back, to a place of memories and longing. Why? she thought. Why should I feel this way? Because it is a return to our earliest memory, the memory of the comfort of the womb, when we are surrounded by warmth and liquid and there is no light to impinge upon the comfort of darkness.

Damp, clad in towels, they left the bathroom and went back into the bedroom. Through the window the evening sun, even at eight, slanted across the cover of their bed, a white Ulster cambric. She loved cambric: *Tell her to make me a cambric shirt / Parsley, sage, rosemary, and thyme / Without no seam nor needle-work / And then she'll be a true love of mine.* She had sung this to Charlie once and he had watched her studiously, his eyes wide, although the words must have meant nothing to him.

Jamie stood in the middle of the room, the towel about his waist. 'I forgot to wash my hair,' he said. 'I was going to . . .'

He was interrupted by the ringing of the telephone. Isabel glanced at him. 'Should we bother?' she asked.

'No, we should. You never know.' At odd times Jamie received requests to play; this could be one.

He went to the bedside table on which the telephone stood and picked up the receiver.

He answered a question she could not hear. 'Yes.'

Across the room, Isabel heard the sound of a distant voice.

Jamie lowered his voice. 'No. I can't.'

Isabel turned away.

'I told you, I can't. I just can't.'

Isabel turned round. He was holding the handset in an odd way, half-cupping the top against his ear, as if to muffle the voice at the other end. But she had heard. Their eyes met.

'Look, we can't talk. I'll . . . I'll speak to you some other time. Tomorrow.' A pause while something else was said, something that elicited a heated response. 'I didn't. I did not say that. Sorry, but I have to go. Goodbye.'

Isabel stood quite still. She heard her heart beating hard within her; her breathing was shallow. 'Who was that?' She knew, of course, but still she asked.

Jamie moved away from the telephone. 'That girl.'

'I thought so.'

'I told her not to phone me. I told her.'

Isabel felt her cheeks burning. 'She's phoned you before? Here at the house? Our house?'

Jamie sighed. 'I told her.' He made a gesture of helplessness. 'What can I do? She's pursuing me.' He paused. 'She told me that she was feeling weak. She wanted me to come round to her flat.'

'This evening? Right now?'

He nodded miserably.

'Right,' said Isabel. 'I'm going to have a word with her. I'm going to go there right now. Right now.'

'Do you think . . .'

She brushed him aside. 'We have to sort this out, Jamie. I know you don't want to do it. You're . . . you're far too kind. And anyway, she's not listening to you. Perhaps she'll listen to me. Women have a way of conveying this sort of information to one another.' Yes, she thought – we do. And she remembered a fight she had once witnessed when walking past a bar in Tollcross years ago: two women had come tumbling out, tearing at one another's hair, scratching at each other like cats, and one had been screaming *Cow! Cow! He's mine, you cow!* She remembered how shocked passersby had been, or most of them: one, a young boy, had shouted out his delighted encouragement until his mother put a hand across his mouth.

'She's dying,' said Jamie quietly.

'We all are,' snapped Isabel. 'Ultimately, we all are. So dying is no excuse. Not for this.'

She was about to add something, and almost did. She was about to tell him about her bizarre idea that charity required of her that she share him, but she did not. She was ashamed that she had even thought it, and she would keep it to herself. Now she was angry, too, and that feeling was even more inappropriate. This girl, with her astonishing gall in telephoning Jamie at home, did not deserve such concern. She deserved what Isabel was going to give her: an unambiguous warning.

She dressed quickly. Jamie said something about being gentle with Prue, but Isabel barely took it in. She asked him the address, and he gave it to her. 'It's in Stockbridge,' he said. 'Leslie Place. It's that narrow street that goes up to St Bernard's Crescent.' He gave her the number. He did not have to look it up, and she wanted to ask him whether he had been there before. Had he said anything about that? Then she remembered that he had.

'I don't expect I'm going to be long,' she said. 'Can you wait for dinner?'

He could. 'I'll cook something,' he offered. 'I'll wait for you to come back.' His voice sounded flat.

She moved towards him. She was clothed now; he was still wearing his towel. There were goosebumps on his shoulders when she embraced him. She did not want to go; she wanted to stay with him. She wanted to lie down with him and forget about this girl, and about everything, really: about being the editor of the *Review of Applied Ethics*, about being a person to whom others came for help, about being one of whom material charity was expected. She wanted to forget all that and think only of the fact that she was a woman singularly blessed with a beautiful young lover who wanted to marry her, and who could play the bassoon, and loved their son and . . .

'I have to go and speak to her. You realise that, don't you?'

He nodded silently.

'Sometimes,' she went on, 'the only way of stopping a mess becoming more of a mess is to . . . gird up your metaphors and lance the boil.'

They laughed together, the tension disappearing.

'A mixed metaphor never harmed anybody,' he said.

'Don't you believe it.'

She walked down Leslie Place, looking up at the numbers painted on the stone above the doors. With one or two exceptions, the doors here led to what were called common stairs – a stone stairway shared by a number of flats that gave off each landing of the four-storey tenement. The flats themselves varied: most of them were spacious enough; others, tucked in almost as an afterthought, consisted of no more than a bedroom and a living room that doubled up as a kitchen. In the nineteenth century, when they were built, even such cramped accommodation would have housed an entire family, that of some struggling clerk, perhaps, battling its way up from more modest housing in a less favoured part of the city. Some of the stairways had now been done up, with new stone treads and refurbished banisters; others remained dowdy, with crumbling plaster where generations of careless removal men had allowed wardrobes to collide with walls, and smelling vaguely of cat.

Prue's flat was up one flight of stairs. The door seemed freshly painted, a lilac colour in contrast to the black of the other two doors off her landing. A small card had been pinned to the door with the name – P. L. McKay – written on it, and underneath: *Mail for Thompson and Edwards.* In pencil, some-body had written alongside the name Edwards: *Owes me ten quid.* Although she was feeling tense, Isabel allowed herself a smile.

She drew in her breath. She could see from light coming through the fanlight above the door that there was somebody within, which would be Prue, as she had only recently made the telephone call. Thompson and Edwards only received their mail there; they would not be in. And Edwards, of course, would be keeping his head down.

She rang the bell, which had an old-fashioned wire pull. Inside there came a muffled clanking sound.

Prue opened the door. She was a young woman in her mid-twenties, dressed in a pair of jeans and a red-flecked sweater. She wore no shoes.

Isabel said, 'You're Prue?'

Prue's lip quivered. Isabel saw this. *She knows who I am.*

'I'm Isabel Dalhousie.'

Prue took a step back. It was not a planned movement, Isabel thought, and for a moment she was worried that the other woman was going to faint.

'Do you mind if I come in?' Isabel moved forward as she

spoke, and reached to close the door behind her. 'I knew you were in, you see, because you telephoned Jamie a short time ago. You telephoned him at our house.'

Prue said nothing. She was staring at Isabel in unmistakable fear.

'I don't think that it's a good idea to . . .' Isabel searched for the right words, remembering that Jamie had said something about being gentle. She would be gentle. This poor girl was dying.

She started again. 'Look, I know that you are very fond of Jamie. I understand that. But Jamie and I are together, you know. We're going to get married. He likes you – don't think that he doesn't like you. It's just that . . . well, he and I are together and that's really all there can be to it. You do understand, don't you?'

Prue seemed to be recovering herself. Her shocked expression was slowly changing; now she was beginning to smile. 'Jamie is very fond of me,' she said. 'Yes, you're right. He is. He's shown it.'

The words hit Isabel with an almost physical force. 'Shown . . .'

The smile widened. 'Yes. Jamie and I are . . . well, we're lovers.'

Isabel stared at her. She could not speak.

Prue continued. 'Has he not told you? I thought he had. He told me he was going to speak to you.'

'When?' It was a whisper, almost inaudible.

'When what?'

'When did you become lovers?'

'Oh, I forget exactly when. A month or so ago. May, I think. Yes, May.'

A door opened. They were standing in a small entrance hall, and the door gave on to a living room. There was another woman, slightly older than Prue. She shot a glance at Isabel and then addressed herself to Prue.

'Prue? Is everything all right?'

Isabel turned and opened the front door. She did not say anything to either woman, but simply left the flat. She felt her eyes stinging with tears. She stopped at the bottom of the stairs and grasped the rail. She looked up, right up through the stair-well to a skylight. There was still a glow in the sky, which was empty, white in the evening, innocent of the insignificant tragedy happening below it.

She heard footsteps on the stone stairs; somebody was coming down. She looked up, prepared to see Prue, but it was the other woman.

'You're Isabel, aren't you?'

Isabel did not answer. She stared at the other woman, uncertain what her intentions might be. She remembered the catfight in Tollcross.

The other woman was before her, reaching out to place a hand on Isabel's arm. 'I'm Prue's sister,' she said. 'And I heard what was said up there. I came round when she telephoned me a few minutes ago – I live round the corner in Danube Street.'

She continued: 'You have to forgive my sister. She's not well.'

There was something in the other woman's manner that reassured Isabel. She started to speak. 'I'm shocked . . . I don't know . . .'

'Of course you are. But listen: it's not true. None of it. It's all imagined.'

It took a few moments. There were words; now there was meaning, and eventually, slowly, there came relief. Isabel felt herself being plucked from the dark place into which she had fallen. 'Not true about Jamie?'

The woman shook her head. 'Certainly not. She's done this before, I'm afraid.'

Isabel winced. 'And she's dying.'

The other woman groaned. 'There's nothing wrong with her – at least, nothing physical. It's a trick she plays. She tells people that she's at death's door. It gets sympathy.'

It took Isabel a moment or two to absorb this. Of course. Of course. It was an obvious trick: if you were dying you could get what you wanted. 'It's a sort of blackmail,' said Isabel.

'Exactly. Look, we're trying to get her to have treatment. I think we're getting there, but it's not easy.'

Isabel felt weak with relief. 'It never is.'

'You've been very understanding,' said the woman. 'And I can promise you there'll be no more of this. She's going up to Aberdeen. Our parents are there and they're taking over. My father's a doctor up there. He's spoken to his psychiatrist friends.'

Isabel felt sympathy for both of them – for Prue and for her sister. There were apologies. The woman told her how embarrassed she was by Prue's behaviour. Not everybody, she said, was as understanding as Isabel.

They made their goodbyes to one another and Isabel walked out into the street. She felt drained, and would need to get a taxi. She saw one at the end of the road, its yellow light glowing. She waved her arms. The taxi turned, the driver signalling with his headlights that he had seen her.

'You all right?' he asked, as she settled into her seat.

'Entirely all right,' she said.

Edinburgh taxi drivers were not just taxi drivers. They were social workers, psychotherapists, and, like Isabel, philosophers. She caught his eye in the mirror.

'You seemed upset,' he said.

'I was,' she admitted. 'A few minutes ago I thought my world was in ruins. Now I know it's not.'

The taxi was making its way up the hill past the end of Ann Street. Down to the right, at the end of a wide road, was the Gothic bulk of Fettes College, another school.

'Well, that's good,' he said.

'May I ask you something?'

He looked into the mirror again. 'Of course.'

'Should we feel ashamed of believing ill of someone we love? When we ought to trust them?'

He thought for a moment before replying. 'No,' he said. 'That's natural.'

'You think it is?'

'I know it is.'

She smiled. 'I suppose you people see all of life in your cabs – and then some.'

'Aye, we do.'

They were now approaching the Dean Bridge; beyond it the dizzy terraces perched on the edge of the ravine. It was called a precipitous city, and it was.

'So I shouldn't feel bad about thinking the worst of somebody I love?'

The driver was clear on the point. 'Not in the least. As long as you're ready to admit you're wrong.'

'I was wrong,' said Isabel.


When she returned, she found Jamie at the piano. She came into the room behind him, quietly, and it was a few moments before he became aware of her presence. He turned round, his hands on the keys, and looked at her. She nodded.

'You spoke to her?'

'Yes.' She crossed the room so that she was standing immediately behind him. She placed her hands gently on his shoulders. 'I think it's over.'

He sighed. 'Poor girl. It's very unfair, isn't it?'

'What's unfair?'

'That she's so ill. That sort of illness – it's unfair, isn't it?'

Isabel wanted to laugh. 'Yes, if it's genuine.'

She felt him react. He twisted round to face her. 'What?'

'Prue isn't dying at all,' she said. 'I spoke to her sister. There's nothing wrong with her – at least not in the physical sense. Mentally, it's a different matter.'

Isabel explained to Jamie what had happened and what Prue's sister had told her. He listened in astonishment that slowly turned to anger.

'Forget all about it,' she said.

'I hate her for this.'

Isabel bent down to kiss him. 'You mustn't. Don't hate her. I don't think it's ever the right thing to do to hate somebody.'

'Isn't it?'

She thought. Righteous anger? Yes, there was a place for that. Hatred? Could that ever be right? 'What's hatred? Wishing ill for others? Wanting their utter negation, their death?'

'Yes. That, and . . .'

'And what?'

'Wanting to see them suffer.'

She stroked his cheek. 'And do you want that for her? Do you really want her to suffer?'

He shook his head. He nestled against her. 'No, I suppose I don't.'

She thought: hatred shrivels you up inside. It's like stoking a fire to burn the other person and all the time it's burning you yourself. She knew that she would have to remind herself of this because she had found it so easy to hate Jamie when she had first heard of the cinema outing with Prue. She had shocked herself over that.

'I interrupted you,' she said.

He turned back to the piano and began to play. She recognised the song and she mouthed the words silently. *I shall build my love a bower / By yon pure crystal fountain / And upon it I shall pile / All the flowers of the mountain.*

All the flowers of the mountain. All the flowers of the mountain. She would gladly bring him all the flowers of the mountain. Gladly, however long it took. Songs did not exist in a world of reality; they made such feats quite possible. Ten thousand miles was not far to walk in a song. Nor was Eternity a long time to endure.

# 15

With all the brisk enthusiasm of one who has at last successfully tackled one awkward task, Isabel set about disposing of the second. She had telephoned Alex Mackinlay to arrange to see him and tell him what she had found out and what her views were. She could not give him a firm answer to his problem, but could reveal what she knew about the three candidates and leave him to reach his own conclusions. She did not relish voicing her suspicions about Gordon, but she felt that she had no alternative. She would put it in as objective a way as she could manage: he might, just might, have written that letter, and the board *might* care to bear that in mind. She had no grounds for attributing the letter to him, yet somehow she felt that this is what had happened. There was something in their conversation that had made her think so: some sixth sense had prompted her to this conclusion. But should one pay any attention to a sixth sense?

When it came to John Fraser, he *might* have behaved less than heroically on a mountain, but once again she was unsure about exactly what had happened. She knew that she should have talked to the family of the other climber, but she had not done so. They had moved to London and were difficult to contact; she had not pursued the matter.

John Fraser was the victim of a campaign of whispers, but perhaps, just perhaps, with good reason. Which left Tom Simpson, a man considered to be none too intelligent by Alex Mackinlay himself. Well, what did that mean? His assessment of the candidate could be based on personal animosity. Sometimes people had strong views on the question of who would be their successor. Harry Slade might have conveyed his dislike of Tom Simpson to Alex and this might have led him to question the genuineness of Simpson's claim to a master's degree. But again this sounded like tittle-tattle, and did the board want even to consider it?

Isabel had expected that Alex Mackinlay might offer to come to the house to hear what she had to say, but he did not.

'We're having a meeting at the school tomorrow afternoon,' he said. 'It's the end of term. We're meeting through lunch and should be finished by three. If you would care to come out, I could show you round and then you and I could have a private conversation.'

She was on the point of saying that this would not be convenient and would he mind coming in to see her, but she did not. It was convenient, as it happened; Grace wanted to take Charlie to tea with one of her friends in Trinity, and Jamie was rehearsing. She had wanted to see what the school was like, and this would give her a chance. So she replied that she would be happy to come out.

'And do you have an answer for us?' asked Alex.

Isabel hesitated. 'Some answers come more in the form of questions,' she said.

He laughed. 'That sounds very enigmatic.'

'Some situations are inherently enigmatic.'

She was not sure whether he would appreciate that. He was a businessman, she remembered – a doer – and he probably thought in terms of certainties. But he appeared intrigued. 'Then let us de-enigmatise them.'

Isabel laughed. 'Indeed.'

The next day, she left the house shortly after two. It would not take her much more than half an hour to get to the school, but she thought that she might walk round the grounds before she had the meeting with Alex. The school had a well-known garden that had been stocked with rare rhododendrons brought from the Himalayas in Edwardian times and Isabel wanted to see this. There were sculptures too – a renowned sculptor who lived not far away had donated some of his unusual works to the school: there was enigma enough there, she thought, in the messages the sculptor carved into the stone.

On the drive out she stopped just after Silverburn to watch a bird of prey hunting over the lower slopes of the Pentlands. It was a large hawk, waiting to swoop down on its victim. She drew up at the side of the road and watched as it was mobbed by a flock of smaller birds and ignominiously chased away. The small birds, like tiny spitfires in some unequal, heroic Battle of Britain, twisted and turned in dizzying aerial combat; the hawk, outnumbered and irritated by the onslaught, suddenly flew off towards higher ground and disappeared. Isabel sat for a moment, the engine of the green Swedish car idling, before she resumed her journey. This little battle was so close to the city and yet belonged so completely to another world – as did the man feeding his cattle in the field a mile further along the road, emptying a sack of food into a metal hopper while the cattle thronged about him, jostling for position at the trough.

She knew West Linton, where her friend, Derek Watson, had his tiny bookshop. She resisted the temptation to call on him; there would be time for that on another occasion. Driving through the village, she followed the smaller road that led into the hills and after a few hundred yards came to the gates of the school. *Bishop Forbes School, an Independent Boarding School for Boys aged 8 to 18*. Eight, she thought, was terribly young to be sent away from home. She tried to imagine sending Charlie off to boarding school in just over six years' time, his possessions packed in a small suitcase. No, she could never do it, no matter what people said about the character-building and the sense of independence fostered by such schools. Those could be developed at home, she felt. *She* would socialise Charlie – she and Jamie – not some stranger.

She followed a sign to the car park, where she left the car. Behind this, beyond a stand of oak trees, she saw the main building of the school, a large stone building, Palladian in spirit, with several wings stretching out on either side. There were wide lawns around it with, at their edges, clusters of other, more modern buildings – what looked like a gym, hostels, a chapel. Here and there small groups of boys moved from doorway to doorway, books under their arms, going, she thought, from lesson to lesson. From somewhere further away the wail of a pipe band split the afternoon air: band practice.

The rhododendron garden was reached by a path that led away from the car park. She followed this and after a few minutes found herself standing before a small notice that explained the history of the garden and listed some of the varieties it contained. Some of the shrubs had lost the blossom of early summer; others were still a brilliant flourish of colour. The paved walkway snaked its way through the shrubs, and she made her way along it, pausing from time to time to read the small name-plates at the side of each plant.

She reached the far end of the garden and found, to her surprise, that she was on the edge of a cricket pitch. Cricket was not a Scottish game, but was played at schools such as this; a sign of English influence. She knew a few Scottish cricket players, and it seemed to her that they took a perverse pride in playing an arcane game that was a matter of such little interest to the vast majority of their fellow Scots. And here were boys being initiated into just such an attitude.

Not far from where she was, a couple of benches had been placed under the shade of a tree, and it was here that the members of the batting team were sitting. Around them was a mess of pads and other cricket paraphernalia: bats, white jerseys with the arms tied in knots, a large blackboard on which the score had been written in chalk. She walked over; the boys acknowledged her politely, one raising his cap in greeting.

She spoke to a boy who was standing at the edge of the group. He was a smallish boy, as they all were – it was clearly a junior team, made up of boys of ten or eleven.

'How's the game going?'

The boy replied politely. 'Very well. We're going to win.'

'And how many runs have you made yourself?'

He looked down at the grass. 'I was out for a duck. None. Bowled. Macdonald did it. He's a fast bowler.'

'Bad luck.'

'Thanks. I'm going to bowl to Macdonald when they go in. I'm going to get him.'

She pointed to a couple of deckchairs that were a little way away from the group. 'Who's sitting there?'

The boy shrugged. 'Two of the teachers. They've gone back in. You can sit there if you like.'

'Would you sit there beside me and tell me what's going on on the pitch? I don't really understand cricket.'

He hesitated, but then agreed. 'If you like.'

They moved over to the deckchairs.

'You have to be careful with deckchairs,' Isabel said. 'They can collapse and catch your fingers.'

'That happened yesterday. A boy called Brodie. He got his fingers caught and he had to go and get plasters put on them. Served him right.'

Isabel smiled. 'Oh? Did he deserve it?'

'He's a bully,' said the boy.

'Ah. And does he bully you?'

'Yes.'

Isabel looked at the boy's face. He had freckles and green eyes. She noticed a small scar on his chin — a recent scratch, nothing serious. Boys were always scratching and cutting themselves, breaking things too.

'Can't you do anything about it?'

He shook his head. 'You can't clype on him. If you do that, they hit you.'

'Who?'

'Other boys.'

It was a jungle. Of course it was. A jungle for boys between eight and eighteen.

'Are you happy here?' she asked.

226

He thought for a moment. 'Yes. A bit.'

Then she asked, 'And are you going to miss Mr Slade when he goes?'

He frowned. 'He's going to Singapore.'

'Yes. To a school a lot like this one, I believe. Lots of cricket there.'

'I like Mr Slade. I'll be sorry when he goes.'

She smiled. 'So you will miss him then?'

'Not as much as Miss Carty will. She . . .'

Isabel waited for him to finish his sentence, but something had happened on the pitch and his attention was diverted. A batsman had hit a ball in the air and a fielder was running towards it. There was a groan from the field as the catch was dropped.

'A near thing,' said Isabel. 'But tell me, who's Miss Carty?'

'She's the school secretary. We call her Tarty Carty.'

Isabel tried not to laugh. 'Not very polite. And may I ask why?'

'Because she's a tart.'

Isabel drew in her breath. He looked so innocent – and probably was. He probably had no idea what he was saying.

'That's not very kind. Do you think you should say that?'

'She's in love with Sladey.'

Isabel said nothing. Miss Carty was in love with Mr Slade. Nonsense. Schoolboy fantasy. Boys made things up; shocking stories dreamed up with no regard to the truth or even to feasibility. They made them up. But then she thought: Miss Carty, unhappy school secretary, in love with Mr Slade, handsome headmaster. Headmaster announces his departure for Singapore; Miss Carty pleads with him not to go. He says he must. She thinks: if I stop them making an appointment, then he might stay, even for a few months longer. And anything can happen in a few months . . .

227

She watched the boy. He had taken a tube of peppermints out of his pocket and had peeled one off. 'Would you like a mint?'

She shook her head. 'How do you know that Miss Carty is in love with Mr Slade?'

He answered nonchalantly. 'I saw him kiss her. He didn't know I was there. I had lost a ball under one of those bushes back there.' He gestured towards the rhododendron garden. 'I was looking for it when they came along the path. They didn't know I was there. I saw him kiss her. Tarty Carty. Yuck! Disgusting. I wanted to be sick right there. Yuck!'

Isabel found the school office by asking a boy where to go. He pointed to a staircase that gave off the main entrance hall. 'Up there. There's a white door that says *Headmaster*. That's the school office.'

She climbed the stairs and reached a broad landing. There were several chairs placed around a glass-topped coffee table, and beyond that the door marked *Headmaster*. Slightly below, there was a sign saying *Knock and enter.*

She knocked and pushed open the door to a spacious room in which there were several desks, a bank of filing cabinets, and a pinboard covered in notices and aides-memoires. At the far end of the room, a woman sat at a desk under a window. She had streaky blonde hair and was wearing a red shift dress. Tarty Carty, Isabel thought.

The woman turned round in her seat when Isabel entered. She looked at her watch. 'Miss Dalhousie?'

Isabel nodded. 'Mr Mackinlay . . .'

'Yes, he's expecting you. He's in the Governors' Room – I'll take you there.'

Isabel followed the secretary out of the room and along the corridor, which was lined with photographs of sports teams. Under-15s Rugby, First Tennis Team, Swimming Team. All schools were the same. This took her back to George Watson's Ladies' College and the headmistress in her black bombazine and the smell of chalk and . . .

'You have wonderful grounds here,' said Isabel. 'I walked through the rhododendron garden.' What do I expect? she asked herself. Blushes at the memory?

'It's very pretty,' said Miss Carty. 'I like it a great deal.'

'Yes,' said Isabel. And then, her heart racing at her effrontery, she went on: 'You'll all miss Mr Slade when he goes off to Singapore.'

She was ready for Miss Carty's reaction – any reaction, but there was none. 'A great loss,' the secretary said evenly. 'But that happens in schools. Popular teachers move on. One gets used to it.'

'You must have worked closely with him.'

'Of course. But no doubt we'll get a good replacement.'

Isabel nodded. 'It's a good field,' said Miss Carty. 'Or so I'm told. I have nothing to do with the appointment process, of course. But I've heard that we've got some strong candidates, whoever they are. I'll be interested to find out when they come for interview.'

'I'm sorry,' said Isabel to Alex Mackinlay. 'I'm sorry, but I'm going to have to sort out my thoughts.'

They were alone in the boardroom. Miss Carty, after having shown Isabel in, returned a few minutes later with a tray of tea, and then went back to her office.

'She's a pillar of this place,' said Alex as the secretary closed the door behind her. 'She's been her for fifteen years or so. She's become the institutional memory.'

'Useful,' said Isabel.

Alex began to pour the tea. 'You said that you needed to order your thoughts: do you want me to leave you for a while to do that?'

Isabel shook her head. 'Do you mind if I think aloud?'

Alex handed her a cup of tea. 'Not in the slightest.'

Isabel took a sip from her cup. 'I've found out a certain amount about two of the candidates,' she began. 'John Fraser and Gordon Leafers.'

'Yes?'

'John Fraser is a climber.'

'I know that.'

'And do you know that he's lost a couple . . .'

Alex raised a hand. 'Let me save your time. John Fraser is no longer a candidate. We don't need to bother about him.'

It took Isabel a moment to take this in. 'You've taken him off the shortlist?'

'No. He did it himself. He withdrew.'

She asked why, and Alex explained that he had received a letter from John Fraser only that morning. He did not wish to pursue his application for personal reasons, but felt that he owed the school an explanation, having made claims on their time. 'It was a rather long and emotional letter. He said that he was being treated for depression, and he felt that he should not conceal this from us. The depression came, he said, from the fact that he felt massively guilty.'

'I was going to tell you that,' said Isabel. 'I think he felt guilty about cutting a rope.'

Alex frowned. 'No. Quite the opposite. *His* rope was cut.'

'I'm not . . .'

Alex put down his cup. 'Apparently his life was saved some-where up near Glencoe. The other climber had fallen and was tied on to him. He was beginning to drag John down into danger and realised that the only way in which he could stop this happening was to cut himself free. So he did, and fell. It was an act of self-sacrifice on the other man's part. Remarkable, really. And John felt guilty that he was alive and the other man was killed. People can feel guilty in that way – survivor's guilt, it's called.'

Isabel looked out of the window. Of course.

'Anyway,' Alex went on, 'he felt that he really couldn't cope with this job in that frame of mind and he pulled out. Understandable. Poor man.'

'Yes,' said Isabel.

'But that still leaves the other two. Leafers and Simpson. What about them? Any skeletons there?'

She was still absorbing the news of John Fraser's withdrawal. There was not much left for her to say, she thought. 'I haven't really paid much attention to Simpson. I formed the impression that you had a lowish opinion of him.'

He nodded. 'I'm afraid so. He's not up to it, in my view. There were one or two members of the board who were keen to give him a chance, so I let his name go on the shortlist. But I'm afraid that that's as far as he'll get.'

'We don't need to worry about him then?'

He shook his head. 'No, we don't. Even if there were to be something in his past, which I rather doubt, it wouldn't matter. He's not going to get the job.' He looked at Isabel expec-tantly. 'And that leaves Gordon Leafers. Enlighten me about him.'

Isabel knew what she must do. 'I must declare an interest in respect of Gordon,' she said. 'He's my niece's current boyfriend.'

Alex listened as she explained that she liked Gordon but that she understood that she had to be objective.

'And your objective assessment?' asked Alex.

'My objective assessment is that there's probably nothing to worry about with him, other than . . .'

He looked interested. 'Yes?'

'I wondered whether he was the writer of the letter. I think he's ambitious and might have wanted to compromise the other two candidates. I can't say why I feel that – I have no evidence.'

'So it's just a feeling?'

'Yes. He knew who was on the list. So he would have both motive and ability.'

Alex thought about this. 'But there were others who knew.'

'Who?' asked Isabel.

'Miss Carty. And another woman in the office. That's where the list was typed up.'

Isabel waited a moment. 'By?'

'Miss Carty, I believe. She's the one who passed it on to me to pass on to you.'

'So she knew I was going to see it?'

He nodded. 'And I think I told her about what we were asking of you. I trust her, you see. She's in on everything here, but she's the soul of discretion.'

And she misled me, thought Isabel. But that was not what she wanted to talk about. 'May I speak to you in absolute confidence?'

'Of course.'

'Do you know of any relationship between Mr Slade and Miss Carty?'

'Beyond an employer and employee relationship?'

'Yes. An affair.'

His eyes widened. 'My goodness! Highly unlikely, I would have thought. I just can't see him getting involved with her.' He seemed amused by the idea. 'Nor she with him.'

Isabel was insistent. 'Why should it be so unlikely? Mr Slade is a good-looking, even rather charismatic man. His wife, if I may say so, is hardly exciting.'

Alex looked embarrassed. 'No,' he said, shaking his head. 'I just don't see it.' He paused. 'Why would you even suggest it? Have you heard something?'

Isabel hesitated. She did not like to lie. But one does not have to answer every question one is asked. So she said, 'One should always be prepared to consider every possibility.'

He shrugged. 'Yes. But some possibilities . . . Still, what about Gordon Leafers. You have your suspicions about him. You think he might be capable of doing something underhand, such as writing an anonymous letter in order to strengthen his chances. Well, maybe, maybe not. I can't see it, frankly.'

He poured more tea. 'There is, however, something I heard about Gordon that makes me think that he might not be our best bet. I heard, in fact, that he's not a serious candidate at all – and never was.'

She waited for him to continue.

'I heard from a very reliable source – somebody at the school he's currently teaching at, that his application is intended purely to enable him to show an offer – if he got one from us – to his existing employer and ask for promotion. Apparently he confessed to a colleague, and it got out. He doesn't want to move at all. He's using us, as people sometimes do in these job competitions. So we're going to tell him that his application is no longer shortlisted. We are certainly not going to let people make use of us like that.'

Isabel hardly knew what to say. All three candidates were out of the running now, which made her wonder why Alex Mackinlay had wanted to see her. Did he think she had nothing better to do with her time than investigate a list of non-candidates?

She drew in her breath. 'I'm surprised that you didn't tell me about all this earlier,' she said. 'I've rather wasted my time, haven't I?'

He looked immediately apologetic. 'I'm very sorry,' he said. 'I would hate you to think that. In fact, I have remained very keen to hear what you have to say.'

She looked at him reproachfully. 'But nothing I say has any relevance.'

'But it does, Miss Dalhousie. It's the letter I'm really interested in. Who wrote it? Can't you see that this is in a way a more important issue for us? Is there somebody here who can't be trusted? That's a very important question for me.'

She understood. An anonymous letter was an acutely destabilising thing. It bred distrust and suspicion; it weakened the normal bonds between people.

He suddenly turned and reached for a file on the table behind him. Taking out a single sheet of paper, he held it out towards her. It was the letter. She saw the green ink and the handwriting – which had been disguised in childish capital letters.

'This bit of paper is potentially very destructive,' he said. 'And I was hoping that you might be able to help us find out who wrote it. Have you any ideas?'

She stared at it. Miss Carty and her assistant knew who was

on the list, but so did the other members of the board. She had no means of knowing what they thought about the candidates and she doubted if she would have the time or opportunity to find out. Any one of them might have written the letter.

'I'm not sure. But perhaps we should consider the obvious suspect.'

'Namely?'

'Well, Miss Carty knew who was on the list, didn't she?'

He laughed. 'You do have it in for her, don't you?'

'Well, she had the information and she had a motive. What if she didn't want Harold Slade to leave? What if she thought that the best way of ensuring this was to prevent, or at least delay, the appointment of his successor?'

His reply was brusque. 'Out of character. As much out of character as . . . having an affair with Harold Slade.'

Isabel considered this. He seemed confident of his opinion, even if he had earlier admitted to her how wrong he had been about that poor man in Glasgow.

'May I tell you something?' she said. 'When I was being shown in here, she – Miss Carty – said to me that she had no idea who was on the list. She said that. Nor, apparently, has she seen any of the candidates. Why would she mislead me?'

He frowned. 'Is that what she said?'

'Yes.'

'Are you sure you didn't mishear her?'

'Positive.'

He frowned again. It was as if he was searching for an explanation. It came. 'Discretion,' he said. 'She's very discreet. What would you do if somebody engaged you in conversation about a sensitive topic – one of which you had confidential knowledge? Might you not say, "I don't know anything about it"? I would. It puts people off.'

He seemed pleased with this, and he looked at her expectantly, as if challenging her to refute what he had said. Isabel said nothing. She looked at the letter in his hand. 'May I?' she said.

He handed it to her. 'Offensive thing, isn't it?'

She noticed that the letter was crumpled where he had been holding it. She felt chilled at the thought of the venom that went into the writing of something like this. Snideness, too. Cowardice.

'Did you show it to anybody?' she asked.

Alex Mackinlay answered in an offhand way, 'Show it? No, of course not.'

'So nobody else – absolutely nobody – saw it? Not even your wife?'

'I certainly didn't show it to Jilly,' he said. 'I put it in that file and that's where it remained. It disgusts me. I feel dirty even handling a thing like that.'

'But you mentioned it to other people?'

'No,' he replied. 'As far as I recall the only person I told was Jilly.'

Isabel felt her breath coming in short bursts. She was getting close. When they had first discussed this over coffee at Cat's delicatessen, Jillian had told her that the letter was written in green ink, and yet she had never seen it. Her mind raced ahead. That meant that . . . No, all that it meant was that her husband had probably told her. Letters in green ink were unusual, and he could well have mentioned that feature of it to Jillian. She felt disappointed: it would all have been so neat.

'Green ink,' she muttered, looking at the letter.

Alex frowned. 'What?'

She gestured to the letter. 'Green ink.'

He shrugged. 'Oh, I see. Or don't, rather. I have the usual male thing – red-green colour blindness.'

She spoke very quietly. 'You can't tell?'

He seemed slightly irritated by her question, as if he wanted to get back to the subject in hand. 'No, I can't. And lots of men are in the same position. It's very common. You women don't seem to suffer from it – or hardly ever.'

For a few brief, delicious moments, Isabel experienced a sense of euphoria. It was akin to the satisfaction felt on solving a difficult crossword puzzle, or seeing the reasoning behind a mathematical proof. This fact established the authorship of the letter beyond question. Alex Mackinlay could not have told his wife that the letter was written in green ink, nor had he shown the letter to her. It was she who wrote it.

He was staring at her. 'You look as if you've had a brain-wave,' he said. 'Care to share it?'

Isabel opened her mouth, and then closed it. No, she thought. No, I don't care to share it.

'Well?'

She handed the letter back to him with a shrug. 'The whole point about anonymous letters,' she said calmly, 'is that we don't know who wrote them.'

He took the letter from her and slipped it back into the file. He was losing interest; she could tell. And that, she thought, was the way this man was; he was interested in those who could help him, but not in others. She had a strong intuition to that effect, and this time she decided to trust it.

She looked at her watch. 'I really must get back to town,' she said. 'I'm sorry that I've been unable to help you very much.'

He was polite, even if there was a lack of warmth in his voice. 'I'm most grateful to you, Miss Dalhousie. I'm most grateful to you for the time you have spent on this matter, even if we are no further forward than when we began.'

But we are, she thought. *We are a great deal further than you imagine.*

'I take it, then, that you'll ask Harold Slade to stay?'

'I shall,' he said. 'In fact, I've already done that, and he was happy to agree.'

'Temporarily?' she asked.

'No, permanently.'

'But what about Singapore?'

Alex smiled. 'Oddly enough, I think they're going to be quite pleased if Harry doesn't go – or some of them will be. I had a chat with my counterpart, the chairman of that school's board. He became quite frank and admitted that they were not exactly of one mind about the appointment. There was a strong faction on their board that wanted an internal appointment – the deputy head. The chairman let slip that he was of that per-suasion himself, but had been out-voted. He'll be pleased when Harry calls off.'

Isabel sighed. 'Well that seems to settle that,' she said. 'I must say again that I'm somewhat surprised that you asked me to look into this in the first place. Everything seems to have set-tled itself rather satisfactorily.'

He said nothing. She turned to face him again. There had been a note of anger in her voice, and he reacted; he looked concerned.

'But I didn't ask you,' he said. 'My wife did. She acted entirely off her own bat and then presented me with a fait accompli. I concurred and let you get on with it.'

Isabel turned away, looking out of the window at the lawn below. Two boys were engaged in what appeared to be a wrestling contest, one throwing the other down and then sitting on his chest. Their hair was dishevelled, their shirts hanging out of the tops of their trousers. The boy on the ground hit the other on the back and rolled him off. Then he kicked him, but only lightly. They were obviously good friends.

'May I ask you,' she said, turning back to face Alex. 'May I ask you this: who does your wife think wrote the letter?'

He hesitated, seemingly unsure as to whether to answer. But then he said, 'Janet Carty.'

'And she voiced these suspicions to you?'

'Yes, she said she was pretty sure it was her. She urged me to take action.' He looked bemused. 'In fact, she seemed to think that your investigation would back her up.'

Of course she did, thought Isabel. And she remembered the evening at Abbotsford, recalling the sight of Jillian mouthing something across the table at Harold Slade; and the look on his face as he responded. Lovers. Of course they were lovers. And what if Jillian had a rival? And this rival was Janet Carty? It would make perfect sense for her to undermine the secretary and at the same time stop, or at least delay, her lover's departure for Singapore.

'I'm confident that Janet Carty did not write the letter,' she said. 'If there's one thing that's clear to me, it's that.'

He looked interested. 'How can you be so sure?'

'Because I know who wrote it.'

She spoke impulsively, and immediately regretted it. *I should not have said that. I can't tell him his wife is having an affair. Why? Because it could bring his whole world down around him and who am I to do that? The affair might come to an end, fizzle out, and Jillian might return to him. And who am I to preclude that possibility?*

He fixed her with an intense gaze. 'But you implied a few moments ago that you had no idea.'

She began to move towards the door. 'That was then,' she said.

'Then who was it?'

She hesitated. She did not trust this man and she could not trust him not to take his anger out on his wife.

'I choose not to tell you.'

He raised his voice almost to shouting pitch. 'You choose not to tell me?'

Perhaps this is why his wife is looking elsewhere, she thought. Perhaps he needs somebody to tell him.

'That is what I said, Mr Mackinlay. You are an arrogant man, I'm afraid. You are used to demanding that people comply with what you want of them. I shall not.'

She walked past him. She half expected him to try to stop her leaving, but he did not.

'I'm sorry,' she said. 'I would normally give people the information to which they are entitled, but I do not think you deserve this information. So I shall not.'

She left the room. He said nothing as she opened the door and stepped out into the corridor.

Miss Carty was outside. You have been listening at the door, thought Isabel; it is quite apparent from your demeanour.

Isabel drove back even more slowly than she had driven there. The road was quiet, and she felt calmer now as she made her way home under the wide sky of late afternoon. To her right, on the horizon were the folds of the Lammermuir Hills, blue against blue. Between the road and the hills were rich stretches of green, squared by hedges and drystone walls that marched off into the distance.

I love this country, she thought. I love it because it is soft and green and the sky is a theatre of white and grey and is so heart-breakingly beautiful in all its moods. I love it because of its people, who are frustrating and interesting and full of joy and sorrow, in equal amounts perhaps; who plot and scheme and yet find time to love one another and make songs and music and plant rhododendrons and write poetry and talk Gaelic and catch fish. I love it for all of that.

As her car picked up speed when the road dipped down towards Flotterstone, Isabel thought about what she had done. She had been asked to find things wrong with three people with whom there was essentially not much wrong: they were simply human. But the people who had involved her in this had more substantial faults. They were schemers, she felt; schemers in a small and contained society. But then were we not all like that, whatever circles we moved in? Were we not all concerned with our reputation? Were we not all intent on securing what we could for ourselves? Did we not all have flaws of greater or less magnitude – all of us?

She had effectively left them to their own devices, but what else could she have done? She could have said to Alex Mackinlay, 'Your wife wrote that letter, you know. Your own wife.' And he would have laughed at the very idea, or reacted angrily perhaps and challenged her to justify the accusation. Which she had decided she could not do because it would have made the whole situation messier and more difficult.

Her thoughts turned to happiness, and its only too common shadow, unhappiness. She hoped that Janet Carty would find happiness somewhere, although she doubted it. She hoped the same for Jillian, whose anguish and anxiety was so vividly attested by the letter she wrote. And poor Tom Simpson, who wanted the job but who would never get it; and John Fraser, in his grief and his guilt; and Gordon, whom she had misjudged in imagining the presence of malice when only ambition was present; and Alex Mackinlay, who was trying his best to defend the reputation of the school, but who could not help, it seemed, being a bit of a bully; and . . . and . . . Harold Slade. Isabel hesitated. It was all his fault, *simpliciter*. But it was never that simple. She made an effort, and eventually she thought: *I wish happiness for Harold Slade too. There, I've thought it. I've thought the thing I knew I should think. And I feel better for it, because although it's harder to love, it's always better.*

The road ahead curved slowly to the left. Off to the right, the land dipped down towards the plains of the coast, to the cone of Berwick Law and the blue haze of the North Sea. Suddenly she thought of the schoolboy with whom she had spoken; she saw his serious expression, his freckles, his green eyes, and she smiled as she sent him a mental message: *Don't worry. You may think you are in prison right at the moment, but the door will open soon enough. Remember that. It will — it really will.*

Back in Edinburgh, and two days later, they did not have far to go for their picnic — only a few paces, really, out on to the lawn behind the house, close to the wooden summerhouse that Isabel had decided she would soon convert into a place for Charlie to play in with his friends, when he eventually found some. There she laid a rubber-backed picnic rug on the grass — a rug in Macpherson tartan — and brought a few of Charlie's toys to keep him entertained: an old wooden truck, green in body, with red wheels, that had belonged to her father and would not have looked out of place in a museum of childhood; his stuffed fox, who might be a familiar for their resident member of the species, Brother Fox; a vaguely sinister woollen spider, knitted by a Morningside widow and sold for charity at a bring-and-buy sale at Holy Corner. These would keep him entertained for hours, as he loaded the spider and fox into the back of the truck and then unloaded them again; interminably, it seemed; fascinated by the whole process.

'Do you think he knows that his stuffed fox is a fox?' asked Jamie, as Isabel laid out a plate of cucumber sandwiches and a neatly quartered Scotch egg pie. 'Or is it just . . . something else?'

'I've been trying to see if he says "fo" when he plays with it,' said Isabel. 'He knows that Brother Fox is a fo, as he calls him. But I'm not sure if he knows that this is a fo.'

'*Fo!*' exclaimed Charlie, pointing to the bushes alongside the garden wall.

'Perhaps,' said Isabel. 'He may be there. But I don't see him, do you, Charlie?'

Isabel passed Jamie a quarter of the pie, and for Charlie she cut off an eighth. 'We bank up so many resentments in our children,' she said. 'As Mr Larkin observed in that poem of his.'

'I haven't read it,' said Jamie. 'What does he say?'

Isabel waved a hand in the air. 'Oh, something about how your mum and dad *confuse* you.'

'Confuse?'

'Well, something like that.'

Jamie looked puzzled. 'Why do you mention that?'

She pointed to the tiny piece of pie. 'Because here I am

giving you a large slice of pie, and Charlie gets one-eighth of a pie.'

Jamie snorted. 'He won't notice. The size of one's pie in this life depends on the size of one's stomach. Charlie has a small stomach.'

'You're right,' said Isabel. 'He seems happy enough.' Words came to her, unbidden, unplanned. '*I never wished for larger pies / A one-eighth pie was very nice / I never yearned for larger pies / My own small slice would quite suffice.*'

She looked at Jamie, and they both burst out laughing.

'Don't expect me to set that to music,' said Jamie.

'I don't.'

They moved on to cucumber sandwiches. Above them, the sky was pale blue, empty apart from a few stately drifts of high, cotton-wool cumulus. Jamie lay back on the rug and stared up into the void; Isabel followed his gaze. They had more than enough cucumber sandwiches; they had all the elderflower cordial in the world; they had box after box of wafer-thin almond biscuits; they had everything that two people and a child could ever want.

'You've been busy, haven't you?' observed Jamie. 'I've been worried about you.'

'You don't need to worry about me,' she said dreamily. 'My life seems to tick over in a satisfactory way. Not much happens, I suppose. I run a philosophical review. I have a little boy. I have a hus . . .'

'. . . band,' he said. 'Or almost. When are we going to get married, Isabel?'

'Soon,' she said. 'We can talk about it after this picnic.'

'We mustn't forget.'

'No, we won't. I promise.'

He turned on to his stomach and, resting his head on his forearm, looked across the rug at Isabel. 'Have you dealt with that business with Professor Lettuce?'

'No,' said Isabel. 'And I don't know what to do. I just don't.'

'Then let me decide for you. You say that he sent in a dreadful review of Dove's book?'

'Yes. It arrived yesterday. They must have fallen out with one another. They've done that before – like squabbling children. He tore the book to shreds.'

Jamie thought for a moment. 'If you don't publish it, then he'll think that you're trying to silence him. He'll accuse you of personal pique because of what went before with Dove and him.'

'Quite likely.'

'And if you do publish it, then Dove will think that you're trying to destroy him – for the same reason: what went before?'

'Yes.'

Jamie thought for a moment. 'All right. This is what you should do. Write to both of them – the same letter. Say that you will not be party to their private rows and that this is the reason why you will not publish the review. Let Dove read the review and he can sort it out with Lettuce. Or not. It'll be up to them.' He paused, judging her response to his suggestion. 'In that way, you'll rise above both of them.'

She nodded her agreement. 'That's the wisdom of Solomon. Thank you. And I have always wanted to rise above Dove and Lettuce.'

'Well, you do. Calmly and elegantly, like a Zeppelin, you rise above them.'

She smiled. She knew it was a compliment. 'You're very kind.'

'Because I love you so much,' he said. 'That is why I like to be kind to you.'

'And that is why I shall bring you all the flowers of the mountain,' said Isabel. 'For the self-same reason.'

She went on to say something else, but Jamie found his attention drifting. He was feeling sleepy, for it was warm, and he could lie there for ever, he thought, listening to the sound of Isabel's voice, in the way one listens to the conversations of birds, or the sound of a waterfall descending the side of a Scottish mountain; sounds for which we cannot come up with a meaning, but which we love dearly with all our heart, and loving anything with all your heart always brings understanding, in time.

**Alexander McCall Smith** is the author of over sixty books on a wide array of subjects. For many years he was Professor of Medical Law at the University of Edinburgh and served on national and international bioethics bodies. Then in 1999 he achieved global recognition for his award-winning series The No.1 Ladies' Detective Agency, and thereafter has devoted his time to the writing of fiction, including the 44 Scotland Street and Corduroy Mansions series. His books have been translated into forty-five languages. He lives in Edinburgh with his wife, Elizabeth, a doctor.